Bewitchingly Hers

Hers

the witches of pleasant grove book 3

JENNIFER CHIPMAN

For the fall girls, who'd rather curl up with a blanket and a hot beverage than go out on the town.

playlist

- Do You Believe in Magic? - The Lovin' Spoonful
- Sweater Weather - The Neighborhood
- Howl - Florence + The Machine
- Dreams - The Cranberries
- then i met her - EKKSTACY
- Wolves - Selena Gomez, Marshmello
- Neon Moon - Brooks & Dunn, Kacey Musgraves
- Rivers and Roads - The Head and the Heart
- Sweet - Cigarettes After Sex
- Sleep On The Floor - The Lumineers
- Kiss Me - Sixpence None the Richer
- Like Real People Do - Hozier
- Eyes on Fire - Blue Foundation
- Too Sweet - Hozier
- Fallin' For You - Collie Caillat
- this is how you fall in love - Jeremy Zucker, Chelsea Cutler
- ivy - Taylor Swift
- Fall Into Me - Forest Blakk

- Hold On - Chord Overstreet
- Lost in the Woods - Jonathan Groff
- Shrike - Hozier
- Make It To Me - Sam Smith
- I Found - Amber Run
- Die For You - The Weeknd
- Work Song - Hozier
- Hold My Girl - George Ezra
- My Love Mine All Mine - Mitski
- Found You - Silicone Boone
- Out Of The Woods - Taylor Swift
- Where You Belong - The Weeknd

contents

prologue

BARRETT

T could smell her. *My mate.*
She was close.

Dragging my body towards the town, a fizzle of magic ran over me as I crossed through a magical barrier. Meant to keep non-magical beings *out.* Discomfort shuddered through me. Like everything was *wrong.* It scraped against my skin, over every cut and bite. I let out a howl with the limited strength I had left.

All I knew is I needed to get to her. That she could fix me, somehow. My body was tired, and losing stamina fast. I couldn't put weight on my back leg. My limbs ached, and my fur was matted in blood. Some of it mine, some of it from the creature that attacked me.

The barriers between our world and *others* were growing weaker, letting beings in between the cracks. Beings that had no place here among the humans. Not that they knew we were here. We'd ensured that for centuries, thanks to wards enacted to keep evil beings away. My town was shielded, much like this place. If it wasn't for my job, I wouldn't even know about them. Wouldn't know about the creatures I fought to eradicate or the beings I sought to protect.

Every moment, every circumstance, every experience had brought me here. To my *mate*. Even the thought felt impossible, but I could feel her presence here.

How was this possible? I didn't understand *how* my mate was here. A whine slipped free from my throat as I put more weight on my front paws, heading deeper into the town.

Pleasant Grove, the sign read.

I knew she was here—her sweet scent drew me to her. Yet everything around me smelled wrong. Gods, I'd never imagined this. *Witches.*

For us, mates were sacred. Finding yours, keeping them, that meant something to us. Would she even understand what we were?

I needed to see her. To scent her fully. To know my mate. To hold her in my arms and—*what?* I was broken. Damaged. In no shape to claim what was mine.

My wolf gave another whimper, knowing we couldn't have our mate. Not in this state. I wanted to shift back, but he wouldn't let me. He knew these wounds would be worse for me than him.

Raising my snout, I sniffed at the air, catching the scent of stale coffee and baked goods. But there was that underlying sweet scent, too. Like apples and cinnamon. Closing my eyes, I inhaled.

Yes. Find our mate, my wolf urged. *She will help us.* Would she? I could only hope.

The trail took me to a back alley, behind the coffee shop. It was stronger here, but there was no one in sight. The sun was disappearing into the sky, and soon it would be dark.

If the creature came after me again, tonight, I wouldn't

survive another attack. I could only hope that the town wards would be enough to keep *it* out.

I whimpered again, dropping onto my paws and staring towards the door. *Where was she?*

If this was the end, I just wanted to see her once. My mate —couldn't she sense me, too? I couldn't wait to find what color her coat was. To run with her in the forest. To learn why she was here, in this town of strange smells and witches.

Please, I begged, letting out a weak howl. *My mate.*

That was my last thought as the world faded to black.

CHAPTER ONE

eryne

A wolf's howl distracted me from my peaceful contentment of watching as the sun drifted lower in the sky. It painted Pleasant Grove in the most beautiful orange and yellow hues, making it hard to look away. I'd always loved fall here—the nip in the air, the leaves crunching under foot—but our sunsets were something else entirely in New England. It made me wish I could curl up on my porch swing with a blanket and a cup of hot apple cider as I watched the explosion of color in the sky.

Maybe one day. I sighed, turning back to the empty storefront. It was the end of the day at the Witches' Brew, the coffee shop and bakery I managed. We'd already closed for the night, and there were only a few things I had left to do before I could head home. There was a box of apple turnovers I'd stashed away earlier—they were my favorite—sitting in a box on the counter, waiting to go home with me.

My broom sat in the corner, since I'd already finished sweeping the floor, and the trash was emptied, the large black bag sitting by the door to take outside to the dumpster. Most of the employees didn't want to close, though I didn't mind the busy work, since it left me a lot of time alone with my thoughts.

As an only child, I was used to that. I'd grown up having to entertain myself, and I'd never even joined a coven. Despite all the invitations from my best friends, I was happy alone.

At least, that was what I told myself.

Most of the time, it was true.

No matter what Wendy and Rina liked to tell me.

These days, between books and making earrings, I kept busy. My job here paid the bills, and the owners—a pair of sisters, Willow and Luna Clarke—had promoted me to manager last year after they'd both fallen in love, so I couldn't complain too much. Plus, I had my familiar, my little hedgehog Nutmeg, to keep me company.

My eyes drifted outside the shop, to the main street of Pleasant Grove. Our quaint little town was cozy, already illuminated with lights, preparations for Halloween in full swing. Decorations were going up everywhere, and everywhere I looked, it felt like couples were walking hand in hand.

Sometimes, I felt a pang in my heart when I saw them cozied up next to each other at the annual pumpkin festival. It was hard not to watch them from the windows of the shop. Everyone was just so *happy* here.

"What's wrong with you?" I scolded myself, sighing as I finished dusting the outside of the display case. I worried my lower lip in between my teeth, glad no one else was around to listen to me talk to myself.

Maybe I could blame my melancholy on my breakup with my boyfriend last year. Sure, we'd been together since high school, but the relationship had gone stale. Much like the day old pastries that I needed to throw out.

At a certain point, it felt like we were just going through

the motions. There was no passion, no *fire*. No spark. Maybe at one point I loved him—or I thought I did—but he wasn't my *person*. My soulmate. Though I knew better than to wish for what I couldn't have. I was only twenty-five... what was the rush?

"Soulmates aren't that common," I tried to remind myself. "Just because Willow and Luna somehow found theirs, doesn't mean—"

A strange scratching sound distracted me from my train of thought, and I looked up from the counter I was wiping down. I froze. A few seconds later, there it was again. Was someone outside?

Pleasant Grove didn't have much crime, something I'd always been thankful for. Which meant it was probably some kid playing a harmless prank. I sucked in a breath.

Or maybe it was some*thing*.

"It was probably just the wind," I mumbled to myself.

If I told myself that enough, maybe I'd believe it. I'd never loved being alone at night—probably why my house had a deadbolt *and* spells cast on it. It was also the reason I refused to watch horror movies. I wasn't taking any chances.

Not moving from the counter, I strained my ear, listening for it again. When I didn't hear anything, I figured it must have been my mind playing tricks on me.

"Just have to take the trash out and then I can go home to a hot bath and a book," I reminded myself, dropping the dirty towel in the basket. Maybe I'd even make a hot cup of cider to relax.

Grabbing the black bag, I slipped out the door, thankful that it wasn't completely dark outside yet as I trudged over to the dumpster. It was my least favorite task, which was why I always saved it for last, then hurried to lock up and head to my car. Tonight was no different. Only now, I regretted it.

Why hadn't I done this before the sun started to set? Especially after Luna had been attacked by demons out there last Halloween. I hadn't even known they were *real* until the Clarke sisters both fell in love with a pair of demon brothers last year. I'd always thought they were a legend, like werewolves and vampires. Things that our elders spun tales about to scare us into obedience, not because they actually existed in the real world.

Though the ones that attacked Luna hadn't been like their mates. They were blood-thirsty and *dangerous*.

What were the chances something like that would happen twice?

It was safe to say, us witches were living in the dark here in Pleasant Grove. Suddenly, that complacency felt terrifying. What was out there that we didn't know about yet? I didn't want to find out.

A full body shudder wracked through my body, and I tried to ignore the goosebumps on my arms. "There's nothing out here," I said the words out loud, more of a reminder to myself than anything else. *Goddess*, when had I become such a scaredy cat? I was a witch, and while I might not know powerful offensive magic, I could defend myself. My affinity was healing, and though I could have pursued a different career—like nursing— I hadn't wanted it to become my entire life. When it had first manifested itself, I'd been slightly disappointing. But overtime, I'd realized how special it was that I could heal with just my touch. That I had this gift of life.

Slamming the lid shut after I dumped the bag in the dumpster, I turned back towards the door. Just a few steps, and then I'd be safe. Maybe I'd call my mom as I walked back to my car. She might laugh at me, but she'd appease me.

Looking up, I found the moon already high in the sky. It was huge, and it felt like an omen. Maybe if Luna was here, I could have gotten her to tell me what it meant. Unfortunately, she was living in the demon realm now.

A whimper distracted me, and chills ran down my back. Because that noise *definitely* wasn't human. I frowned, knowing I couldn't ignore the sounds of distress coming from any living thing. It just wasn't how I was wired. I'd spent my childhood healing dozens of injured animals—and friends. Broken arms or scabbed knees were just the beginning.

"Hello?" I asked, looking for the source of the noise, poking around the side of the dumpster. "Are you... okay?" I cursed internally, reminding myself that an animal wasn't going to answer me.

There was a trail of red down the alley, and a pool of blood underneath the furry creature that gave another cry of pain. I blinked as I realized what exactly I was looking at. It was a large red wolf, lying there and whimpering.

"Oh my goddess." Had it dragged itself from the street? I probably should have been scared, but the unsettling feeling from earlier was completely gone. The beast was in no position to harm me, and I was pretty sure it wouldn't, even though I couldn't explain why. "Oh, you poor thing," I cooed, crouching down to check its wound. "Who did this to you?" He had a large slash in his abdomen, the cut still bleeding, and what looked like sharp teeth marks in his hind legs.

What could have made those bites? I didn't want to find out.

The wolf turned his head slowly, his eyes meeting mine. They were amber, and I had the faintest sense that I was looking at a pair of human eyes, ones that blinked at me as I ran my hand over the animal's muzzle. It was a large creature —the biggest wolf I'd ever seen, almost as big as me—so I assumed it was a *he*. Not that I was going to verify that by poking around down there. I might not have felt uneasy, but that didn't mean I trusted him not to snap his extremely sharp canine teeth at me.

"Can you walk?" I asked him. A groan was my only response. "Hmm." I looked around, not finding anything that would help me get him inside, and worried my lip into my mouth. "Wait here."

The wolf gave a little snort, like he was rolling his eyes.

"Sorry," I offered. "I guess it's not like you can go anywhere else." The wolf's paws twitched as I did one more glance over before standing up. I couldn't explain why I had this feeling that he understood me.

Goddess, I was losing my mind, sitting here and talking to a wolf.

I hurried back into the bakery, grabbing my phone and a handful of clean raggedy towels we used for spills. They weren't much, but maybe I could stop the bleeding, and fasten some sort of sling that would help me get him inside to help him. Though I hadn't really figured out what I was going to do after that.

Only that I *needed* to help this poor creature that was in pain.

I'd always loved animals, and though I couldn't talk to them—not directly—I felt a deep connection to their feelings and needs. Sometimes, I liked to think they understood me, too. Growing up, everyone had thought I would end up working at the animal shelter, or becoming a vet—especially with my healing abilities—but I'd never had any interest in the field. I was too tenderhearted to lose patients or perform surgery.

Managing the coffee shop suited me just fine.

Rushing back out with the towels—and a large tablecloth I

found in one of the cabinets—I crouched back in front of the wolf. Pressing one against the biggest gash on his side, I kept applying pressure. I needed to heal him—the blood was already matting to his russet fur, turning it a deep, angry red. He was still bleeding, and I knew I needed to act fast. Trying to do it outside in this grimy, dirty alley seemed like a way to get it infected. Plus, what if whatever did this to him was still lingering around?

I struggled to move him onto the tablecloth, wiping the sweat from my forehead off on my arm once I had finally completed the task.

"I'm sorry," I said, hearing the creature cry out as I started to tug him into the coffee shop. "I'm not exactly the strongest. You probably could have found a better alley. Like, maybe behind the hardware store." Lou, the man who ran the place, was older, but he could still lift things I couldn't even fathom. Being blessed with superhuman strength would have come in handy right now.

Finally, after a lot of huffing, I succeeded in dragging him into the back of the shop.

"You're really big, you know," I said to the wolf, who hadn't moved from his spot. He lifted his head, stared into my eyes, and then dropped it again. "I think you might need stitches after I clean you up. And I might need to pack the wound with some gauze. I think we have a first aid kit somewhere around here..." I bit my lip, running over to the spot where we kept it. There were bandages and ointment—burns and cuts were common in a bakery and coffee shop if you weren't careful—but I didn't know if it was enough to help.

I grabbed all of the supplies I thought I needed—plus a basin of water, and sat down in front of the beast.

"This might hurt. I'm sorry." Talking to him like he was a

person was helping distract me from the severity—and insanity—of the situation.

Grabbing more clean towels, I worked to clean his wounds, trying to infuse my magic in the hopes that it would speed up the healing process.

The wolf let out a howl, and I winced. "Hey, it's going to be okay," I told him, worried he'd bite me if he got too agitated. "Please, try to stay calm." Though, that was more for *me* than it was for him. "If anyone hears and finds you, I have no idea how I'm going to explain this."

I was fully aware that I was talking to myself, that this babbling nonsense wasn't something you'd normally say to an animal, but I was out of my depth here. I'd never helped an animal this big before. Certainly not one with teeth that could rip out my throat if he desired it.

Surprisingly, he settled down, only letting out a few whimpers here and there as I worked across his body, paying attention to each spot where he'd been attacked, cleaning and healing as I went. When I pulled the towel away, the bleeding had slowed significantly, though I couldn't see just how deep the cuts were.

"What could even do this to a wolf of your size?" I wondered out loud as I took another clean cloth, dipping it in the water before wiping the wound. I repeated the process until they looked clean.

"Do you think an antibiotic ointment would help?" I asked the wolf. "Probably not. I don't know why I'm still talking to you." Probably because my hands were shaking, and I was trying to ignore the fact that I'd let a wild animal into the back of Willow and Luna's shop. "I think I'm just nervous." Taking a deep breath, I covered the wounds with gauze. He didn't seem to be able to move much, so I didn't have to worry about how I was going to wrap them. "I've never healed anything of your size before. Mostly just some small birds and cats." And the occasional rabbit.

Standing up, I took the bowl of bloody water to the basin and washed my hands.

"We'll probably need to change those again in a few hours," I muttered, propping my hands on my hips as I looked at the wolf. "Otherwise, it might get infected." That was my biggest fear at this point. Though, what was I going to do with him? I couldn't exactly leave him here, and there was no way I was going to be able to drag him up the stairs to Luna's apartment. It was hard enough just to get him inside.

"I'm just going to have to get help," I said, more to myself than the wolf. He needed to be somewhere where I could check on him—without worrying about anyone else finding him or what a potentially wild animal might do as he healed.

Biting my lip, I pulled out my phone, desperately texting two of my friends. Maybe it was a little crazy, but what was I supposed to do?

ERYNE

SOS. I need help.

RINA

Where are you? I can head over in 5.

ERYNE

Still at the Witches' Brew. Something happened.

WENDY

I'm on my way! Hang tight, E.

RINA

Copy that. Grabbing my broom.

I snorted at the mental image. Most witches didn't use

brooms to get around anymore, but even I had to admit that it was quite a handy mode of transportation.

Unless, of course, you had a wolf to take home with you. Luckily, my car was parked on the street outside.

I busied myself doing some organization and prep work for tomorrow, making notes of what I needed to order next time I did inventory. Though we'd hired a new baker, Luna still loved to pop in occasionally and make a random batch of something, and I liked to make sure the bakery was always well stocked just for her.

Staying busy was the only way to keep my mind off what I was going to do with the wolf in the kitchen.

Less than ten minutes later, my friends walked in. They couldn't have looked more different if they tried—Rina was a brunette with longer hair, a tan complexion and hazel eyes, while Wendy had shoulder-length blonde hair and bright blue eyes.

Witch magic manifested differently in all of us, giving almost every witch a different ability and affinities. While I knew Wendy was clairvoyant, I also knew she resented her powers. The ability to see, and speak to, spirits couldn't have been easy. She was also incredibly perceptive, a skill I definitely needed now. Rina, on the other hand, had been extremely secretive of hers. Almost every witch in their coven—thirteen total—possessed a different ability.

I gave them both a guilty smile as they stood in front of me.

"Alright, we're here. What's up?" Wendy asked, smoothing her hands down her red velvet overall dress. She had a white long-sleeved t-shirt on under it as well as star patterned tights and a pair of short black booties.

Rina, on the other hand, was wearing a pair of black ripped jeans and a deep purple flannel shirt over a black corset top. She'd probably come from the Enchanted Cauldron, if I had to guess.

"It's probably better if I just show you."

I led them back into the kitchen where I'd left the beast. Thankfully, he hadn't moved.

"Eryne." Rina propped her hand on her hip as stared between me, Wendy, and the wolf currently on the floor. "What did you do?" The wolf responded with a rumble in his chest, like he was clearly not happy I had brought others around. "You brought a *wolf* in the bakery?"

"He was hurt!"

Wendy just blinked. "And we were your first call, because?"

I scrunched up my nose. "Because I trust you both. And I'm a little terrified of Olive." She was in the coven too, but we weren't close. Olive ran the vet clinic in town, made easier by her affinity with animals. I couldn't explain why, but I didn't want to lose my furry patient. "So... yeah. He's heavy. Probably close to two hundred pounds. He was in the alley and I couldn't just leave him there. Something attacked him, and I just—"

Wendy shook her head. "You and your bleeding heart. How'd you even get him inside?" She looked out the back door, her skin looking even paler than usual.

"It wasn't easy."

"Those look like teeth marks," Rina said, unfazed, crouching down and inspecting his wounds.

"You think something *bit* him?" Wendy asked, incredulous.

"It looked that way to me, too. I have no idea what could cause this sort of damage, though. It seems like it just... tore through the skin. Maybe a bear?"

"That would have been one hell of a fight. What wolf would go after a bear?"

I shrugged. These were all questions I didn't have answers to, since, unfortunately, wolves couldn't talk. "So what attacked him? I'm open to theories."

"Or maybe the better question is... *who*?" Rina asked.

"*Sabrina*." Wendy shot her a look. Rina hated her given name, saying it didn't fit her.

Our brunette friend shrugged. "What? It's plausible. Demons exist, after all. Who knows what else is out there that the elders never told us about?" She picked at her black manicure.

"I was just thinking the same earlier," I said. "There's no way they didn't know, right? If it wasn't for Willow and Damien—"

"We'd never know," Rina finished my statement. "I know. That's what has me so uneasy. If they've known all this time, *why* did they choose to keep it from us? We have no idea what's out there. Our whole lives, we were taught Pleasant Grove was safeguarded, warded, to keep humans out. To keep *us* safe. But maybe there's more to it than that?"

Wendy was ghostly white now, all blood having drained from her face. "Like what?"

"You're the one who sees ghosts, babe. I feel like you should be the expert."

I crossed my arms over my chest. "Enough, you two. We can ponder this later. I need to get him home."

They both blinked. "You're taking a wild animal to your *house*?"

"What else am I going to do with him?" I looked at the wolf. *Goddess*, I could only imagine how beautiful he was running through the woods. "I can't leave him here. He needs to heal, and I can help him."

Rina bit her thumbnail. "True. Okay, well, I guess we're doing this." She approached the wolf, who let out a low growl. "Um, Eryne?" Her head turned back to look at me. "Are you sure he's not going to bite us?"

I frowned, stepping up close to him. "That's weird. He was fine earlier." I reached out, stroking my hand down his muzzle. The rumble in his chest immediately stopped.

Rina tried to touch him again, and he bared his teeth. But whenever I did...

Somehow, with my hand on his head, petting between his ears, he stayed calm enough to let the girls approach him.

"This is freaky." She looked between the wolf and I, shaking her head. "Alright. You stay there in his line of sight. Wendy and I will lift from back here."

I nodded, and we each grabbed different corners of the blanket, heaving him up before heading out to the parking lot, where my small car waited. It was much easier with three of us, but he was still heavy. Opening the back, I was suddenly grateful my seats were still down after transporting decorations to the Witches' Brew earlier this week.

"Thank you both," I said, looking at my friends. "I seriously owe you one." He took up most of the back of my car, but luckily, we got him in. Which meant now, I just needed to get him home.

"I'm happy to take payment in pastries," Rina said, grinning as she tucked her hands into the pockets of her jeans.

They were always happy to be fed.

Wendy rolled her eyes. "We're always happy to help, girl. Don't listen to her." She straightened her red dress. "But I *would* happily take some cinnamon twists if you have any left over."

I laughed. "It's on me next time. Promise."

Waiving goodbye as they both set off, I got in the front seat of my car, turning over my shoulder to look at the wolf. He raised his head, blinked at me, and then laid it back down. I let out a breath. "Well, you're not out of the woods yet, but hopefully the hardest part is over."

I had to hope. Because I really didn't know what to do if he took a turn for the worst and those wounds got infected?

All I could do was pray to the goddesses that my healing magic would be enough.

CHAPTER TWO

barrett

My mate's hand was pressed against my face, and I was keenly aware that nothing had ever felt as right as her touch. *How was that possible?* I'd always heard of what it felt like, but never imagined...

Pain radiated through me as I tried to move, despite every fiber of my being telling me not to. Everything was agony.

But I wanted to see my mate. My body was on fire, a relentless wave of torture that crashed over me again and again.

It was hard to focus as she fretted over me, dressing my wounds, pressing poultices to my body and brushing my fur.

The witch was healing me, mending each broken bone and gash slowly.

And she was a witch. However that was possible, I didn't understand. Wolves always mated wolves. But I could see the gold, faint thread between us, could feel her at the other end of the bond. And she smelled like... she smelled like mine.

I wanted to tell her, but I couldn't shift.

Everything *hurt*. Everything except for where she was

touching my coat. She was so careful. From the moment she'd found me, her voice had soothed me. *Calmed* me.

The beast was letting her do it all willingly, because she was our mate.

How was this possible?

Maybe I was just delirious. Maybe none of this was real, and I was still lying in that dirty alleyway. The fates couldn't have been so kind to me as to let me see my mate before I died, could they?

That was probably what it was. I was in the afterlife, and this was my penance, and my torture. Getting to see my mate but never touch her, speak to her. To never really know her.

This didn't make any sense. Neither had the attack. I hadn't seen it coming, and the pain made it too hard to think about it too clearly. I'd been looking for something, but what?

My head ached, my wounds throbbing as she ran her hands over my body.

I closed my eyes, everything fading back to black as sleep took me under once again.

The next thing I remembered was her sweet voice murmuring to herself as she checked my bandages, warmth radiating over my skin. But not the same burning pain as before. This was a soothing warmth. Like lying in the sun or cuddling under a blanket. A comforting warmth. I let it ripple through my body, easing aches as it went.

I didn't know how much time had passed—I was in and out of consciousness—but she was always there. Stroking my muzzle, taking care of me. Checking on me, all while she babbled away. It amused me that she was constantly talking to herself. Cute, even.

She might have been a witch, but she was nothing like I'd imagined.

"Are you feeling better?" Her voice was soft as she ran her fingers up my muzzle. "Does it still hurt?"

I lifted my head—surprised that the pain had ebbed—and took her in.

She was pretty, my mate. Her hair was red, cut into a short bob with bangs, and she was wearing a cozy sweater and leggings. I was laying in the middle of a plush bed, the remnants of her healing scattered around the bedside table.

I still wasn't sure how she'd gotten me into her house by herself, considering my weight. Alpha wolf shifters tended to be larger than even the biggest of regular wolves—part of why I was so good at my job. At least, normally. Unfortunately, every once in awhile, something got the better of me. Though not normally like *that*.

The attack... I winced. The wounds would have been fatal on a human. I was lucky.

Even luckier, considering it had somehow brought me to my mate. I couldn't figure out how my wolf had known to find her, but I was glad he had. I wished I could speak to her, but it was clear I was not going to get my body back. So as much as I wanted to talk to her, for her to know my name, I was stuck like this for now.

"You've been a little touch and go," she said as I turned my head back to look at my fur. It had been shaved in spots, though I was sure it looked better than it had before she found me. "You were so hot, and shaking. I was worried an infection was going to take root." She let out a breath. "I had to go into town, and thankfully Sophie's shop was open, but I felt horrible leaving you." Listening to her sweet voice was a welcome distraction from the discomfort that still itched at my skin.

I sniffed at it, wondering what she had applied. "It's a combination of healing herbs I got from one of the other witches." She seemed to realize my uncertainty, and rubbed between my ears, like I was some sort of house pet. "Sophie's a friend," she clarified, still petting me. "She had some poultices and salves made from the best ingredients. I'm a healer, but I'm not an herbalist. Willow would have been a good option too, but she's not making potions right now. Still, it had been two days, and I was worried—"

Two days? I had been out two whole days? I tried to sit up, but the movement pulled a cry from my wolf. *Fuck.*

She winced. "Don't move. You're still not fully healed yet."

I shut my eyes. *Clearly.* This was fucking awful. I let out a puff of air through my nose.

It had never taken me this long to heal before. Wolf shifters had accelerated healing, and I should have been right as rain within twenty-four hours. Whatever had attacked me was clearly not a monster I'd ever dealt with before. But for the life of me, I couldn't remember any of it.

Like it had stolen my magic, my memories.

Once I was better, I would have to call Ezra and warn him. Maybe he'd been right, that I shouldn't have gone out on this job alone. But what was the alternative? Putting others into danger?

I was a lone, alpha wolf. I didn't have anyone depending on me—no mate or wife at home, no pups to care for. My family and friends didn't even know about my job, or the risks I took on a daily basis. It was the only way I could leave them without having them worry about me all of the time.

But I *did* have a mate now. The room smelled like her. Like apples with a hint of cinnamon and something *sweet.* My wolf decided it was his new favorite scent, and I knew if he was feeling better, he would be trying to get it directly from the source.

I winced as I shifted, trying to roll onto my stomach so I could lay my head on my paws and continue to stare at her.

"Oh—" my mate said, sounding surprised. "Hi." She gave me a small smile, and then shook her head. "I cannot believe I'm actually talking to a wolf. But... You *can* understand me, can't you?"

My eyes met hers, and I nodded my head. Her eyes widened as she scratched at my ears. "I thought so. You're a very smart wolf."

If only she knew that I wasn't just a wolf at all.

CHAPTER THREE

eryne

T he first few days of having the wolf in my house had felt... precarious. Like at any moment, I might lose him, succumbing to his wounds. I couldn't explain *why* I cared so much that he survived. Only that he was connected to me in a way I didn't understand. How he seemed to understand me, and those strange eyes that almost felt like I was looking back at a person, and not a wolf.

As much as I would have liked to stay home all day, fretting over my newfound animal companion, I had to work. Unfortunately, I couldn't stay away from the bakery for more than a day or two. Luckily, the wolf seemed to sleep most of the time anyway, so I let him be.

Not even a perfectly cooked apple pastry could distract me right now.

Well, maybe. It was worth a shot, wasn't it?

It was getting harder and harder to only refer to him as *the wolf* in my mind, but naming him felt... strange. He wasn't my pet. And maybe he could understand me, but I knew he was a wild thing.

Once he was healed, he would be gone.

The bell chimed as the door opened, and I looked up, surprised to find Willow Clarke slipping inside, wearing a pumpkin orange sweater dress and a black hat. It looked cozy, and adorably complimented her pregnant belly.

I couldn't help but grin. "Willow!"

"Hi, Eryne." She gave me a small smile as she padded towards the counter to meet me.

"What's up? Is everything okay with the shop?" I asked her.

She was a few years older than me—I was a year younger than her sister, Luna—and had always been nice to me growing up. Working under her had been a dream. Now, I had the most hands-off bosses I could have asked for. They practically let me run the shop however I wanted, only popping in to check on the books and how things were going every so often.

Willow laughed. "I should be asking *you* that. You've taken over so many of our responsibilities."

"I don't mind," I said. The shop had never been Willow's passion, though she'd helped her sister open it, but I loved working here. "Besides, you've got more important things going on." She was due in December, so she still had a few months to go.

She snorted, rubbing her belly. "Yes, and one very overprotective mate. He's hardly let me out of his sight ever since we found out I was pregnant." It sounded sweet to me, though from what I knew about Damien, it probably drove Willow absolutely crazy. Still, it was obvious they were deeply in love with each other.

"How'd you get him to let you come here?" I asked, leaning against the counter as she flitted about, using the coffee maker to brew something that smelled heavenly.

She winked, a mischievous smile curling on her lips as she handed me a cup, and then took a sip of her own. "It's decaf," she said, with a shrug. "And... I didn't. Thought I'd sneak out while he thought I was napping. I've been craving a pumpkin chocolate chip scone so badly."

Luna used to make them all the time, though she'd just given birth to twins last month. Her and her husband hadn't made it back to Pleasant Grove yet, and I wasn't expecting her anytime soon. Luckily, we had a stack of her recipe cards, and our new baker had been experimenting with some twists of her own.

"Those always sell out so fast, but I stashed a few in the back." I'd had a feeling we might need them. Good to know my witchy intuition was still correct. "Come on."

I waved to the witch running the counter, letting her know we were going into the back.

"Gladly." She followed me into the kitchen, taking a deep inhale. It always smelled delicious back here—even when nothing was in the oven—like baked goods and sweet sugar. Sometimes I wondered if we had the scent pumped in, it smelled that good. "This baby is always wanting sweets. It drives Damien mad. You know I had to force him to try candy corn last year? I'm pretty sure he only puts up with my obsession because he knows it makes me happy." Willow smiled, like she was thinking about the demon she now called her own. "And it makes the baby kick." She grabbed a scone from the box, plopping it in her mouth and letting out a moan as she chewed the first bite. "*So good.* I swear, I could eat these all day."

I took another sip of the coffee she had made me. While I wasn't a bad barista in any sense of the word, nothing compared to Willow's coffee. Mostly because of her affinity with making potions, and what was a cup of coffee but a brew of caffeine? They were like magic, pepping you right up.

"I don't know how you and Luna do it all, honestly," I admitted.

"Pregnancy?" She asked, raising an eyebrow.

I shrugged. *Everything.* Mates and relationships and..." I waved my hand.

Somehow, even though it wasn't an answer, Willow seemed to know exactly what I meant. "It's easier when you have someone you love. I mean, we weren't exactly expecting to get pregnant this soon. Damien and I have only been together a year now, after all. But I'm almost thirty, and I'm looking forward to meeting our little one and starting our family. It feels like the rest of our lives are just beginning, you know?"

Did I know? Not really. I'd never experienced that for myself. My life felt a little stagnant. I gave her a hesitant smile. "I guess I've just never met the right person."

"You will," she promised. "They're going to come into the coffee shop and sweep you off your feet, and you won't even know what hit you."

I finished the cup of coffee as she scarfed down another scone. "Maybe."

"Just look at me. I never thought the love of my life was going to be my *cat.* Sure, it was a little non-conventional, but..." She snorted. "I wouldn't trade it for the world." Willow gave me a once over. "Maybe we should call the coven together have a little manifesting circle."

I rolled my eyes. "We don't need to try to manifest a love interest into reality. I'll be just fine. Besides, I have Nutmeg." And a wolf in my house, who was surprisingly great at keeping my mind off any lack of potential suitors.

"Well, you know the coven invitation is always open. Especially now that Luna is with Zain, we're down one."

Thirteen was a lucky number for witches. It was one we

associated with powerful energies, which made it the ideal number of members in a coven.

I fidgeted with the ring on my right hand. "I don't know." I'd always been a bit of a loner. Being part of a group sounded...

Actually, it sounded pretty great. But I was just scared that I wouldn't fit in. That something would happen and I'd find myself alone again. Except the second time, it would be even worse, because I would know what it felt like to be a part of something bigger than myself.

"Everyone is in agreement. We'd love to have you join us. Especially Rina and Wendy." Willow winked, like my friends hadn't been wearing me down on the same topic for the last few months. I was just being stubborn.

Dammit, she knew my weakness. "Okay," I whispered out. "I'll think about it."

She stood up, stretching her back. "Good. I'll send you the information for our next meeting. You just missed one last week during the full moon."

The full moon had been the night I'd found the wolf. I bit my lip. "Speaking of..."

"Hm?" She was busy wrapping up scones into a box to take home.

I pondered what to say, how to ask for what I needed. "Do you have anything that would aid healing?"

Willow raised an eyebrow. "Is something wrong?" She looked me over, like she was searching for any potential injuries.

I shook my head. "Not for me. I just..." Fiddling with my favorite broom earrings, I thought about the best way to phrase my little predicament. *I brought a wolf home.* Probably not the best thing to say to my boss, especially considering he'd been inside the bakery. Sure, I'd cleaned it thoroughly afterwords, but still. "I'm just helping a friend with some injuries, that's all. I've used some poultices and salves, but I'm worried about the internal damage, and infection. There's only so much my magic can do." I looked down at my hands. Even I had limits.

No matter how much I wanted to, I couldn't bring a creature back from the brink of death in just a few days.

"Well, I *think* I have something back at the house that could help. But I'll have to consult my book of potions. It's been awhile since I brewed a healing one."

"That would be amazing. I'd really appreciate it." I felt a bit of relief course through my system. Things were fine, and the wolf would be fine. I'd get him back on his feet, and then the lingering worry would dissipate. All would be right again.

She smiled. "Then consider it done."

Without warning, Damien entered the back room, his eyes flaring red for a moment before they faded back to brown. "Willow." He let out a sigh of relief. "There you are." He wrapped his arms around his mate's stomach. "I was looking everywhere for you."

"Damien." She chuckled. "I've only been gone for..." Willow looked over at the clock on the back wall. "An hour."

He rubbed his nose on the crook of her neck. "Doesn't matter. You know how much I worry about you and our little witchling."

Willow blushed, turning to me. "We should go."

I laughed. "It was really good to see you, Willow. Thank you for the help." I held up my empty cup. "And the coffee."

"Any time." She placed her hands over Damien's, who seemed content to hold her in his arms. "Thank you for the scones."

I nodded. "It's still your shop, you know. You never have to thank me for anything."

She winked. "I know." Turning to her mate, she stepped up

on her tiptoes—a feat, considering Damien was a foot taller than her—and whispered something in his ear. He scooped up the box on the counter before interlacing his fingers with hers.

"Bye, you two," I called out.

"Goodbye," Damien said, not even looking back, like he was too eager to get Willow home.

And yeah—I couldn't deny that I wanted something like that for myself. A doting husband, someone who loved me and fretted over me.

Maybe one day.

For now, I'd be going home alone.

Or, at the very least, to the wolf in my bed.

He was still sleeping as I entered my bedroom, pulling off the clothes that smelled like stale coffee. I tried not to wear any of my favorite outfits to work, as even with an apron on, I ended up spilling on myself.

Sure, I didn't *have* to work the front counter any more as manager, but I still loved the energy of the shop. I wasn't a witch who was skilled in auras, but there was something about the general cheeriness at the Witches' Brew that always seemed to energize me.

After quickly changing and pulling on a comfy crewneck plus a pair of leggings, I sat on the edge of my bed to check on the wolf.

He'd clearly changed positions since I left this morning, which was a relief. Though he didn't seem too apt to walk yet, at least if he could move, the worst of it was over. At least, I hoped. I wasn't a doctor, nor was I a vet, but his injuries were healing well and seemed less red than before.

Now that I had the potion from Willow—she'd dropped it

off before I'd left for the day—I hoped it would help with generating new, healthy tissue and helping him feel less lethargic. Though the brew was definitely formulated more for a human than a wolf. I wasn't sure exactly how I was going to get him to drink it, but that was a different problem.

I smiled, watching him sleep. His russet fur was growing back in from where I'd had to shave it, thank the goddess. It was soft—and I was honestly obsessed with how cuddly he was. I'd gotten used to sleeping next to him. Originally, it had been because I was worried about leaving him alone. The first few days, it felt like I'd woken up every few hours to heal him. Now, it was that I liked his body heat—even if his giant form took up most of my queen-sized bed.

One eye blinked open, looking at me as I ran my fingers through his pelt. "Hi," I said, wishing I could read his mind. It would be nice to understand animals and to know what my wolf was thinking. "I'm home," I said. "Obviously."

He perked his ears up, tilting his head to the side as he looked at me.

I ran my finger down his spine. "My friend Willow—she's my boss, actually—she made you a potion to drink. It should help aid your healing. I know you might not trust me, but I hate seeing you hurting." I continued petting him, because it seemed like it helped.

And okay, maybe it just helped me.

Here was this big, giant animal that I'd always been told to be afraid of, and he was simply laying on my bed, letting me pet him. Every day, I felt like I was letting down my guard a little bit more.

He wasn't going to hurt me. Honestly, he felt more like a dog than a wolf right now.

"Will you drink it?" I grabbed the to-go cup. It just looked like soup, honestly. It didn't even smell bad. Witches all over town came to Willow for her potions—for everything from memory potions to sleeping draughts."Please?" The wolf's eyes dragged from the cup up to mine, like he was trying to parse out whatever was inside of it. "I promise, I wouldn't have gone through all this work to keep you alive just to poison you."

The wolf snorted. Again, I had the distinct feeling that if he'd have been human, he would have just rolled his eyes.

"Please?" He brought his head closer to me, finally, and I set the cup underneath his maw, watching him as he opened his mouth and began to lap up the liquid, that giant tongue sucking it down. He scrunched up his nose at the taste, but didn't stop drinking.

"That wasn't so bad, now was it?" I asked, scratching between his ears when he finished.

He gave me a look that said, *you've got to be kidding me.*

I giggled. "I'm sorry. But if it helps, then it's worth it, right?" Tomorrow, I'd have to see if I could get him outside. He'd been cooped up in my bed for days, and that couldn't be good for his joints.

His only answer was to lay his head on his paws, curling up next to me.

I yawned. There were a few things I had left to do around the house before bed, but all I wanted was to cuddle with this giant animal and sleep.

All of those things would be a problem for tomorrow.

For now, I just laid my head down on my pillow, content with this giant, wild animal to serve as my cozy blanket.

CHAPTER FOUR

barrett

There was something wrong. I couldn't shift back to my human body.

And my wolf was too damn comfortable letting our mate pet him to care.

Dammit, I needed to get back out there. At this point, the trail was probably cold.

I'd spent too many days lazying away in her house, sleeping as my body stitched itself back together. Licking at my wounds, I hoped my saliva would help. I was almost fully healed—I knew it. And yet, there was a tightness to my body that hadn't existed before. Each step I took still felt like needles in my side.

But I knew I needed to do it.

My mate had left me this morning, heading to her job. I'd deduced that she must have worked at a bakery, because she came home smelling faintly of coffee and baked goods every day. I had a faint recollection of collapsing outside of one, of being brought into a large kitchen filled with appliances, but all of the memories from that night were hazy.

The memory of her was the strongest.

Still, she was so sweet to me, considering she thought I was a wild wolf. There was no fear in her eyes—not as she stroked my head or told me what a good boy I was as she continued to feed me those disgusting potions. At least they were working, even if it was slow. Whatever had attacked me had messed with my shifter healing abilities, and whatever the witch had sent was doing its job.

How many days had passed? I couldn't keep track. I didn't have my phone or any of my belongings. All of my stuff was still at the inn I'd been staying at before I'd caught the trail of the reported monster living in the woods.

I was stranded here. No clothes, no way to contact anyone.

But... *she* was here, so maybe this was where I was supposed to be.

With each painful step, I padded around the house, using my nose to smell around. I couldn't explain why I wanted to explore my mate's house, only that I wanted to get to know her better. To understand the person the fates had decided to bless me with.

Her sugary smell was everywhere in this house—like it had seeped into the very walls. I didn't smell any other males here, which satisfied me more than it should have. Nor had she brought another man home in the last week or so since she'd rescued me.

I preened at the thought. It shouldn't have made me happy that she seemed to be single, but I was glad I didn't have to fight someone else for her. An alpha wolf who found their mate was prone to jealousy and was known be quite possessive.

We didn't share. When a wolf bonded with their mate, it was for life. Not that *we* were anywhere close to bonding. Especially when she didn't even know who—or what—I was.

There were plants scattered everywhere, small pots that

looked healthy and well loved. Collections of crystals, dried flowers, and a pile of books sat on the table next to her couch. The entire house was full of rich, warm colors, obviously well taken care of.

The only other smell in this house belonged to whatever animal lived in the large cage in her living room. I stared at it, sitting on my hind legs. The creature burrowed under the bedding of what looked to be paper shredding, poking its head as it took me in.

It was a hedgehog, who wiggled its little nose at me as it seemed to sniff the air. I wasn't a threat to her pet—though my senses told me this was a deeper connection than just of a pet and owner. The way the little beast stared at me, as if trying to parse out my intentions, felt different.

I'm not going to hurt her, I wanted to tell it. *I'm going to keep her safe.* My little healer was precious, and there was no way I could ever let her come to harm.

We were in a staring contest, the hedgehog and I, and I refused to be the one to break.

Finally, I looked longingly outside out the sliding glass back door, feeling the urge to run unfold under my skin. My wolf wanted it—no, *needed* it.

But we were in no shape to run. And I knew our mate would give us a scolding if we split any of the wounds open and ended up bleeding again.

Plus, I didn't want to ruin her bed. The comforter was cozy, and it was ten times better of a sleep than I'd ever gotten at home.

Maybe that was just her.

Finally, I gave up, curling in a ball in front of the front door so I could wait for my mate to return to me.

"I'm home," my mate called. "Sorry it took me longer than I expected, I stopped by the general store to pick up a few things, but the line was long, and..." She blinked, like she just realized I was sitting on the floor and not on her bed where she'd left me. A little gasp left her lips. "You got up."

I couldn't help the involuntary wag of my tail at the sound of her voice. At seeing her sweet form in front of me.

Her shoulder length ginger hair with those blunt bangs was wavy, and she was wearing a pair of black denim jeans today—along with the pair of black combat boots she wore most days—and a cozy dark green turtle neck. She'd even done a little bit of makeup, highlighting her blue eyes.

"I hope you didn't get into anything while I was gone." She narrowed her eyes at me as she carried her bags over to the kitchen counter, and then turned back to look at me. "Do you want to... go out?" My mate looked almost embarrassed, a little pink blush blooming over her cheeks. "It's been awhile."

Yes. I did want that. My wolf let out a bark of confirmation.

Standing up, I hobbled over towards the door and sat, waiting for her to open it for me.

"I'll take that as your answer," she laughed, letting me out the door. I trudged out to the yard, relieving myself behind a tree before padding back to her, sitting in front of her. "Good boy," she praised.

I wagged my tail. I *was* a good boy, wasn't I?

Wait, fuck. What was I doing? I wasn't a dog. I was a human, dammit. And I needed to get back to my human form. It wasn't good for shifters to spend this much time in their animal form.

I knew some shifters who had spent so long as their wolves that they'd gone feral, and I was *not* having that happen to me.

Leaving me sitting, she walked over to the cage, reaching her hand in and pulling out the small creature, who curled itself into a small ball. "Hi, Nutmeg, my sweet girl." My mate scratched under the hedgehog's chin. "How was *your* day? Our big scary wolf friend didn't try to scare you, right?" Her eyes drifted over to me.

Nope. I was a perfect gentleman.

Nutmeg—the hedgehog—climbed into her shoulder, cuddling up against my mate before giving me a discerning look.

I was a little jealous of her, because she could nuzzle against my mate, while I couldn't. Pouting, I let out a few whimpers as she lavished the tiny creature with attention before returning it to the enclosure.

Gods, I was acting like a pup right now, not a full-grown adult.

Following her to the kitchen, I tried not to get in her way as she unpacked the bags from the grocery store.

"I brought you a steak," she said, and I wagged my tail at the thought of a delicious, juicy steak. "Thought maybe it might cheer you up after all those potions." A whine left my throat at the thought of drinking that bitter concoction again. "Don't worry. You're mostly healed, so I don't have another one today."

Letting out a sigh of relief, I watched her as she opened up the packaging with the raw steak, and then looked down at me. "Should I cook it, or..."

While I'd had my fair share of raw meat as a wolf, I definitely was still a human who preferred it cooked. *Please.*

She nodded to herself as I perked up my ears. "Okay, then.

Guess we're cooking a steak." She muttered under her breath. "For a wolf. Goddess, when did my life get so fucking weird?"

I yipped once in agreement.

If she knew how truly bizarre this situation was, what would she think? Would she accept me? My mate had a tender heart. I could see it in the way she took care of me, even when she didn't have to. She could have left me in that alley to bleed out and die. She could have taken me to a veterinarian, someone who had a lot more experience treating dogs and wild animals.

But instead, she'd taken one look at me, and jumped into action. Yet, I still knew that there was a chance she wouldn't accept me when she found out what I was. Though I'd only heard bits and pieces of her conversation that first night with the witches—it was evident that this town didn't even know about us.

What had happened that this city had closed itself off from the world?

I needed to find out.

After I got my strength back and could *shift*. I missed my human body, my ability to speak. I couldn't communicate with her like this—not until we'd bonded. So, for the moment, I was stuck.

It wasn't all bad living with her. Her presence calmed a piece of me that had always been restless. I was still trying to figure out how the fates had matched me with a witch, and not a wolf. In the beginning, I'd thought maybe I'd just been hallucinating, but her scent wasn't like any shifter I'd ever met.

She was a witch.

I watched her move around the kitchen, doing things I'd never even imagined—and with my job, the unimaginable was my specialty. But seeing her float things through the air, to summon something from the cupboards without even batting an eyelash was... incredible.

There was no doubt about it. I was in awe of my little healer. The mate who didn't even know we were destined. I couldn't deny the pull towards her though. The faint thread that kept us tethered. Every time she left the house, I wanted to go with her. To be by her side. The way she was taking care of me—nursing me back to health—was like nothing I'd ever experienced before.

A whimper slipped free from my wolf at the thought of leaving her unprotected. She was small—five foot two, maybe —and though she had beautiful curves, her body wasn't covered in muscles, like mine.

I licked my paw at the thought. We were strong. *We can protect her,* my wolf insisted. *She has us now.*

"I'm sorry," she said, putting the now-cooked steak onto a plate and setting it onto the floor for me. "I'm sure you're starving."

Dipping my head down, I sniffed the meat. It smelled like the best thing I'd had in months.

Being out on the road meant I didn't often get a home cooked meal, living off of fast food and diner meals. I gobbled it down in a few bites, glad for my extra sharp canines that helped me rip through the meat. The steak was juicy, tender, and perfectly cooked—still a little rare, which my wolf was happy about. He didn't like it when the meat was too done.

Damn bastard was perfectly happy wagging his tail as we ate, and I knew our mate was watching us with amusement.

Settle down, I scolded my wolf. *She's going to think we're some sort of trained house pet.*

I really hoped with how comfortable she was with me in her house that she didn't make a habit of picking up injured animals off the street and nursing them back to health. What would I do if I came home one day and found her cuddling an *actual* dangerous animal?

Pushing the plate towards her with my nose, I watched as she cleaned up the kitchen before sitting down at the table to eat the meal she'd cooked for herself.

I nuzzled my head into her hand, brushing up against her before laying at her feet. I had a good vantage point of the door to watch for intruders.

She scratched between my ears. "You're just my little protector now, aren't you?"

Yes, I was.

When she finished eating and got up to stretch, I hopped up on the couch, laying my head down on one of the pillows as my mate cleaned up the kitchen.

I was mostly healed, and there was no reason I needed to sleep next to her. Only that I *wanted* to—but was that a good enough reason? I wasn't sure. Not when she didn't know who I was. Dammit, she didn't even know my name.

Her footsteps were soft as she padded over to me, kneeling down on the furry rug until we were eye level."Are you coming?" She looked towards her bedroom.

Raising my head, I looked at her and then back down at the couch.

Did I want to sleep out here, separated from my mate? *No.* No I did not.

So I hopped up, following behind her, padding across the wooden floor till we reached her bedroom. I hopped up— ignoring the slight sting pain that still radiated through my muscles from jumping—and curled myself into a ball on her bed as she changed into her pajamas.

But I didn't look—because I was a good wolf who was not trying to catch a peek.

When she came out, sliding under the covers, my mate

wrapped her arms around me. She burrowed her face into my fur, cuddling against me like I was her own personal heater and blanket in one.

For once in my life, I couldn't complain, because my mate was wrapped around me, and the rest of my problems, well... they were later problems.

Tonight, I was just going to enjoy this.

CHAPTER FIVE

eryne

T'd never slept so peacefully. Warm and surrounded by the coziest smell of all time—like spice and leaves—I was more content than I'd ever been. Nuzzling my head further against my pillow, I let out a happy sigh.

Apparently, I should have adopted a wolf as a pet way sooner, if it meant I was getting this good of sleep. Last night, he'd been so cute, wagging his tail when I got home and perking up his ears as I made him the steak. I was probably getting too comfortable, inviting him into my bed like he was my new dog, but what did I care? He was so soft, and... *wait*.

Something hard pressed against my back. My eyes flew open, and I held my breath as looked down. I wasn't wrapped around the fuzzy, soft wolf this morning.

At some point in my sleep, I'd rolled over, and there was an arm wrapped around my stomach. A very *human* arm, coated in a fine dusting of reddish hair. I sucked in a breath.

Okay, Eryne, I tried to calm myself down, breathing in deep. *I'm sure there's a simple explanation.* My mind raced, but I couldn't come up with any ways to explain what was happening.

There was a man in my bed—in a spot where I knew the red wolf had been when I'd fallen asleep. A man who was spooning me, which meant that—*oh, goddess.* I turned my head just a little bit, confirming my fears.

He was totally, completely naked. My cheeks burned, and I tried to wiggle out of his grasp, but the arm around me was tight.

I had to look at the facts.

Last night, I'd fallen asleep next to the wolf. This morning, there was a very *naked* man in my bed. A man with dark auburn hair and a loose bandage wrapped around his leg.

What did this mean? My heart stuttered in my chest. It was almost like I couldn't accept the reality that was staring me in the face.

Maybe Rina was right, and our elders had been keeping something from us. After the Clarke sisters married a pair of demon brothers, nothing should have surprised me. But this *did.*

I didn't move. Didn't breathe.

The man groaned, rubbing his nose against my neck, and I held in my gasp. He was still sleeping, but if I moved even a fraction of an inch—

All I could do was stare at the muscular arm curled around me. I was wearing a large, oversized t-shirt and panties, but no shorts. It didn't really seem necessary to wear super thick pajamas when the wolf kept my bed nice and toasty. Only now, I was regretting the decision. My t-shirt had ridden up, and there was only a thin piece of cotton covering my bikini area.

His hand creeped lower down my abdomen as he continued to bury his face against me, and I didn't know what to do. My face flushed. Was he going to... touch me?

And why was I watching all of this in slow-motion, like it was happening to someone else? Like I was powerless to stop it. Like I didn't *want* to.

I let out a small exhale.

Was he having a dream? His fingertips reached the waistband of my underwear, and then they... stopped. *Froze.* I could instantly hear his breathing change behind me.

"*Fuck.*" His voice was thick—*deep*—but hoarse, like it hadn't been used in a while. I supposed it hadn't. It had been almost two weeks since the night of the full moon. The man sat up, looming over me. "I'm sorry. I didn't mean..." He cleared his throat.

"You're—" I blinked at him, my brain finally accepting what I'd been struggling with the last few minutes.

He wasn't just a wolf at all. All the confirmation I needed was staring right back at me in those amber eyes. Those *human* eyes. Somehow, I'd felt it all along.

"You're the wolf?" I stuttered out.

I felt my eyes practically bug out as I took him in. His immense size... *everywhere.* His gaze followed mine, looking down.

"Godsdamn." He grabbed a pillow, covering his well-endowed erection, like he'd only just realized he was completely naked. "I know this may be hard to believe." His chest was muscular, covered in a thin layer of red hair, and he had freckles *everywhere.*

"You think?" My jaw dropped. "I-I've been nursing you back to health. You were a human the whole time? How is this possible?"

He swallowed roughly. "I'm not a human—not really." He tilted his head to the side, and I could almost picture his wolf form doing it the same way, those ears perked up on the top of his head. His nostrils flared. "But you're not either. You're a *witch.*"

"You don't have to say it like it's a bad thing," I said, wrapping my arms around myself, hoping to hide my body's reaction to his naked one. I wasn't wearing a bra, and my nipples were hard, poking through my thin shirt. "If you're not a human, and you're not a wolf, what are you?" My eyes widened. "You're not a demon, are you?"

"Did I say I *wasn't* a wolf?" The man raised one auburn eyebrow. "I'm not a *demon*, no. Though I'd love to find out how one of those made your acquaintance." He let out a bark of a laugh, like that idea was preposterous. "I'm a shifter." He looked at me expectantly, but I just blinked. "A wolf shifter. You... don't know about us, do you?"

I shook my head. "I've never heard of anyone with that ability. Though, to be fair, until last year, I didn't know demons existed, either." I frowned, a thought popping into my head. "It's like the town founders chose to ward us off from the outside world instead of telling us what, exactly, was out there."

He winced. "Well, guess that's why getting through the wards hurt like a bitch." His hand reached up, massaging his neck. I wasn't really sure what he was talking about—the wards were supposed to keep us safe and keep humans out, so why would they *hurt?*

"What attacked you?" I asked, reaching out running my fingers down the scars on his bare chest absentmindedly. I couldn't help it. His abs were rock-hard, and even though there were still some cuts and bruises, he looked like he'd never been hurt at all.

Realizing what I was doing, I pulled my hand back, clutching it against my chest.

"Honestly, I don't know." The man sighed. "That night... My memories are hazy at best. All I can remember is flashes of black, and teeth, and then dragging myself towards this sweet scent."

"Oh." The bakery, I supposed.

I had no idea why I wasn't freaking out right now. Why I felt comfortable around him. It must have been because of all of the time I'd spent with him in wolf form—at least, that was what I was going with.

He reached up, tucking a strand of hair behind my ear. "You are so..."

My cheeks were even redder now, and I scrambled to find something else to say. "I-I'm Eryne, by the way."

"Eryne." He said my name like he was tasting it on his tongue, and I decided I loved the way it sounded in his deep voice. "I'm Barrett. It's nice to finally meet you. Officially, I suppose." He chuckled.

Barrett. After so long of just calling him the wolf, I finally had a name. And gods, he was beautiful. It was hard not to ogle his naked chest. All of him, really.

"Should we maybe..." I looked away. "Finish the rest of this conversation when you're not naked?"

"Oh." Barrett looked down at the pillow he was clutching over his waist. "Well, I uh... I actually don't have any clothes?"

I stared at him. "What do you mean?" I mean, logically, I should have assumed that, but I was still a little dumfounded.

"Kind of the thing about being a shifter. You lose your clothes when you change forms." He tilted his head. "Everything I have is back at the motel I was staying at. I'll need to get back there to get my stuff." He ran a hand through his auburn hair.

It was the same color as his fur.

"Huh." I mused out loud, staring at him. He was handsome, with a sculpted jaw and freckles that dotted his face, shoulders and collarbones. Though handsome didn't begin to describe Barrett. He was simply... *gorgeous.*

He grunted. "What?"

"You know how people always ask, *does the carpet match the drapes?*" I asked, fiddling with a strand of my hair.

Barrett blinked. "You—*what?*"

I pointed at his hair. "Your hair is the same color as your fur."

"Yeah. That's kind of how it works." He thrust his hands in his hair—and gods, they were big—and tugged at the ends. "So, do you want me to—" He gestured down *there.*

Oh my goddess. I turned around, hearing him get up off the bed. "Right. I'll leave you alone. If you want to shower, there's towels in there. In the meantime, I'll..." I turned to look at him and lost my train of thought.

He was *tall.* Definitely over six foot, and that shouldn't have surprised me, given how massive his wolf form was. But I was still mesmerized. Struck stupid. Dumfounded.

Unable to make a single cohesive word come out of my mouth.

"*Wow.*" Shit, had I just said that out loud?

Barrett kept the pillow over his waist, but his thighs were thick, corded with muscle, and my mouth was dry.

"Um. There's probably a pair of old sweats in my closet you could wear," I squeaked. They were way too big on me, so I had no idea why I'd kept them all these years, only that they were cozy in the cold winter months.

He made a grumbling sound. "Don't look at me like that," he said, still holding the pillow in place. His voice was rough—like gravel, and it scraped over my skin.

I tried to ignore the way my nipples pebbled at the command.

Sure, he was attractive, but it wasn't like I was actually going to *act* on that attraction, right? Even if he was hot as sin, and he'd had his erection pressed up against me this morning. I was trying not to think about what it felt like, how *big* he was.

"I'm gonna go." I needed to get out of here before I did something stupid. "I'll be back with... clothes." I grabbed a baseball cap from my closet, pulling it over my hair, as well as a pair of jeans and a baggy sweater. Grabbing a pair of socks and my favorite boots, I hustled it out of there, needing some air.

Fanning at my warm cheeks as I stood on my front porch, I was grateful for the cool air to aid me in cooling off.

I pulled out my phone, thinking about my options. I really only had one, unless I called a friend and asked them to bring me their brother—or boyfriend's—clothes. And the thought of doing that was mortifying.

Even more mortifying than buying men's clothes from Dark Moon Fashions—the biggest clothing boutique in town.

But I could pull my big girl panties on and go find him something.

/

"And you had *no* idea?" Rina asked, blinking as we thumbed through the racks at Dark Moon an hour later.

I'd just finished summarizing what all had happened with the wolf—Barrett—to them. Well, I'd left out a few key details, including waking up to him wrapped around me, *naked,* and the very generous package he was, um, packing. Also that I'd gotten attached to said wolf enough to let him sleep in my bed.

They'd definitely think I was pathetic and lonely if I revealed that.

"Of course not," I said, letting out a huff as I pulled a jacket off the rack, inspecting it. So far, we'd found a few pairs of pants I was pretty sure would fit him—though I was really guessing at the size. "You think I was caring for an injured wolf because I knew he was actually a *shifter?*" I whispered the last word, though it still came out louder than I intended.

"She's got a point, Rin," Wendy said, nudging Rina out of the way as she pulled out a soft gray henley. "We were there that night. He really did seem like a wolf." Wendy was wearing a sports bra and matching leggings, like she'd come right from the yoga studio. She always looked put together, even after a workout, which was much better than the sweaty mess I became.

I bit my lip. "Mostly. He certainly had some... quirks." Like following me around like a dog. And the way he whined at me, but growled at Rina and Wendy that night. "Either way, I need to get him clothes, and then I'm going to take him back to wherever he was staying, help him get his stuff, and then send him on his way. After that, he's not my problem anymore. Clearly he's all healed now." Saying the words felt almost cruel.

There was part of me, however small, that felt bonded to the wolf I'd spent night after night caring for. The one I'd checked on just to make sure he was still breathing. It hurt to think that I was just going to kick him out and send him back out there.

What if whatever had come after him did again?

But he wasn't from here.

Our little town had enough drama last year after Willow and Luna had revealed that they'd fallen in love with two demon princes. If everyone discovered that there was more than we knew outside, who knew what sort of cataclysmic reactions it would set off?

I thought about his comment about the wards. Maybe everything we knew was a lie.

But was it my job to expose that? *No.* Though the little voice in my head couldn't quite agree.

"You should find out what really happened first," Wendy said. "We need to know if we need to protect the town from whatever it was that attacked him. It could still be out there."

It was like she was reading my mind. "Do you think we can really go after it? I mean, Barrett's a *wolf.* A giant wolf. And you saw what happened to him."

"Yeah. It looked like someone used him as a chew toy," Rina retorted.

I glared at her. "If that happened to a witch, they'd be done for—*instantly.* None of us can survive that, and you know it." Even with an entire coven, what hope did we have against something with claws or sharp teeth?

"So we ask for help. If there's more people out there like him, wouldn't they be willing to lend a hand? Isn't it worth it to at least try?" Wendy crossed her arms over her chest. She was ever the pragmatic one, while Rina often jumped to fighting with her fists first and asking questions later. Between the three of us, we balanced each other out.

She had a point. "But can I ask him to do that? To put himself in danger all over again?" My heart clenched at the thought.

Even if I didn't know the man, I'd become attached to the wolf. I loved the way he would follow me around, the way he'd tilt his head to the side and perk an ear up, and the way he curled up at my feet. Maybe I liked the way my loneliness had been cured, even if just for a bit.

Wendy and Rina both shrugged. And I knew what that meant, too.

Carrying the pile of clothes we'd found to the register, I sighed. "Alright, I'll ask him. But no promises."

I didn't even really know him. It was a reminder that I needed to keep my walls up. He might have not been a wild wolf, but he was still a stranger. A stranger who needed my help.

And now, I needed his.

CHAPTER SIX

barrett

It was amazing how much better I felt after a hot shower after so many days trapped inside my wolf's body.

I felt like a human again. I wasn't sure how I'd shifted back in the middle of the night unconsciously, though it wasn't unheard of. My guess was I'd felt comfortable in bed with my mate, and it had been an involuntary change.

Being wrapped around my mate when I woke up had been the best feeling of my life. At least, until I realized that it wasn't a dream, and I'd been two seconds from dipping my fingers under the waistband of her tiny panties. I'd been harder than I'd ever been in my life, having her curves all pressed up against me, her sweet smell in my nose. I was losing it.

When I got out of the shower, I wrapped a towel around my waist, not bothering to look for the sweats she'd mentioned earlier. Honestly, I just hoped that she found something that actually fit. After I had clothes, I needed to find a way back to my things. I needed to call Ezra and talk about what I'd found. Though I didn't fool myself into believing we were *friends*, I knew he had my back.

And I needed to know if he had experienced anything similar up in his neck of the woods.

The door to the bedroom opened, and then my mate was there, her little hedgehog curled on her shoulder as she carried in a large plastic bag.

Eryne. Yes, I liked the way her name sat on my tongue. I still couldn't believe I'd found her. That she was mine. My wolf let out a grumble of appreciation as he watched her.

And she had no idea.

It had been clear when we'd woken up that she didn't know we were mates. But she hadn't completely freaked out, either, so maybe that was good? I wasn't sure what the proper protocol was here. For shifters, when we found our mates, the second we locked eyes, the bond was there.

And we *knew* we were meant to be together.

Did witches not feel that? Was it possible this was completely one sided, and I was wrong about her being my mate? I hated that thought. It made my mouth taste fill with bile.

No, my wolf insisted. *She is ours.*

"Here," Eryne said, handing me the bundle of clothes as she diverted her eyes. Our hands brushed, and sparks ran down my arm. "Hopefully there's a few things in there that you can wear. I wasn't sure what you'd like, so I got a bunch. We can return the rest."

"Thank you," I said, truly taking this moment to look at her. I had earlier, but not like this. Not when I could appreciate how much smaller than me she was, how that ginger hair perfectly complimented her skin. "I'll go change."

She dipped her head, and then looked at the bathroom. "I'm going to shower now, and then after I'm finished, maybe we could go get something to eat? I'm starving, and this feels like a conversation we shouldn't have on empty stomachs."

I swallowed.

She was going to tell me to leave. I could see it in her eyes. She was kicking me out already.

My mate didn't want me.

Well, what she didn't know is that I would fight for her. No matter what it took, I wasn't giving up—not yet.

The little diner in the middle of town was quaint. It was covered in halloween decorations—despite it still being almost a month away—but I supposed that was part of the charm. It felt like the entire town was here, crowded into booths and chatting at tables.

It also seemed like everyone was looking at us.

But maybe they were all just staring at the beauty across the table from me, who didn't seem to realize just how gorgeous she was.

Her short copper hair had dried into loose waves, and she'd pulled on a pair of dark jeans with those boots she seemed to wear, along with a cream colored turtleneck. Her earrings were a pair of shooting stars. I'd stared at her collection in her room —she had dozens of pairs, all different dangly earrings, that she seemed to rotate her way through. I wasn't sure I'd seen her repeat a pair yet.

What did I look like, sitting across from her? Luckily, the jeans and gray henley she'd found for me fit, and the coat, while on the larger side, wasn't too shabby. They didn't smell quite right, but I was trying to ignore that fact, knowing my shifter senses were sharper than the average humans. She hadn't even attempted to find a pair of shoes, not wanting to guess my size, so we'd stopped at the second-hand store before heading into the diner. I wiggled my toes in the pair of work boots I'd found, thankful they were decently broken in.

"What attacked you?" Eryne asked once again, after we'd ordered our food.

At least this time, we could have this conversation while fully clothed.

It had been hard to pay attention earlier. Waking up next to my mate, my body reacted, and it had been hard to control it. Even though I'd hated when she'd left, it had been the right call.

It was too soon to touch her.

She barely even knew what I was.

"I don't know," I said, even though I had my suspicions. I wanted to protect her—the worst thing that could happen was her getting in the middle of it and getting hurt. Plus, if I had to leave her soon, I didn't want to leave my mate unprotected. I'd been sent here for a reason, and I still had to finish my mission.

She raised an eyebrow. "You don't know?"

I shook my head. "I told you, my memories of the night of the attack are all jumbled. It was unexpected." I remembered her, her scent, her soothing voice. But the actual incident was nothing more than disjointed flashes of information.

"But..." her voice dropped to a whisper. "Those were *teeth* marks, weren't they?"

My wounds ached at the thought of the being ripping into my skin. I'd seen things she couldn't even imagine. I changed the subject, not wanting to talk about that feeling of cold, of emptiness. "You mentioned demons before, right? If you don't know about shifters, how do you know about demons?"

I'd met a few demons in my time, and they were smart. Cunning. Capable of deceit on scales humans couldn't even comprehend.

Eryne bit her lower lip. "My boss—Willow, the one who gave me the healing potions for you—she fell in love with a demon last year. His name is Damien. He's not a *bad* demon though. He's a good guy. Loves Willow. They're expecting their first baby together."

My eyes widened. "They are?" That was... something.

"They're soul mates," she offered, tapping her fingers on the table. "It's hard to argue with fate, don't you think?"

If only you knew.

"That still doesn't answer my question about how you didn't know shifters existed."

Eryne pinched the spot between her eyebrow. "It's like, you know, growing up, how your parents tell you tales about all the things that go bump in the night to scare you into being a good kid? Because they want you to be scared of the monsters under your bed so you don't act out?"

"Sure."

"We had stories. Legends. But they were just that. Until Damien and his brother showed up, this town has been a sanctuary for witches for the hundreds of years. The only people who can come here are witches, for our own safety. The wards were supposed to be impenetrable." Eryne frowned at me. "How did *you* get through, anyway?"

I shrugged. "Must be weakening." Though that was only part of my theory.

She furrowed her brow, but continued on. "Our elders taught us that these other beings—demons, vampires, *were- wolves*—were ghost stories. Things to be feared, sure, but not something any of us ever expected to come face to face with. I guess we just took it at face value since it seemed so far fetched. None of us had ever seen any of those things, so of course it wasn't true. And yet..." She gestured towards me.

"And yet it is," I concluded. "I'm not a werewolf, though. Just a shifter."

My little healer scrunched up her nose. "What's the difference, exactly?"

"Werewolves aren't wolf *or* human. They're something *other*. Forced to change during each full moon, feral and rabid. Shifters were... blessed, if the stories are true, by a coven of witches many millennia ago. In exchange for use of our lands for their ceremonies, they gave us the ability to shape-shift into our wolves at will. No full moon needed."

"If that's true, why didn't we know about *you?*"

I gave her a sad smile. "Maybe more things have been lost to time than either of us truly know." I rested my hand over hers. "But I think it's our responsibility to figure it out. To right the wrongs of our ancestors. We're all being persecuted by humans. Isn't it better to have strength in numbers? To have a town like this be a safe haven for all?"

She scrunched up her nose. "That's pretty deep for ten o'clock in the morning, Barrett..." She looked at me, a question in her eyes. "You know, I don't even know your last name."

"Lockwood," I answered. "Barrett Lockwood."

"Eryne Fowler," she said in response, before holding out her hand. "Pleased to make your acquaintance, I guess."

We shook, and something unfurled in my chest. I couldn't explain why I instantly felt better, but I did.

"How old are you?" Eryne asked, studying my face. I looked scruffier than normal, in desperate need of a shave and a haircut, so it was a fair question.

I chuckled at her blatant perusal. "Twenty-seven. How old are you?"

She let out a breath. "Twenty-five. I thought you were going to say something crazy, like you were hundreds of years old."

I ran my hands through my hair. "No. We age much in the same way that humans do—as witches do."

Our lifespans were similar as well, though both of our species would outlive humans.

Our food came, and we were silent for a few minutes, taking bites of our food.

I was *ravenous,* and after barely eating for the last two weeks, I knew why. My metabolism was ten times faster than a regular humans, part of how we managed to heal so quickly. It also meant I had ordered *way* more food than the witch opposite me, and I was quickly gobbling down dish after dish.

When I finished most of my first plate, I looked up at her. She'd ordered a cinnamon roll with a side of apples, and it was so *her,* I almost smiled. Watching her was proving to be an enjoyable pastime.

"I never thanked you for taking care of me," I said, pausing eating to stare at her.

"Oh." Eryne blushed, dragging a forkful of food through the puddle of icing on her plate. "It was no problem, really. I couldn't just leave you there to bleed out and..." *die.* I heard the unspoken word.

"You could have. For all you knew, I was some big, scary wolf, who could have just as easily snapped your neck with my jaw."

"I did consider that," she admitted, not making eye contact. "But only for a moment."

Hmm. So she wasn't scared of me, then? "What changed your mind?"

"Your eyes. From the first moment I saw them, I thought they looked so human. Now I know why." She giggled to herself. "You also acted more like a domesticated dog than a wild animal."

"Blame my wolf," I said, rolling my eyes. "He likes you."

Her eyes widened. "Your wolf? Is he like... a separate being that lives inside of you? Can you talk to each other?"

I shook my head. "He's an extension of myself. I *am* the wolf, and the wolf *is* me, but it's more than that. I don't know how to explain it, other than we're two sides of the same coin."

"That's..." Eryne twirled a piece of ginger hair around her finger.

"Insane?"

She snorted. "I was going to say incredible. But sure, Wolf-Man, we can go with that, too."

I chuckled. It was so nice to be able to talk like this, instead of being forced not to speak to her in wolf form for all those days.

"About my stuff—" I started. I'd come here on foot, and I really needed to get it. Otherwise I'd need to buy a new phone and set up a secure connection to contact Ezra.

"Oh. Right." She looked down at her plate. "I can take you there, if you want. I have a car, and I'm happy to drop you off—"

I cut her off. "I wasn't going to—"

"It's fine."

A growl left my throat. "I'm not leaving," I said, making sure she understood. "I just need my phone, and some of my equipment. But whatever brought me here, I think I need to see it through."

She just didn't know that part of what I was talking about was *her*.

"Oh." Her blue eyes held mine. "Are you sure?"

I nodded. "Plus, I need to repay you for the last two weeks. And this meal."

Eryne waived me off. "You really don't have to do that. I don't mind."

"I insist."

"Fine. But only because I think you're right. We do need to figure out what's going on around here." She dropped her voice. "And I don't think I can do it alone."

"You don't have to," I promised.

She'd never have to be alone again if I had anything to say about it.

"*This* is where you were staying?" Eryne asked, pulling into the parking lot. She'd insisted on driving, so I was currently in the passenger seat. Her car was small—just like her—and I was looking forward to having a moment to stretch before I drove back to Pleasant Grove.

I shrugged, looking at the run-down motel. Sure, it didn't look great on the outside, but the bed had been clean, and that was all I really cared about after a long day of tracking. "It got the job done."

"Wow."

We got out of the car, doors slamming shut. "That's my car," I said, pointing across the parking lot to the retro sports car I drove.

"Wow. I didn't peg you for a car guy."

I chuckled. "To be fair, a few hours ago, you didn't even peg me for a *guy.*"

"The fur was very convincing." Eryne stuck out her lip in a fake pout. "Who could blame me?"

I liked this. We were almost... flirting? It felt so natural. I laughed, and the sound felt like something opening up inside of me. A chance to not be alone.

After all these years, I never could have imagined how good it might feel to know the possibility was there. We had an easy rapport—a comfort that felt almost too good to be true. I didn't want to ruin it by saying something stupid.

What if I told her the truth, and everything changed? I couldn't risk it.

"They probably emptied the room since it's been a few nights. I probably need to go check in with the front desk." I'd left my car keys and everything in my bag that night before I'd shifted.

"Okay." Eryne stayed by my side. I liked that she wanted to be next to me, instead of choosing the easy way out and waiting in the car. "Let's go get it."

An hour later, we were back on the road. I'd successfully managed to get all my things back—it only took going a little alpha male at the front desk guy, and some growling. My car was, thankfully, in working order. If I'd waited a few more days, it would have been towed.

Eryne was right in front of me as we drove back to Pleasant Grove, and I was doing everything I could to keep her car in sight. I would have much rather had her with me in mine, but at least things could change now.

As I drove through the wards, the sensation fizzling over my skin but not burning this time, I wondered if what we talked about earlier was true.

Were the wards weakening? Or were they failing entirely? Unless it something else entirely. If the town had been set up so only witches could get in and out, that didn't explain how two demons had found this place. Magic from that many witches was powerful. Eryne was right. Something was going on here.

She pulled into her driveway, and I took the time to really appreciate her small house. I'd been a wolf the first time I'd entered her house—and passed out from the blood loss—and this morning, I'd had too much on my mind. But it was cute.

There was a porch swing on the front deck, and even though the house only had one story, it had a charm to it.

Honestly, this place reminded me so much of Walnut Ridge. Even though we were a few hours from the town I'd grown up, it felt comforting.

Though maybe that didn't have anything to do with the town, or the house. Maybe it was all my mate.

CHAPTER SEVEN

eryne

I didn't know why I was filled with so much apprehension as Barrett followed me home in his car. Maybe it was because he didn't have to stick around anymore, despite saying he would.

Still, I let out a breath of relief when he pulled into my driveway, parking his car next to mine.

He wasn't leaving. At least, not yet.

Though I was still holding my breath as he climbed out of his car, trying not to appreciate the view. He looked *good* in the clothes I found for him—stylish, even. Like those things had always been meant to go together.

"Why do you look so surprised?" Barrett asked, throwing his bags over his shoulder. "I told you I wasn't going anywhere. I'm going to help you find out what happened."

I gnawed on my lip. "I know. It's just... I was worried, I guess."

He was healed, but I could still tell that he was limping a little from the gait of his walk. He was favoring his left side— the one that hadn't been mauled as badly—and there wasn't much I could do for him at this point. The only thing he needed was time.

After following me inside, he dropped his bags on the floor, and then looked at the couch. "I'll sleep here tonight," he announced.

I leaned against the wall. "You're barely going to fit on that, Barrett." His eyes flared as I said his name, and it made me want to say it again and again. "Even when you were a wolf, it's not that big of a couch."

He crossed his arms over his chest. "I'm going to protect you. And that means I can't let you out of my sight. So, I'm staying here."

I frowned. "Am I in danger or something?"

He avoided my gaze. "You might be."

"I think I can take my chances."

Barrett let out a small growl, and then cleared his throat. "Sorry. Like I said, my wolf likes you. He, uh... doesn't want to be apart from you." He grimaced. "I'm sorry if this makes you uncomfortable."

It didn't. And I couldn't quite explain that out loud. "Barrett?" My voice was soft.

"Yes?" His head perked up—just like it did when he was a wolf.

"You can share my bed, if you want to. I only have the one, but we can both fit on it." Part of me knew what I was offering. After this morning, it felt insane not to acknowledge that this was crazy. But I couldn't help it. He'd told me his wolf liked me, so maybe it didn't hurt to admit this. Maybe I was a little attached, too. "I don't think I can sleep without your wolf anymore. He's like my own heater."

Maybe that was the wrong call. Maybe asking him to share my bed was just temptation after this morning. But I really did only have one bed in my house, and the idea of forcing him onto the couch when he was still a little banged up didn't sit right with me.

There was a rumbling sound that seemed to come from his chest, and he rubbed over the spot, like he didn't understand it himself. "Okay," he finally said. He picked up his bags once again. "After you, sugar."

Sugar. That was new. I was glad to be in front, because at least he couldn't see the blush on my cheeks. There was something about Barrett as a human that unsettled me—though maybe that wasn't the right word.

The man was a mystery, and I wanted to unravel him.

I wanted to understand what had brought him here, to Pleasant Grove.

To *me.*

After setting his bags down at the end of my bed, he looked around my room, like he was seeing it with a whole different set of eyes for the first time.

I was trying not to think about this morning, when I'd been all pressed up against his body. Was it wrong to ask him to do that again, just for science?

"I have to go to work," I blurted out. "I normally close." Even though I didn't need to. The café could operate just fine without me.

"Okay." He nodded his head, once, like that was totally fine.

"You'll be okay here?" I asked, hesitantly.

He furrowed his eyebrows. "No."

"No?"

"I'm coming with you."

My jaw dropped. "*What?*"

Barrett crossed his arms over his chest. "I've been stuck in this house for days. Besides this morning and getting my car, I've hardly even set foot outside."

"But..." I frowned.

He stepped closer to me, my entire body practically buzzing from the close proximity. I could feel his body heat, and it was hard to focus on anything else.

"Let me come with you, Eryne. Please. I need to see the town, too. Get a feel for what's going on."

"*Fine*," I relented, letting out a sigh. "But you can't get in my way."

He raised his hand. "Scouts honor. I'll just bring my laptop and stay at a table in the corner."

"Were you *actually* a Boy Scout?" I raised an eyebrow, crossing my arms over my chest.

The man just hummed. "We had our own version in Walnut Ridge. Wolves only." He winked. For some reason, I could picture little Barrett, dressed up in a uniform, running around with the other kids on a camping trip, and the thought made me smile.

"So... that's where you're from? Walnut Ridge?" I asked, wanting to know more about the mysterious man in front of me. I'd never heard of it before.

Barrett nodded. "Yeah. It's up in Vermont. Just a few hours away from here, actually."

Vermont. My heart sank. I knew he wasn't from *here,* but something about knowing he was so far away just drove home the fact that at some point, he would leave. It wasn't like I *really* expected him to be my knight in shining armor, here to sweep me off my feet, but I guess I'd just hoped that somehow...

I shook the thought away. *Not the time, Eryne,* I reminded myself.

"That's great," I said, turning my back to him as I grabbed my work bag from the spot I always left it. If I looked at him now, well... my face would betray my feelings.

And considering I hadn't even known the man before this morning, it made no sense.

He'd been a *wolf,* for goddess's sake. A wolf I'd been taking care of, who had been sharing my bed and letting me snuggle with him, because I'd thought he was an animal. Maybe I still hadn't fully processed that yet. He'd been stuck inside all along. A man who looked like he could bench my weight or run a four minute mile didn't need to be treated like... well, a dog. Heat crept into my cheeks, thinking of the way I'd babied him, telling him how he was a *good boy,* plus of all the conversations I'd had with myself.

There were some things you just didn't need a guy like that to know. Gods, I'd changed in front of him. What was wrong with me?

"Ready?" I asked, turning back to him. My broom was in the corner of my room, though on a day like today—the fog had burned off with the afternoon sun—I was perfectly content to walk to the shop.

He slung his bag over his shoulder. "Yeah. Let's go."

Barrett was sitting in the corner, just like he'd promised, though I noticed he seemed to be doing more staring at me than actually working. Though I wasn't exactly sure what he was working *on.*

I drummed my fingers against the countertop, aware that I was guilty of the same thing.

What was his job? Was he some sort of *paranormal investigator?* I didn't know why he had even been nearby, or what he was searching for by staying in town. I assumed he had a plan, but he hadn't shared it with me.

I made another coffee order—a shaken espresso for one of

our regulars, Olivia—and then turned back to the counter, finding a familiar looking man standing in front of me. The problem with living in such a small town—with such an involved community—is everyone knew everyone.

"Hi, Eryne." He pushed his glasses up his nose as he stepped up to the counter.

"Hey, Simon." I gave him a warm smile. "How's it going?"

We'd gone to high school together, and he was harmless, but also a shameless flirt with the girls. Though I'd never really paid much attention to guys when I was younger.

Now... I looked over at Barrett.

There was a scowl on his face, those amber eyes locked on mine.

I turned back to Simon, who was prattling on about his day and what had happened to him. Poor guy had definitely been hit with a bad luck hex, and I suspected I knew exactly who had done it, though I couldn't exactly *prove* it was Cait.

Still, she was the master of hexes, better than anyone else in her coven—or in Pleasant Grove in general.

"That sounds awful," I told him. "I hope you can get it figured out." I really meant that—but I also wasn't going to sell Cait out when I had no idea if she was the culprit.

"Thanks. You going to come out to the Enchanted Cauldron one of these nights?"

I hesitated. When was the last time I'd gone out? The last two weeks, I'd been so busy taking care of the wolf—of Barrett, I corrected myself—that all I'd done was work, eat, sleep, and check on him. There had been no time for a moment to myself.

"Maybe," I offered. Ghoul's Night was Friday, and it wouldn't be hard to convince my friends to go out with me. But... what about Barrett? Would he want to go? I worried my lower lip into my mouth. "We'll see."

He smiled, like he knew that was the most he was going to get. "Hope to see you around."

My phone lit up with a text on the counter next to me after he walked away, sitting at a table as he waited for his order.

> ???
> Who is he?

I frowned, looking up, only to find Barrett typing on his phone.

> ERYNE
> Barrett?

> Yes.

> When did you get my phone number?

> When you were in the shower.

> ... You did what now?

Scowling at him from across the room, I changed his name in my contacts as I waited for another text to come in.

> BARRETT
> Listen. Be mad at me later. Now, who is he?

> Just an old friend. We went to high school together. Relax.

> I don't like the way he was talking to you.

I could practically hear the growl rumbling in his chest from here.

> Good thing I didn't ask.

Shoving my phone into my pocket, I ignored him as I

continued working, taking orders, making drinks, and grab-bing pastries from the case.

What did it matter what he thought? We weren't together. He didn't get to feel possessive over me. I'd only just *met* the guy! He could fuck off, as far as I was concerned. Maybe I *should* tell him to sleep on the couch tonight.

My phone buzzed a few more times, but I ignored it until I slipped into the back room.

BARRETT

I'm sorry.

I told you, my wolf is attached. He's a little possessive.

A little?

I rolled my eyes.

I have to work. Tell him to chill. It's none of his business who asks me out.

There were other unread texts on my phone, too—a few texts from Rina and Wendy, and I quickly opened those next. Goddess knows they were like flies to honey.

WENDY

Eryne, we need an update.

RINA

How's it going with your wolf man??? I need answers!!

ERYNE

I'm at work now.

WENDY

And... you left him at home?

> No, he came with me. He insisted.

RINA

> So, has he peed on you yet? Marked his territory?

I blushed, because they weren't too far off.

ERYNE

> No. Gross.

> ...but he did almost growl at Simon who was just in here getting a coffee.

RINA

> Oh he *likes you* likes you.

> It's just his wolf. He says he's attached.

> Honestly, I think I might like the wolf better than the man. He's just confusing.

WENDY

> Hmmm...

RINA

> Are you thinking what I'm thinking, Wends?

WENDY

> I could use a cookie, if that's what you're thinking.

RINA

> Perfect. Meet you there.

Sighing, I stashed my phone away, grabbing another tray of sugar cookies and carrying them out to the case. There was no stopping those two once they had an idea in their heads, something I knew too well. Ever since they were little, they'd been best friends, always getting into trouble wherever they went. It wasn't surprising to me that they were still single— even if we were all passing the mid-twenties point. Neither of them seemed interested in meeting someone or settling down.

They didn't waste any time, and a few minutes later, I saw them both peeking in the front window, past a pair of paper bats I'd hung in the beginning of the month.

I rolled my eyes, surprised it had taken this long for them to ask me about Barrett.

This morning felt like a week ago, so much had happened today, but there was something about him meeting my friends that had me anxious in a whole different way. What if he was a jerk to them? I didn't know how I'd handle that.

My friends had never met a boyfriend before. Not that he was my boyfriend. Far, far from it. But it felt like we were more than just friends, too. Maybe it was my hormones. I was all jittery, and I'd only had one cup of coffee at breakfast.

"Is that him?" Wendy whispered, leaning across the counter after they'd finally come inside. Barrett was using his laptop, focused on the screen in front of him.

Crossing my arms over my chest, I glared at them. "Yes. Now, if you're done gawking, I have to get back to the actual *paying* customers." They both rolled their eyes at me. "Also, don't you have, I don't know... jobs to do?"

"Oh, shut up," Rina said, fanning herself with her hand. "He's *hot*. You should definitely go for it." She gave me a thumbs up. "Get that wolf man D, girl." She'd pulled up her long, brunette hair into a ponytail on the top of her head, wearing a tight black top and a pair of jeans.

"I..." I blushed, glancing over at him. He had an eyebrow raised as he stared at us, and I wondered how good his hearing was. Could he hear what we were saying from across the room? I hoped not. Goddess, that would be *mortifying*.

"Rina," Wendy scolded, adjusting the slouchy white sweater dress on her shoulder. She'd also tied a red ribbon in her hair as a headband. It was her signature color, and it was rare to see her not wearing it.

Rina, on the other hand, stuck to dark colors and edgier patterns.

Meanwhile, I just liked whatever was cute and comfy, though I did own a dozen different pairs of boots.

"What?" My friend shrugged. "It's true."

Wendy let out a sigh of exasperation. "I'm not denying it's true. But have a *little* tact."

Rina narrowed her eyes. "You agreed with me. You think she should fuck him too."

"Guys," I hissed. "Why are you talking about my sex life like I'm not even here?" Yep, mortifying.

A throat cleared, and I looked up into a pair of amber eyes.

"Do you think he heard us?" Rina whispered to Wendy. The two of them looked so comical that I had to hold in a laugh.

Wendy tugged on her arm. "Yeah, I think so." She looked back at me. "We should go."

"Uh-huh." I watched them turn and run out of the shop and resisted rolling my eyes as they left. When I looked back at the man at my side, he had an amused look on his face.

"So, those are your friends, hm?"

I grimaced. "How much of that did you hear?"

He chuckled, and the sound went straight between my thighs. He leaned closer, so close that I could feel his breath ghost over my neck. "All of it."

A squeak slipped from my lips.

Yeah, I was so fucked.

CHAPTER EIGHT

barrett

I couldn't stop the low rumble in my chest. He was leaned over the counter, reaching out to touch her arm.

Who did that? Touched someone *else's* girl like that.

Of course, she wasn't really mine. Not yet.

Even though every fiber of my being was begging for it. But I couldn't *touch*. I needed to remember that. The implications were too high. What was at stake was too large to risk it all.

But then she *smiled at him*. And my wolf was ready to fight to the death. Like he'd throw down over some invisible gauntlet, over the small witch who had the other half of my soul. She tucked a strand behind her ear, looking visibly annoyed as she typed back and forth with me.

Tell him to chill. It's none of his business who asks me out.

I scowled again at Eryne's text message. She said that like it was so easy to control myself around her. I tried to remind myself that she had no idea.

Fate was playing a cruel trick on me that she didn't recognize what we were to each other. My growl rumbled deep in my chest, and I watched as the skinny guy leave with his coffee cup in hand.

That's right, my wolf said. *Leave our mate alone.*

I rolled my eyes internally before returning to the task at hand. Since my phone had been dead when I'd gotten it, I'd had to charge it before I could call anyone back, and I had eighty seven missed calls. That didn't even count all the unread texts. *Fuck.* I massaged my forehead, scrolling through the notifications on my phone.

After sending a quick text to my family, assuring them I was fine and had just been backpacking in the wilderness for two weeks without service, I dialed Ezra's number.

He picked up on the second ring.

"It's me," I said without waiting for him to say hello, holding my phone up to my ear as I watched Eryne flitter around the coffee shop.

The entire place was decked out in halloween decor, from little black bats taped to the windows to small tissue paper ghosts hanging from the ceiling. Someone had clearly gone through the trouble of carving pumpkins and hanging lights for the coffee shop as well, giving it a cozy, warm vibe.

What must have been the entire town seemed to have stopped by this morning. I'd lost count of the amount of people that had asked for the famous pumpkin chocolate chip scones, or the sugar cookies that had me licking my lips.

And that didn't even count the coffee that smelled absolutely divine.

I was only a little distracted taking it all in. It felt like I'd been coming here my whole life, instead of seeing it fully for the first time today.

"Oh, Lockwood." Ezra's voice, deep and slightly old-fashioned, came through the phone, bringing me back to the issue at hand. "I wasn't sure you were even still *alive*. Two weeks, and you failed check in once."

"I was sort of... otherwise incapacitated." I winced, thinking about how I'd been slowly bleeding out before Eryne had found me, and how long I'd been letting her take care of me without a worry for all the people I left behind. "Sorry. I didn't have my phone back till this morning."

He made a strangled sound, the one he gave when I knew he was frustrated. "What happened?"

"There's something out there. Something big. I was tracking it, but—"

Ezra cursed. "I told you not to go alone. I could have come down."

"Dammit, I know. I made a rash decision, and I paid the price."

"What happened?"

I hesitated, but I knew he needed the truth. "It almost tore me limb from limb. Took a few chunks out of my skin. Luckily, my wolf's stronger than I am. Unfortunately, I didn't get a good look at it. All I know is that it's massive, and those teeth..." I shuddered. And it had somehow knocked out my healing abilities.

"You're damn lucky to even be alive. What the fuck were you thinking?"

My eyes drifted over to Eryne. "I have no clue. But that's not all."

"There's *more?*"

I dropped my voice to a low whisper. She was far enough away that she couldn't hear me, but I didn't want anyone else in the coffee shop to be listening in, either. "I found my mate."

Silence. Then, "You *what?*"

"My mate. She's here." I rubbed my jaw, knowing I needed to shave. And maybe get a haircut. Both things were on my itinerary for tomorrow. "She was the one who found me. Nursed me back to health. I couldn't shift back until this morning."

He whistled. "What are the odds? You go off on your own and find your pretty little mate, and I'm stuck here, not getting to see any of the action."

"I didn't say she was pretty," I muttered.

"Is she?"

"Well, *obviously*." I wasn't blind. She was gorgeous. Even covered in coffee grounds and exhausted from a long day at work, I thought she was the most beautiful thing I'd ever laid eyes on. "But you're not allowed to even *look* at her."

"Possessive, much?"

I grumbled a few choice words under my breath. "You know how shifters are, Darkmire."

He chuckled. "Ah. Just as you know how my kind act with our own. I won't go near your female, Lockwood. You have my word." I could almost picture him bowing, wearing the three piece suit I wasn't sure I'd ever seen him go without. The man was a walking enigma. A puzzle I wasn't sure I'd ever solve.

"She's a witch," I added, almost an afterthought.

"A witch? Now, that is interesting..." He trailed off. "Why do you think that's the case?"

I shook my head, even though he couldn't see me. "I think I was meant to be here. Something about this place isn't *right*. And I'm going to figure out what that is. To right the wrongs of our ancestors." I caught Eryne's eye, and she gave me a soft smile, curling her finger around one of the short, copper strands of hair.

My lips curled up in a smile of my own looking at her, my beautiful little healer.

"So, you're staying."

"For now, yeah."

"Alright. Where did you say this town was again?"

"Pleasant Grove," I answered, still looking at my mate. "Massachusetts. About an hour away from Salem."

Ezra hummed into the phone. "Figures."

"I'll call you again when I know more," I told him. It seemed like Eryne's friends were here, two scents I found familiar. They were there that night, I realized quickly. Even though I didn't remember much, I knew they helped her get me into the car. "Listen, I have to go," I said, watching them at the counter. "Talk soon."

Hanging up without another word, I listened to their conversation across the room. I was intrigued by her friends, because I wanted to understand her. Who she was. The things she liked. Everything.

They looked over at me, giggling, and I sat up a little taller in my seat as I pretended to be engrossed in my laptop.

"He's *hot.* You should definitely go for it," her friend said. "Get that wolf-man D, girl."

Eryne's cheeks went pink and she looked over at me. I raised an eyebrow, and she looked away, back at her friends, who were still prattling on to her about how she should sleep with me. I was out of my seat before I could think better of it.

"Why are you talking about my sex life like I'm not even here?" Eryne said to her friends, clearly exasperated.

I cleared my throat from behind them, and she turned to look up at me, eyes widening.

That's right, little mate, I wanted to tell her. *I'm right here.*

Both of her friends scurried off without introducing themselves, and I shoved my hands in my pockets as I studied her. "So, those are your friends, hm?"

She made a face. "How much of that did you hear?"

I chuckled, leaning in closer, knowing exactly how much I was affecting her. "All of it."

Eryne swallowed roughly. "All... of it?"

Humming, I twirled the piece of hair that had come free from behind her ear. "Yep. Every. Last. Word."

"Barrett..." Her voice was barely above a whisper. "We hardly know each other. That would be..." She stumbled on her words. "A bad idea."

I pulled away. The words stung. Would it? Maybe to her. "You're right," I muttered. "It would be a mistake." But not in the way she thought it would.

"Yeah." Her voice was all breathy.

Shaking my head, I looked out the door. "I should go."

"Go where?" She frowned. "I'll be done in an hour, and then we can—"

"No." The word was more of a grunt than anything. "I'll meet you back at the house."

Fuck me, I was fucking everything up. What was I even doing?

I grabbed my bag, hoisting it onto my shoulder, before hightailing it out of the coffee shop. My senses were riding me too hard, and I needed out. Out of this place, where her smell surrounded me. Out of reach, where all I wanted to do was pull her against me. Out of sight, where I could stop thinking about the witch who'd saved my life.

The witch who didn't know she was my *mate*. Who had no idea why seeing other men around her was making me go out of my skin. Who had no idea what hearing her talk about sex was doing to me. How badly I needed her. How badly I *wanted* her.

I'd just met her, and I knew it was irrational. But it felt like I'd known her my entire life. Like something had clicked into place that night when she'd found me, broken and bleeding, and my heart was now a little lighter. But what was it about her that had me in such a trance? That had me truly *bewitched?*

Shutting my senses down, I focused on inhaling the clean, fresh air. It wasn't quite the same as home—there, the air smelled of mountains, like pine and spruce trees. Here, it smelled earthier, with more oak trees, elm trees and beech trees dotting the skyline. I didn't mind it though.

There was something about the feeling of the world under my feet here that settled me.

"*Fuck*," I groaned. This wasn't what I was supposed to be doing here.

I was supposed to be figuring out what had happened for the witches to close themselves off, why the fate would give me one as a mate, *not* trying to figure out how to get her to want me too.

Stripping off my clothes, I left them in a bundle on the back porch, and headed towards the woods. I needed a run to clear my head. The shift happened almost instantaneously—one second, I was running on two feet, and the next, on four paws. I turned around to look at Eryne's cute little house, thankful it bordered the woods. Letting out a short howl, I dove into the thick underbrush.

After not running for weeks, feeling the air through my fur and the ground under my paws felt freeing. Like back there, everything was muddled. Complicated. Out here, surrounded by forests and nature, there was just me.

Letting my legs take me wherever they wanted to go, I headed towards the mountains at the edge of town. There was something strange about the town wards. About how they'd cracked and fought against my skin as I entered.

If Eryne was right—that this place was supposed to be protected against those who weren't witches—they weren't working. They were failing, as if there was something *wrong* with the magic. It felt *bitter*, like it tasted wrong. It grated against my senses.

Something sinister was festering here. The better question was *why?* Why had this community closed themselves off from the rest of the world? And did it have something to do with the creature that attacked me outside the town limits?

My wolf whimpered. He knew something was wrong, too. I ran the perimeter, along the ring where I could feel the witches magic at its highest, until something *foul* hit my nose. Like the lingering smell of rot and decay. I dug at the barrier, unable to stop until I realized exactly what it was.

Death.

I needed to get back—to tell Eryne what I'd found.

To tell Ezra that there was something bigger going on than I'd expected before. Something that I couldn't handle alone. Which meant operating as a team.

Wolves were good at that. Hundreds of years ago, we used to live in packs. We thrived on alpha hierarchies, though those had long since been dismantled. Now, our towns functioned much like most human towns did, with governments, town councils, and a bunch of red tape that made it immensely hard to do my job.

Luckily, I operated outside of town limits.

Outside the law.

There was a reason my entire family had no idea what I did. To protect them, I had to hide the truth. But how much longer could I hide it from Eryne?

Our mate deserves the truth, my wolf reminded me.

If only it was that simple.

Because everything had just become a lot more complicated.

CHAPTER NINE

eryne

My house was empty when I got back, after the shop was locked up and closed for the night. I frowned. Had he left? Maybe he'd changed his mind from earlier. Maybe it was something I'd said.

Had Rina and Wendy's comments upset him that much? Or had mine?

He'd rejected me without even blinking, and I didn't know why it hurt so much when I was the one that brought up that sex wasn't a good idea.

"Barrett?" I called, even though I'd already checked every room. His stuff was still here, though, sitting at the foot of my bed, so I figured that was a good sign.

Why did I care? I had to confront the idea that I hardly knew the man.

Before this morning, I'd thought he was a *wolf*, for crying out loud. And yet, the idea of him leaving didn't sit right with me. I could use any excuse I wanted—that he wasn't healed enough, that I was just concerned about his well being—but I knew what it all boiled down to. For the last two weeks, I'd had a purpose besides my job. Taking care of someone else.

Nursing him back to health had given me something to do. And to go back to before, to a cold, empty house, just felt... *lonely.*

I wrapped my arms around myself. It was hard to admit out loud. Maybe because the last year of my life, overall, had been amazing. I'd gotten this new job. Moved into my own place. Kept myself entertained with making earrings and new friends.

But was it enough? Was I... happy?

Frowning, I headed towards Nutmeg's cage, opening the door and waiting for her to scurry over to me. After she crawled onto my hand, I scratched under her chin with my free hand, the motion soothing me. Witches believed in the familiar bond, that it helped strengthen our magic. There was something incredibly powerful about our connection with animals.

"That's my sweet little Nutmeg," I cooed as she looked up at me, twitching her tiny little nose.

A lot of the witches in Pleasant Grove had cats for their familiars—including the Clarke sisters. Though I wasn't sure Damien really counted as her familiar anymore, but *semantics.* Still, when it had been time for me to pick mine, I'd taken one look at the tiny little hedgehog and I'd known she was supposed to be mine.

Lifting her up, I let her crawl onto my shoulder as I walked towards the kitchen.

Movement outside caught my eye as I walked past my glass sliding door, and I froze.

Was that?

I opened the door in time to watch as the huge, dark red wolf bounded through the air—and then it's form shifted, turning back into man. The transformation was surprisingly graceful in a way I would have never expected.

Some werewolf lore described it like all of their bones were breaking, reshaping to create the new form, but this? This was completely different. Mesmerizing, even. I couldn't look away.

Barrett walked out of the woods, heading back towards my house, running his hands through his wind-swept hair. The most perfect shade of auburn I thought ever existed.

I took the moment to admire his body before he realized I was there. Tall—well over six feet—muscular, and covered in freckles. How was it possible for a man to have that many abs? He was heading toward me, and he was *completely* naked. How did this keep happening to me?

"Oh." My cheeks flamed. I was openly gawking at him as I stood on my back porch.

This the second time today this had happened to us. Except unlike this morning, he didn't cover up with sheets or a pillow. Which meant I could see *everything*.

"Enjoying the view, little healer?" He smirked, flexing his muscles.

My mouth was dry, *again*. Or maybe I was drooling. I wasn't sure.

"Oh, goddess. I'm so sorry." Looking away, I scratched under Nutmeg's head as I stood at my sliding door. I could almost make out his reflection in the glass, and I was trying to avoid looking at anything. Especially between his thighs, at what I knew was definitely an impressive package. And he hadn't even been hard this time.

I bit my lip, trying to ignore the way my heart was thudding in my chest. Had a man ever incited a reaction like this in me before? Had I ever wanted to strip my clothes off and throw myself at—

He cleared his throat. "Sorry. I just went for a run. I needed to—" I heard rustling, and then he was closer to me, his breath practically ghosting over my neck. "You can turn around now, sugar. I'm dressed."

I turned around, finding him dressed in the same clothes he had earlier, sans jacket. His muscles looked even better now, somehow, which should have been a crime.

"I'm sorry," I murmured, still averting my eyes. "I didn't mean to—"

Barrett shook his head. "It's fine." He looked back towards the forest, and a worried look came over his face.

I frowned. "What's wrong?"

His nose twitched, like he'd just smelled something bad. "The wards around your town. How do they work, exactly?" It wasn't exactly a secret, but I wasn't sure if it was something I should tell an outsider. I looked around at the trees, and then nodded with my head for him to follow me inside.

There was something unsettling about having this conversation outside as the sky grew darker.

"I don't know all the details, honestly." I didn't pay that close of attention, something I now regretted. Maybe if I was more in tune with everything happening around me, I might have had more answers. "Every full moon, we do a spell that's supposed to recharge them. It combines all of our energies— all of our magic—to renew what was cast centuries ago."

"To keep you safe."

I nodded. "Yes. But we *can* leave, you know. Plenty of witches choose to live outside Pleasant Grove." It was a life that required you to lose your connection to magic, however, because we all knew what would happen if we were caught by humans. Persecution. Fire. Trials and thousands of our sisters lost. Thousands of innocent lives, because humans were scared of what they didn't understand.

"Did you?" Barrett asked, shaking me from my thoughts of pyres and witch hunts.

"Did I what?" I tilted my head to the side.

"Leave."

Oh. "I thought about it, for college." Wendy and Rina both had, and I knew they didn't regret their years of playing human. I shrugged. "But... I love this town. It's always been home. Even if I've spent most of my life on the outside of society, I can't imagine living anywhere else. Losing what makes you a witch... sacrificing that to be among the humans... it just sounds awful."

"I agree." He rubbed his chin, at the reddish stubble already growing in. "We feel the same in Walnut Ridge."

It was the second time he'd mentioned his hometown. "But you left, didn't you?" I asked, rubbing Nutmeg's chin one last time before putting her back in her large enclosure.

"Left is a big word. I travel a lot for work, but it's always home. Wolves are pack animals, after all."

I nodded. *Home.* "Right. And your job is... what, exactly?"

Barrett turned away, like he knew exactly what he'd been keeping from me. His mouth formed a straight line, and I could practically read the turmoil on his face.

What was so bad that he didn't want to tell me?

"Why did you come here, Barrett? To Pleasant Grove. What attacked you?" I looked back outside. "What did you find out there?"

His amber eyes flashed to mine, darkening like the eyes of a predator. "Are you sure you want to know, Eryne? Because once you do, you can't go back. You can't unlearn everything I'm about to tell you."

"I want to know," I insisted. "No, it's more than that. I need to know. So please. Tell me *why*. Because I don't understand why I feel so connected with you. Why I..." *don't want you to leave.* It was on the tip of my tongue, but I held back.

Barrett sighed. "Okay. But maybe you should sit down."

I complied, sliding onto the couch and resting my legs underneath me, grabbing one of my pumpkin pillows and holding it against my middle for support.

Pacing back and forth, he raked his fingers through his hair, messing up the dark red strands. "I'm a huntsman."

I was pretty sure I'd heard him wrong. "A what?"

"A monster hunter."

Guess I'd heard him right. "That's a real thing?"

He shot me a glare before continuing. "Yes. We're a small team, but our focus is keeping people safe. Both the paranormal communities and humans who don't even know we exist. We eliminate threats before they become a big enough problem for humans to notice. And then we make them go away."

"So the thing that attacked you..."

He cursed. "I got a report. And I was the closest, so I was investigating. I should have waited, but I didn't want to lose my lead. The scent trail was running cold, and I knew I only had a few hours... But I was rash. And look what happened." Barrett gestured to his body, and I could still picture the way I'd found his wolf, bleeding and crying out.

"So, what was it? A vampire?"

Barrett froze, turning to look at me. "A *vampire?*"

I winced. "Those marks on you could only have been made by teeth, and I just thought maybe—"

His voice was a grumble, and when he spoke, it was in a different voice than I thought I'd heard him use before. Commanding. *Alpha.* "Don't go anywhere near vampires, Eryne."

Sucking in a breath, I couldn't take my eyes off of the man

in front of me. The man who took up so much space in my living room, he felt bigger than life. "Okay," I whispered.

Barrett nodded to himself, like that satisfied him. "Anyway, I told you the truth before. I don't know what it was. Nothing I'd ever seen before. Everything from that night is still a bit blurry, but it was wrong. And the smell, the *rot*—"

"You think whatever attacked you has something to do with the barrier failing," I guessed.

Finally, he sat down next to me on the couch. "Yes. I needed the run to clear my head." He looked guilty as he looked over at me. "I'm sorry, by the way. For how I left earlier."

I bit my lip. In the grand scheme of things, it seemed stupid for me to be upset about. But also, he didn't owe me anything.

"What about the barrier?" I squeezed the pillow tighter to my abdomen, trying to ignore the way his commanding voice had left me achey all over. Crossing my legs, I hoped he didn't notice my reaction.

His eyes dilated, and his nostrils flared as he looked at me. "I... What about it?"

"You *were* looking at it, weren't you? You found something wrong with it."

He groaned. "Yes. It has the same traces as the creature that I was tracking. It feels unnatural. *Wrong.* I think it's causing the barrier to break down."

"But why would it come after our wards?" I asked.

"Do you want my best guess?" He scratched his head. I nodded, encouraging him to continue. "It wants to consume the magic. These things... they don't stop until they've devoured everything in sight."

My eyes widened. "So, not a vampire."

He chuckled. "*No.* Definitely not a vampire. I don't know the name for what they are. Not yet. But I suspect that they're creatures from the very depths of the underworld. They only leave death in their wake."

I waited a beat for him to laugh. To reveal this was all some sort of funny joke. But he didn't. He just stared at me, like he was waiting for me tor process that piece of information.

"I need to lie down," I said, rubbing my forehead. "Today feels like the longest day of my life," I admitted. "Was it really only this morning that I found out who you are?" I couldn't look away from his eyes. Those beautiful amber eyes, just the same as his wolf. They were captivating, swirling somehow, full of emotions I couldn't even begin to describe.

He reached his hand over, tucking a loose strand of hair behind my ear before cupping my jaw. "It feels like I've known you forever," he said, voice a low murmur.

It made my heart flutter, bats practically erupting in my chest.

His lips were so close to mine. My eyes fluttered shut. I *wanted* this.

Was that insane? I couldn't describe what was pulling us together, but whatever unseen forces had drawn us to each other, I wanted to pursue it. Wanted to understand. Wanted to *know*.

I leaned in towards him, knowing that all it would take was just another inch or two for our lips to meet.

My heart pounded in my chest, and I wondered if he could hear it. Wondered if he knew how badly I wanted this. Wanted *him*.

Barrett cleared his throat. "We should go to sleep." In the blink of an eye, he was off the couch, standing on the other side of the room.

"Oh." The mortification stung, the implication burning at my cheeks. He didn't want me. "Right."

Of course, he didn't want me. We'd just met.

Why would he want to kiss *me*? I was just some witch in a town that was just a blip on his radar. Just another case as he went around hunting monsters.

I couldn't compete with that. I couldn't compete with *home,* a place he spoke of with such open affection.

So I stood, heading back to my bedroom without another word.

Trying to ignore the pang of loneliness in my heart.

CHAPTER TEN

barrett

S he'd wanted me to kiss her.

Eryne had made it obvious. She'd wanted me to kiss her, and I hadn't.

Every bit of me wanted to, but I'd stopped myself before I could let it happen.

She wasn't ready for this. Ready for *me*. I knew it when I saw the way her face drained of color when I was talking about my job—about the sick creatures I hunted for a living. It unsettled her.

I sat back on the couch as she walked into her bedroom, no doubt ready to strip off her clothes and pull on her pajamas. My cock was practically standing at attention any time I was around her, and this line of thinking wasn't helping.

Earlier, I hadn't expected her to be waiting for me to come home. But when I'd seen her on the porch, and had shifted back to my human form, she was the only thing on my mind. Not my clothes or my lack thereof. Just getting back to her.

Fuck, even now I could smell her arousal, and it was so hard to hold back.

The mate bond was urging me to take her, to claim her, to make her mine, but I couldn't. She had no idea what was between us. I felt like an absolute dick for keeping it from her, but would she still want to be around me when she knew the truth? I still hadn't figured out how it was possible that we were mates when she *wasn't* a wolf.

I'd never heard of mates being different species until now. Though it was possible for shifters to procreate with humans, they didn't normally share a mate bond. Not like this.

Maybe it had something to do with the witch magic that tied us together. I needed to find out more about the witch and demon that were mated.

That was a good distraction from thinking about the sweet scent of my mate and how desperate I was to taste it directly from the source.

"It's been one fucking day, Lockwood," I scolded myself. "Keep it in your pants."

I was going to sleep on the couch. Or maybe the floor.

Next to her, my wolf urged.

Like he knew, just as much as I did, that I wouldn't be able to sleep without her in my sights.

"You're the worst," I grumbled, rubbing at my chest, where the bond ached for completion.

But I couldn't. I *wouldn't.*

Not yet. Not until I knew that this was what she wanted.

Till she could reassure me that all of this—us—was enough for her. I'd never be able to give her the life of a normal witch. I wasn't built for that. Wolves were built for the open road, for forests and pack life and the great outdoors. That was all I'd ever known. I'd spent more of the last decade sleeping in motels and in my car than I had at home.

I didn't know how this would work.

But I knew I didn't want to leave, either.

Tomorrow, I promised myself.

Tomorrow, I'd call Ezra and start investigating this thing for real. Maybe I'd go down to the newspaper or the library to find the history of this town. Something had to have been left behind—a reason *why* the wards were enacted in the first place.

Eryne didn't seem to know the full *how,* but I could be persuasive. I could find out the answer.

And still, I couldn't deny that regardless of all of that, I didn't want to leave because I didn't want to leave *her.*

Maybe that was the biggest problem of all.

/

"Did you really sleep outside my door all night?" Eryne asked the next morning as I rubbed at my neck while cooking a pan of bacon on her stove.

I grunted my answer, not ready for this conversation.

Yes, I'd slept outside her door, curled up in a ball in my wolf form, teeth ready to rip apart anyone who dared to open it. My wolf was ready to tear them limb by limb if anything happened to her.

The witch in question was wearing a cozy two piece pajama set, complete with fleece pants that were covered in leaves and pumpkins. It was cute how much this town loved fall. Her hair was pulled back into two tiny French braids on either side of her head, and it reminded me of my sister.

I wondered what Freya would think of Eryne. If they'd get along.

Stop getting ahead of yourself, B, I reminded myself. It was too soon for that. Sure, we were mates, but none of that changed the decision I'd made last night.

Eryne took one look at the coffee pot where I was brewing

coffee—black—and scrunched up her nose. "I *can* make you coffee, you know." I frowned.

No one had ever taken care of me before. At least, not until she'd rescued me. I liked the idea. It warmed my insides, and I tried to ignore it. How good it felt to have someone that cared that much.

"I really don't mind," she added, voice sweet.

Raising an eyebrow, I flipped the bacon over. "Please tell me there's not any hidden potions inside this promise of coffee." My voice was gruff, but gods, the idea of drinking that nasty concoction again had me near retching. I'd had enough of those for an entire lifetime.

She raised her hands. "None, unless you include the spell for extra energy." She pursed her lips. "And good vibes." Eryne twirled her finger, a little spark of magic bursting through the air.

"Fine," I said, grunting out a response as I collected all of the crispy pieces of bacon while I continued to cook the rest of the food. There were eggs frying in another pan, and toast in the toaster.

"What's all this?" Eryne finally asked as she took over the coffee maker, clearly not using any of the buttons I had before. I had a hard time keeping my eyes off of her, even though I had to look away a few times to make sure I didn't burn the food.

"Breakfast."

She rolled her eyes, grabbing the milk out of the fridge and steaming it with the frother. "Well, I can see that, Captain Obvious."

"You need to eat."

Eryne glared at me. "I normally eat at the shop." She finished the coffee, sliding over a mug to me.

I crossed my arms over my chest. "You don't go in until the afternoon. And then you're there until closing, and I'm pretty sure you don't eat dinner half the nights either." I'd memorized her schedule when I'd been stuck in her bed, day after day in wolf form, unable to move or talk as my body stitched itself back together.

Eryne pouted. "Fine. You caught me." She grumbled something under her breath about me having her daily routine committed to memory.

Plating up the food, I handed her a full dish. "Appease me." I flashed her my best pearly-white smile, keeping my canines retracted.

She sighed, sitting down at the island as I piled my plate high with the rest of the food. I could wolf down a *lot*—and I needed to, with the amount of calories I burned from my high metabolism. After how long I'd spent recovering, I needed the food to help me maintain my physique.

I'd never really cared about it before, but something about seeing her eyes flare last night at my body made me want to look good for *her.*

I sat down next to her, shaking pepper onto my eggs before finally taking a sip of my coffee. I groaned. "Damn, sugar. That's good."

Her cheeks had the cutest tinge of pink to them. "I'm not as good at making coffee as Willow, but I'm not half bad."

"Not half bad?" I took another gulp. The flavors were perfect, with just a dash of cinnamon that somehow perfectly balanced it out. I closed my eyes and savored it. "I'd find it a lot easier to get out of bed every morning if I knew I had one of these to look forward to."

The compliment seemed to make her glow. She fiddled with the end of one of her braids. "So, any fun plans for the day?" Eryne asked me, bringing a bite of food up to her mouth before looking over at me. "Or are you going to stalk me to the shop again and growl any time a man gets close to me?"

A low rumble built in my chest. *Yes,* I wanted to answer.

"Do I need to?" My voice was low.

She bit her lip. "No." The word was a whisper.

"Then... I have research to do," I answered instead. "I want to look into the barrier and find out the history of your town wards. I was thinking I'd see if I can access the town archives at the library. Maybe the newspaper, too."

"Oh, good idea." Eryne's head nodded along. "There's so many old books in there, you could probably be in there a week and not find anything. And I might be able to help with the latter—I know one of the witches who works for the Pleasant Grove Gazette."

"You think she'd be able to find anything for us?"

"If I tell her what's going on—the whole coven, actually—I know they'd all be on board. Ever since Damien and Zain came to Pleasant Grove, there's been a shift in the energy here. I think we'd all like answers." She took another bite of her eggs, finishing off the plate.

"And that's... your coven?" I asked, wanting to know more about her. "Are your friends from yesterday a part of it?"

She blushed. "I was hoping maybe we could forget about that."

I leaned in close. "Not a chance."

Eryne just sighed as she stood up, setting her plate in the sink before turning on the faucet. "Yes, they're a part of the coven. My coven now, I guess." She looked a little in awe. "That's the first time I've ever said that out loud. It's... new. I was never a part of one before."

I tried to imagine what it would be like to be a wolf shifter without a pack, but the idea sent a pang of loneliness through my heart. Was that what Eryne felt like before? All alone, without anyone to call her own?

Finishing my own plate, I stepped beside her, practically

pinning her against the counter, towering over her with my much taller form.

"You're not alone anymore," I promised.

Her eyes held mine. Those beautiful blue eyes seemed to swirl with a myriad of emotions—ones I couldn't even dare to try to understand. But the longing on her face was unmistakable.

"I know," she whispered.

I wanted to wrap my arms around her, to hold her tight. To whisper sweet nothings in her ear and tell her that I'd never let her be lonely again.

But I couldn't.

That wasn't what this was.

I stepped back, clearing my throat. "I guess I'll head out then. See you after work?"

Eryne nodded in response, focused once again on the dishes in front of her.

Heading for the door, I shoved my feet into my boots and grabbed my coat off the front rack where I'd left it yesterday. I pulled it on, pausing for a moment to find Eryne with her hip propped against the counter, watching me.

She gave me a small smile. "Barrett?"

I stopped in my tracks. "Yes?"

"Do you want to get a drink tonight?" She wet her lips. "With me?"

A grin split my face, and my relief was palpable. "Thought you'd never ask, sugar. I'd love to."

Hours later, I was sitting at the bar at the Enchanted Cauldron, nursing a glass of whiskey that had seemed like a better idea when I'd gotten here then it did now, waiting for Eryne to arrive.

I'd spent my day digging through dusty books at the library, though she was right that I could be researching for a week and not find anything. So far, I'd found a few leather-bound history books that talked about the founding of Pleasant Grove—how they'd made the town as a safe haven for witches to avoid persecution—but nothing about the wards or the magic that powered this place. If they'd known about shifters, they hadn't left any indication in their writings.

Something had to explain what was going on here. And I was determined to find it.

Even without my wolf senses, I would have known the exact moment Eryne entered the room. It was like my body came to life with awareness, a prickling against my skin that couldn't be denied. That golden, shimmering thread between us strengthened.

I sat up straighter, as her eyes met mine, unable to hide my smile at the sight of her.

She'd changed since I saw her this morning, and it felt like my tongue was stuck in my throat. Fuck, she was beautiful. Her hair was in loose curls, a pair of spiderweb drop earrings hanging from her dainty ears, a short black dress that formed a deep v in the front. Her legs looked a million miles long in a pair of black leather heeled Doc Marten boots that seemed so perfectly *her*.

It was hard to deny my attraction to her. It was more than that, though. In just a few days, I couldn't ignore how adorable I found all of her little quirks. The way she babbled, talking to herself. Her sense of humor. The way she always smelled sweet, like sugar. The twinkle in her eyes when she found something amusing.

How much I *wanted* her.

I cleared my throat, standing up as she walked over to me, unable to take my eyes off of her for one single moment.

She tucked a strand of hair behind her ear. "Hi."

My hand itched to follow the same path, to caress her cheek, to feel her soft skin under mine.

"Hi," I said back, giving her body a long, blatant perusal. Fuck, I hadn't let myself look at her this long before. And it was a problem, considering how my dick was already reacting to the sight of her. "You look..." I trailed off. "*Wow*."

Eryne did a little spin, her eyes lighting up. "That good, huh?"

I took another sip of my drink. "Mmm. Very."

She smiled, sliding onto the stool next to mine. The bartender, a witch with bright blue hair, came over, quickly taking Eryne's order. A few minutes later, her drink slid across the counter, unassisted.

Shaking my head, I almost laughed at the absurdity of it. I still hadn't gotten used to how they used magic for such mundane things.

"How was your day?" I asked, leaning my chin on my hand as I watched her sip the cocktail.

"Mmm." Her tongue darted out to catch a drop on her lip. "It was good. Quieter than normal, but that's a relief. And I didn't have to work the counter, so I just worked on inventory and ordering." She looked up at me, then wrinkled her nose. "This is weird."

"How so?" I rotated my glass in my hands.

Eryne shrugged. "It's like you said last night... it feels like I've known you forever. Not only a few days." Her eyes met mine. "I don't know why I feel so comfortable around you. It's just so... easy."

I placed my hand on her thigh, slowly rubbing my thumb across her skin. "I know what you mean," I said.

Her eyes fluttered shut as I continued caressing her thigh. Now that I'd started touching her, I couldn't stop. "What are we doing, Barrett?" Her words were barely a whisper.

"Having drinks," I answered, leaning over to brush my lips over her ear. "What else would we be doing, sugar?"

She let out a little whimper, and I sat back up straight, deciding to change the subject in an effort to control myself. "So, you like it? Your job?"

Her eyes darted over to me, a little hazy. "Huh?" She blinked. "Oh. Yeah. I do." She traced the rim of her drink with her thumb. It was a shimmering, purple liquid that looked sweet. Just like her. "When Willow and Luna had first offered me the promotion, I didn't know anything about running a business, let alone a coffee shop. But it turns out... I'm pretty good at it. I like being out there, serving customers and chatting with everyone in town, but I like being in the back office even more." That stubborn curl sprang free from her ear, and she tucked it back again.

"Healing, coffee making, business running—what aren't you good at?"

Eryne blushed, like she didn't see how amazing she was. "Enough about me. How was your day? Did you find anything out in the library?"

I ran a hand through my hair. "No. A lot of dusty old books that hadn't been opened in a century, though."

She looked disappointed.

"Hey." I reached out, squeezing her shoulder. "I'm not going to give up. Don't worry—we'll figure out what's going on. And how to keep the town safe."

She finished her drink, and I signaled for the bartender to bring us both another. As we both sipped on our second drinks, she told me all about her new coven and the twelve other witches that belonged to it, including Iris, the bartender.

"We should go to the Gazette tomorrow." Eryne announced. "Constance will help." She shuddered. "I only find her slightly terrifying, but she'll help."

I frowned. "Why?"

"Why do I find her terrifying?" The redhead next to me laughed, then gave me a deadpan look. "Have you ever met a necromancer?"

"No." I shook my head. And I wasn't really sure I wanted to.

She bit her lip. "She digs up all the best gossip though." Eryne leaned over. "Pun intended."

I let out a howl of a laugh. "You're just fucking with me, right?"

"Oh, no. She actually does terrify me." She lowered her voice. "Don't get on her bad side."

"Noted." I took a deep pull from my glass. "Are there any other members of your coven I should be scared of?"

"Scared of? No. Cait's particularly good at casting hexes, though, so watch your back around her. And then Rina and Wendy are..." She winced. "Well, they're the closest thing I have to best friends, and I love them, but they're really nosy. Particularly about us."

"Us?" I asked. "Is there an us?"

She turned to look at me, and her knees slotted in between my legs.

It wasn't lost on me that she fit perfectly.

Like that was where she'd always been meant to be.

"I don't know," she murmured. "Is there?"

"You tell me." I reached out, tucking that piece of bright copper hair that kept springing free back behind her ear.

"*Barrett.*"

"Eryne," I said, my voice rough as I rubbed my thumb across her cheekbone. "I don't know what we're doing here."

She clutched the sides of my jacket. "I don't know either."

Her voice was barely above a whisper. "All I know is that I want you." Her eyelashes fluttered and her lips were *right there.*

All I had to do was lean down and take it.

How could I hold back anymore, when she said those words? I couldn't.

"Fuck it," I growled, bringing my lips down to meet hers.

It was hardly more than a slow peck, but it felt like something inside of me was rearranging at the touch. Like there was a before Eryne and an after Eryne, and I would never be quite the same man—or wolf—ever again.

Her arms looped around my neck, and she pressed her lips to mine again. A low rumble of satisfaction burst through my chest as I kissed her.

Yes, my wolf agreed. *Kiss our pretty little mate.*

I wove my fingers through her hair, tugging her closer to me, knowing there was no way in hell I was going to be able to stop. Not when I wanted her this badly.

Too badly to want to stop.

eryne

My heart was beating a million miles in my chest, and for once, I didn't want to think anymore. Didn't want to list all of the reasons why we shouldn't.

I just wanted to think about all of the reasons why we *should*. Because I was desperately attracted to this man. I felt safe with him. And maybe some part of me had let what Rina and Wendy said the other day get into my head. But I wanted to know what it would be like.

If it would be as explosive as this heat between us felt.

His kisses were soft caresses against my lips, enough to leave me wanting more. His hand slid into my hair, bringing our lips closer, and I was seconds away from straddling his lap right here in the middle of the bar, to beg him for more.

A sharp tooth dragged against my lip, and I almost moaned. We weren't even kissing with tongue, and I was already more into it than I'd ever been with anyone else.

"Fuck," Barrett said, resting his forehead against mine. "We should stop." His fingers brushed against the back of my neck, his thumb brushing over the top of my spine over and over.

I blinked up at him, coming back to my senses. "Yeah," I whispered back, looking around us, as if just remembering we were in the middle of the bar. "Probably."

Pressing my lips against his one last time, I sat back against the barstool, feeling the heat rise to my cheeks as he settled his hand back on my thigh. It was warm, and I wanted him to slide it higher.

Calm down, horny girl, I scolded myself.

Part of me still preened, thinking about his reaction when he'd first seen me walk in. Maybe some part of me had invited him here tonight hoping this would happen, because I couldn't get him out of my head.

I'd been a mess all day at work, until my employees had finally kicked *me* out after I let one too many shots of espresso die. Yeah, I was *not* ready to look at that too deeply.

Barrett waived Iris over, handing her a card and paying for both of our drinks before I could even speak. Then he stood up, discreetly adjusting himself—I tried not to notice the bulge in his pants, since we were clearly not talking about how affected either of us were—and then extended out a hand to me.

Wordlessly, I slipped my hand into his, interlacing our fingers together. I took that moment to admire how big his hand was.

Really, he was huge *everywhere.* He was over a foot taller than me—making me feel even smaller than I normally felt—and there was no mistaking how muscular he was.

He guided me out into the night, and I tried to ignore the way it felt like bats were flying around in my stomach. Each one lighting a fire burning low in my stomach. A need building in between my thighs.

I was nervous. When was the last time I'd been nervous

around someone? I didn't know. But I also didn't know when the last time I *liked* someone this much was either. Maybe it was quick to feel like this—only a few days had passed since I'd woken up in bed with his human form wrapped around me. And yet, I didn't care about any of that.

Barrett's thumb brushed over my knuckles. "Did you walk or drive?" He looked around, no doubt trying to find my car.

I tried to imagine what it was like to see this place for the first time through his eyes. Main Street was illuminated by string lights and flickering pumpkins, because the moment September came to Pleasant Grove, Halloween was in full swing here. We *loved* it. From the pumpkin festival next week to All Hallow's Eve and even the weekly Ghoul's Night in the bar, everything was all Halloween, all the time, until the end of October. I'd grown up here, and yet I still loved when the decorations went up every year.

The only thing that might have had Halloween beat was when winter hit our little town. When a coating of snow settled across the rooftops and the horseless sleighs pulled by magic could be found traveling down Main Street. Christmas in Pleasant Grove was something else entirely.

"I walked," I said, giving him a small smile. "It's nice out tonight."

He nodded, squeezing my hand. "Then, let's walk back." Perks of living in a small town—even my house, at the edge of the forest, was only a few blocks away from the town center.

"Okay."

Barrett pulled me in close, dropping a kiss to my forehead. "Okay."

I leaned my head against his arm as we walked, enjoying the comfortable silence. Maybe we both needed this moment to cool down.

This was one of the first nights I felt like I'd really gotten to appreciate the decorations since they'd went up. It was already the end of September. It felt like I'd blinked, and then the month was over. Of course, every day meant we were one closer to Halloween, so I couldn't help but be excited.

A little shiver ran through me, and Barrett frowned at my side. "Are you cold?"

I shrugged. "A little." It wasn't anything I couldn't handle, however. Fiddling with my pendant around my neck, I avoided eye contact with him. There was something too real, too raw in his gaze.

Without another word, he took off his coat, draping it over my shoulders. It was warm and cozy, and I was instantly surrounded by his woodsy scent. God, he smelled delicious. I buried my nose in the neck, inhaling deeply. When I looked up, I found him smirking at me, and I knew I'd been caught.

"What?" I asked him as the corners of his mouth tilted up.

"You're cute," he said, lifting our adjoined hands and kissing the back of mine.

I blushed. "Barrett." I looked around, like someone might possibly catch us.

He squeezed my hand. "I'm sorry. I'll control myself." I giggled as he dropped his head down, his lips brushing over my ear as he whispered, "For now."

The sensation of his lips on my skin made me shiver in anticipation.

"That's what I'm counting on," I said back, batting my eyelashes at him. He let out a little growl—not one of aggression, but frustration.

I giggled as we reached my house, taking the few steps onto the porch. He stood behind me as I unlocked the door, and I could almost *feel* the heat from his body seeping into mine. After it clicked shut behind us, I stepped into the living room, all too aware of the man behind me.

His presence was intoxicating in ways I couldn't explain. In ways I didn't want to think about too deeply.

Barrett wrapped his arms around my middle and holding me tight. Shutting my eyes, I tried not to moan as he nuzzled his face into my neck.

"Fuck," he grunted. "Eryne. You smell so good."

I tilted my head back to look at him, sniffing at my collar. "Don't I just smell like you?"

He let out a groan. "With my coat? *Yes.* But it's not enough." He pressed a kiss to the sensitive skin between my neck and shoulder.

"No?" I whispered.

"Uh-uh." Barrett nibbled on my ear. "My wolf wants you to smell like me *everywhere.*"

This time, I did let out a moan as he sucked on my skin.

But I wanted his lips on mine. Wanted to do what we had left unfinished from the bar. I reached backwards, sliding my hand into his hair. Much like his wolf's fur, it was soft, and I raked my fingers through it.

"Take me to bed," I begged.

But we didn't make it that far. He shuffled us over to the couch, sitting down before pulling me on top of him, my core pressed over his.

"Is this a good time to mention I'm not wearing any under-wear?" I asked, sliding my hands up his chest.

He let out a strangled sound, his hands reaching up to cup the swells of my ass, squeezing gently. I made a satisfied humming sound as I leaned in, pressing soft kisses to the corners of his lips, his cheeks, and his jaw. I traced his freckles with my finger, feeling like I was creating constellations on his skin.

"Eryne," he groaned, the word coming out almost as a pant. For the first time, I noticed he didn't look quite right.

Sweat dripped down his forehead, and his skin was flushed.

I frowned, climbing off his lap and sitting down on the couch next to him.

"Barrett?" I touched his forehead. "What's wrong with you? You're burning up."

He let out another pained sound at my touch. Was there an infection? Had I missed something?

"I'll... be... fine," he gritted out. "Don't worry about me."

"You're definitely *not* fine. How can I help?"

Barrett shook his head. "You can't."

"How long have you been feeling like this?" I could tell there was something he wasn't telling me, but I didn't know how to convince the stubborn wolf-man that I was willing to take care of him.

Resting my hand over his heart, I leaned closer to him. He moaned, dropping his head back. "Just... since earlier." That was odd, but maybe something he'd drank had just disagreed with him.

Except at the bar... he'd been fine. He'd seemed perfectly normal until *after* we'd kissed.

"Is it... me? Am *I* somehow the one affecting you?" I asked, my eyes dropping to the bulge in his jeans. He was hard, straining against his zipper. It looked painful, and I didn't know how I could fix it, but I'd try.

"'S not your fault," he said, voice strained. "I can... control myself."

"But what if I said you didn't have to?" Straddling him once again, I traced his freckles with my thumb, staring into his eyes that were almost black. "What if I said I wanted you?"

He shook his head. "You don't know what you're asking me for, Eryne."

I ground down on his cock. "And what if I do?"

"Oh, fuck," he said, shuddering. "I can't decide if I should tell you to stop or do it again."

I wrapped my fingers around the back of his neck, pressing my lips against his flushed skin. He was clearly fighting against whatever urges were driving him right now. But I didn't want him to hold back. I wanted him—all of him.

"I want you, Barrett," I said against his ear. "Please."

He surged up, groaning as his lips met mine. There was no method to this kiss—it was messy, *needy*. I couldn't stop rubbing against him, desperate for some friction as his tongue stroked over mine, over and over. My insides ached, and I wanted relief. Maybe as badly as he did.

"Are you in heat? Is that... what this is?"

"No—*fuck*." Barrett let out a grunt as I rocked over him, moving my hips. "Not exactly." He shook his head. "Females go into heat. Males, we..." His hands grasped my hips, nails digging into my skin. "Males go into rut when they don't mate with their partner."

My eyes widened. "That's what this is? You're going into... *rut?*" I didn't fully understand, but I was trying to.

He nodded. "I won't be able to control myself. I won't be able to be gentle."

"And this will help? If we..." My eyelashes fluttered shut as he ran his mouth down my neck, his mouth hovering over the spot where my neck and shoulder met.

"If we fuck?" He rasped. "*Yes*. I think. I've never—" I reached down between us, cupping his erection and massaging it. Barrett cursed again. "This has never happened to me, baby."

I froze. "Never?"

He shook his head. "I don't want you to regret this."

"How could I ever?" I whispered. Not with him. Not when I'd seen the kind of man he was. When I knew he was *good*. The idea of him leaving still broke me inside, but I knew I didn't want to waste a single moment we had together.

I unzipped his pants, ready to free his cock. Needing to help give him relief. Though I didn't fully understand, I wanted to make him feel good. Wanted to relieve the ache, to get rid of the pain.

Barrett reached out, grabbing my hand. Stilling me. "Before we go any further, there's something you need to know." He swallowed roughly. "Wolf shifters... Our anatomy is... different."

I was pretty sure from what I'd already felt that he still had all the same working parts. And he was big, if what I'd squeezed was any indication. But maybe there was something I was missing. "Are you saying we wouldn't be compatible?" I frowned.

"No." He shook his head, his hands running up and down my sides. "No. It's not that. But female wolves are made to take it. And I don't want to hurt you."

"*It?*" I asked, raising an eyebrow as I pushed down his pants, letting his cock spring free.

"My knot."

My eyes widened as I took in his length. "Your... knot?" Right there, at the base, was a swollen bulb. I ran my fingers down it, mesmerized by the differences between our bodies.

"*Fuck*, Eryne." He shuddered under my touch. "You're going to kill me." Barrett pressed his forehead to mine. "My knot's primary function is to keep us connected." A light blush dotted his freckled cheeks. "*After.* To, uh, ensure successful fertilization."

"Oh." I blinked. And then the realization of what he was saying hit me. It would be okay though, right? I was on birth control, and my pendant was charmed to protect against pregnancy. I bit my lip, deep in thought.

"I don't have to knot you, though." He shook his head. "As long as I don't, I won't hurt you." Barrett nuzzled into my neck.

"You won't. I trust you." I wrapped my arms around his neck, combing my fingers through the hair at the base of his neck. "It might be a little crazy, because we barely know each other, but I feel like I know you." All those hours taking care of him, looking into his eyes when he was a wolf, feeling that deep sense of connection... it all made me feel close to him.

Barrett pressed his forehead against mine, bringing us closer together. "I know exactly what you mean," he murmured, brushing his lips over mine.

I didn't hold myself back this time.

I didn't want to.

I just wanted him.

CHAPTER TWELVE

barrett

"Are you sure?" I asked her, nipping at her neck, running my canine teeth over that spot I longed to sink into, to fully claim her as mine. To put my scent there, my mark, so everyone knew whose she was.

Mine.

My witch tipped her head back, granting me easier access, and I held back another groan.

She didn't know what it meant, giving a wolf access to your throat. She didn't know anything about shifters—that was even more evident when she saw my cock, her eyes widening as she took in my knot, the hardened bulge at the base that practically begged to lock inside of her.

Not that I would be knotting her tonight. It wouldn't be enough, but I couldn't risk it when she didn't know the truth. But my senses were riding me *hard*, and holding back was getting more painful.

Especially when she kissed me so sweetly.

Her fingers ran through the back of my hair, and I explored her mouth with my tongue as we kissed, ignoring the way she rubbed her bare pussy against my cock, rocking her hips and driving me absolutely insane.

I was barely anything more than a beast, with one mission in mind. All I wanted was to be inside of her.

Fuck, I wanted to fill her with my cum so it was dripping out of her, to breed her till she grew my pup in her belly. To keep her barefoot and pregnant and bring her home to Walnut Ridge. To feel the full extent of the mate bond flowing through both of us.

"Barrett," she whimpered as I held on to her waist, keeping her still.

"I know." I pressed a kiss to the spot between her breasts where the fabric dipped, before reaching down and grabbing the hem, pulling it up over her head. "*Fuck*, look at you."

She still had those heeled boots on that made her legs look sexy as fuck, but otherwise, she was completely naked, her nipples practically begging for my mouth. Her teeth raked over her lower lip, like she was slightly self conscious over me seeing her like this. I tried to think about something else, but my brain went completely blank when she reached between us, undoing the buttons before tugging the hem of my shirt. I helped her get it off my shoulders, and she sat back, giving me a heated perusal.

I wondered what I looked like from her eyes, with my freckled shoulders and torso. No part of my body lacked definition—thanks to the amount of time I spent as a wolf—but I didn't know what my mate would think. I wanted to be enough for her. Wanted *this* to be enough for her.

Eryne raked her fingernails down my abs. "Gods," she whispered, her fingers softly tracing over my freckles. "You're *unreal*."

I slid my hand in between her hair and face, cupping her cheek. "That's you, sugar."

She made a sound of disagreement, and I bent my head down, running my tongue over one of her nipples before lightly sucking it into my mouth, lavishing it with attention before switching to the other ones.

"*Oh.*" Eryne shut her eyes, letting out a small cry.

"See? You're fucking perfect." I cupped her perfect tits with my hands. "How did I get so lucky to find you?"

Her lips found my neck, and she pressed a few kisses down my chest, over my freckles, and I had to reach out, cupping her jaw and tilting up her head till her eyes met mine. Eryne wrapped her hand around my cock, stroking it lightly. She ran her thumb around the crown, and I shuddered at her touch.

"Baby. You have to stop," I pleaded, letting out a groan. I could feel the heat rising within me, and this time, I knew I couldn't hold back. "I need to be inside of you."

Her lips pressed against my ear. "I don't think you're going to fit."

She was small, my pretty little mate, but she was perfect. "We'll make it fit. But first I need to get you nice and wet for me." I dipped my fingers down to her entrance, circling my thumb around her clit before pushing an index finger inside. "Fuck, you're soaked," I groaned as I slid a second finger inside her wet heat.

She let out a small gasp as I crooked my fingers. Her fingernails dug into my shoulders as I continued to slowly pump inside of her, feeling her slowly relax around me. Eryne let out a small cry as her release finally coated my hand, and I couldn't look away from her face when she came.

"So pretty," I praised. "But now I need you to come sit on my cock."

Eryne licked her lips as she raised her hips, helping me guide my tip to her entrance. I watched as she sank down onto my cock, her pussy taking each inch until all that was left outside was the base—and my knot.

I'd promised her I wouldn't knot her tonight, and I meant it. She wasn't ready for that.

Though I wasn't sure *I* was ready for that either, considering what it meant to knot your mate. I was already having such a hard time holding back from her, but that? That was crossing a line I couldn't come back from.

I wrapped my hands around her thighs as she dropped her head back. "Oh, *fuuck,*" she gasped. "You're so big. I'm so full."

Pressing a kiss to each of her perfect nipples, I tightened my hold on her, helping guide her up and down my length. She was so tight, and it felt so good inside of her, the way her insides wrapped around my length, squeezing my cock.

"You feel so good," I said, groaning, knowing I wouldn't be able to last long enough to make her come again if I didn't do it soon.

She felt *perfect.* Like everything was right, and I was exactly where I was supposed to be—inside my mate, with her body pressed against mine. I'd never been inside anyone without a condom before, and it felt *incredible.* Having my mate like this was everything I'd ever imagined—and more.

She clenched down around me as she kissed me again, her tongue intertwining with mine as she rocked her hips back and forth, grinding her clit against the base of my knot.

"Fuck." I repositioned us, rolling her over so her head was on a pillow and she was lying down on the couch, and held myself over her. "I can't hold back anymore." I kicked off my pants, needing them off my body.

She nodded, like she knew exactly what I meant. "I want you," she whispered. "All of you. Whatever that looks like."

I groaned as I pried her thighs apart. Next time, when I wasn't so desperate, I wanted to put my mouth there. To have her sweet taste on my tongue. To hear her scream out my name as she came on my face. But that would all have to wait.

"I can't promise I'll be gentle, but I don't want to hurt you."

Eryne reached up with her hand, rubbing the stubble on my jaw. "You won't. I know you won't." Her words echoed her earlier sentiment, and it was all I needed to hear.

Sliding back inside of her, I groaned at the feeling of her pussy taking me in, the feeling of fucking her bare almost too much to handle. My wolf was riding me, so close to the surface, but I held him at bay, needing this to just be about *us* for our first time.

She let out a moan as I began thrusting in earnest, and it was like something unleashed inside of me as I moved, a guttural noise ripping from my throat as I buried myself inside of her, over and over, careful not to let my knot slip inside.

"Need you to come again," I grunted, reaching down and rubbing her clit with my thumb as I kept up the pace, slamming into her over and over again as I brought us closer to the edge. Every noise that slipped from her lips spurred me on even more.

Eryne wrapped her legs around my back and squeezed her cunt around me, and I groaned. *Dammit*, it would be so easy to knot her right now, so needy and pliant underneath me. Every instinct screamed for me to mark her, to claim her fully. To not let her slip away.

"You're trying to kill me, aren't you?"

My beautiful witch fluttered her eyelashes, her arms sliding down my back, fingers tracing the muscles. "I want you to feel good too."

I kissed her again. "I already do." I let my eyes drift shut, just savoring the feeling of being inside my mate. "I don't want this moment to end."

She slid her hand around, cupping my cheek and pressing a kiss to my jaw. "I'm not going anywhere, B."

I brushed her bangs back, running my thumb over her cheekbone. She had no idea what that meant to me. How much hearing it calmed me, calmed this restless beast inside of me that wanted everything with her.

Eryne's back arched off the couch as she let out a strangled cry, her pussy clamping down around me as her orgasm ripped through her. "Barrett," she whimpered.

"*Fuck*," I groaned, feeling the telltale signs of my own release. My knot was pulsing, begging to be locked inside of my mate, but I couldn't. I wouldn't, not yet. Not when this was so new. "You're so perfect. So sweet." I leaned down to kiss her softly as I thrust in again, slowly, not ready for this to be over.

Eryne kissed my neck, sucking on the spot where wolves bit each other to mate, and I was gone.

My orgasm hit me harder than it ever had before, and I pulled out at the last second, wrapping my hand around my knot and squeezing as I painted her skin with my cum, covering her in my scent.

My wolf was satisfied—for now, at least—and I felt the need to rut her slowly fading from my body.

Our heavy breathing slowly turned calm, and I let myself take in my mate underneath me, soft and supple, looking like *mine*. Eryne's cheeks turned the most adorable shade of pink.

"That was..."

I hummed. "We should probably clean up, huh?" We'd made a mess of her couch.

She blushed harder.

I stood up, lifting her into my arms, not caring that I was naked in her living room as I carried her to the bathroom. Setting her on the counter, I turned on the tap for the bath, making sure it was not too hot.

Eryne watched me with rapt fascination. "What are you doing?"

"Taking care of you," I answered instantly. "Don't tell me no one's ever taken care of you before, sugar?"

She bit her lip as she watched me test the water. "No," she finally said, barely a whisper. "Not like this. Not like you do."

That made me want to find anyone who'd ever hurt her and make them regret not making her feel special. Because she deserved to feel cared for, to be taken care of. She deserved the world.

I walked over to where she was sitting, pressing a kiss on her forehead. "You have me now, Eryne. And I'm not going anywhere."

It was the same words she'd said to me, and they felt like more than just that. The words felt like a vow, something sacred between us.

She leaned forward, her lips pressing to my biceps, wrapping her arms around me into a hug. I rubbed her back, holding her tight against my body, burying my nose in her hair and inhaling her sweet, sugary scent.

Hugging Eryne felt like coming home. Like I was where I was supposed to be. Like everything was exactly as fate had meant for it to be. I had no idea where this road would take us, but it didn't matter. No matter what the fates had in store for me and the redheaded witch they had chosen for me, I couldn't deny how right it all felt.

Sliding my hands under her ass, I lifted her up from the counter, keeping her wrapped around my body as I carried her over to the bathtub before lowering both of us into the warm water.

Eryne let out a contented sigh, nuzzling her face into my neck as we stretched out in the tub, neither of us bothering to let go of the other.

I wanted to clean her up, but that would wait for later.
For now, I was content just to hold my mate, just like this.

CHAPTER THIRTEEN

eryne

F or the second time this week, I woke up wrapped in a pair of strong arms, nestled against the front of a firm, warm man. Only this time, I didn't want to move. Didn't want to even breathe, in case I found out this was all just a dream.

Last night between us had been... *incredible.* I'd never felt so taken care of, like I was the sole focus of someone's affections, as I did with Barrett. He'd put my pleasure first, even when I could tell he'd been in pain. Slowly turning around so I wouldn't wake him, I took in his sleeping form, amber eyes covered by long, thick red eyelashes that should have been illegal. It was almost unfair how beautiful Barrett was.

Every inch of his body was toned and muscular, yet his skin was covered with thin white lines and scars that I could only guess came from his job as a huntsman. I wondered how many times he'd been hurt and alone, and the thought made my heart ache.

I barely knew him, and all of this should have scared me. But it didn't.

Maybe it was just my witch intuition telling me that he was *good*. That I could trust this wolf who had found his way into my life by bizarre circumstance, and now seemed content not to leave. I wanted to trust him. Wanted to trust in *this*.

Even if I knew it might leave me with heartbreak when he did, eventually, leave. Because at some point, he'd realize I wasn't worth staying for. Didn't everyone? It was why I'd kept my circle so small. Why I'd broken up with my last boyfriend before he could break up with me. I was just shielding my heart to keep it from hurting.

My hand reached out involuntarily, and I ran my thumb over his lips, so soft and perfect. I couldn't get over how good of a kisser he was—how much I wanted him to do it again and again. I'd never really liked kissing anyone before. It had felt awkward—sometimes there was too much tongue, or teeth, or it was just wet, but with Barrett it was different. *Intimate.*

Like he was using his mouth to tell me all the things he couldn't with words.

"Morning," came his gravely morning voice as I traced my thumb over his cheekbones.

I hummed. "Good morning."

He chuckled. "Indeed, it is." Barrett wrapped his hand around my neck, pulling me closer to him till our lips met, so he could kiss me softly. I smiled into it, into the lazy exploration of each other's bodies as he ran his hands down my sides. Even when I'd been in a relationship, I'd never experienced this level of closeness so easily.

Barrett squeezed my hip. "We should get up, or we'll never make it out of this bed." He spoke the words against my ear, lips pressing against the skin. A shiver ran down my spine.

He was right, even though I liked the sound of that, too.

I sat up, and let out a wince. *Fuck*, I was sore. It felt like I could still feel him everywhere. Last night, I'd been so wet and it had felt amazing to have him inside of me, but he really was *big*.

"Are you okay?" Barrett was instantly behind me, his warm hand resting on the small of my back.

"I'll be fine," I answered. Though I'd definitely be feeling him anywhere we went today. I laughed, because he'd probably like knowing that. "I just need to take some painkillers, and I'll be right as rain." I gave him a small smile. "It's just been awhile for me since I... you know."

He nodded. "Me too." My chest warmed at the expression on his face. At the concern pinching the corners of his eyes, and how he was looking at me like he'd do anything to make sure I was okay. Barrett brushed my bangs back on my forehead, pressing another kiss there. "Want me to kiss it better?"

I blushed, the erotic image of him eating me out unfolding in my mind. *Yes*, I wanted that.

"Do you want to shower while I go make breakfast?" He stood up, brushing his hands through his dark auburn hair before finding a pair of boxers and pulling them on.

I pouted like a child who'd had her favorite toy taken away.

He saw the expression on my face and laughed. "Sugar, you're in pain. As much as I'd love to have you screaming my name again, I'm not going to touch you while you're hurting."

I sighed. "I know."

He rubbed my shoulders. "Shower. I'll go make us food."

Us. I liked the sound of that.

I stood on my tiptoes, wrapping my arms around his neck and pulling his head down till his lips met mine. "Thank you. For last night."

"I should be the one thanking you, baby. You were..." He shook his head, squeezing my hip. "I should say I'm sorry, but I'm not. Being with you was incredible."

I felt the same way. "So, neither one of us regrets it." I

kissed him again before untangling myself, walking into the bathroom to turn on the shower.

He'd washed my body last night in the bathtub before we'd crawled into bed and fallen asleep in each other's arms, but a nice warm shower would do wonders for all of the aches currently plaguing my body. I turned around, finding him watching me with rapt attention, not having moved from his spot.

"Breakfast." I reminded him. And if I swayed my hips, knowing his eyes were glued on my ass, who could blame me?

He nodded, running his hands through his hair and tugging on the ends. "Right." Barrett swallowed roughly, and I traced the motion with my eyes.

"Feed me, Wolf-Man," I said, blowing him a kiss.

That made him laugh, and he shook his head as he made his way out of my bedroom as I stood under the warm water, letting it wash all of my fears and pain down the drain.

The whole time, I couldn't keep the smile off my face. This thing between us might have been crazy, but I didn't regret a single second. I definitely didn't regret *him*.

After we were both dressed—me in a turtleneck, one of my favorite plaid skirts and a pair of black tights with my trusty pair of combat boots, and him in a cozy knit sweater, jacket, and black jeans with his own pair of boots—we headed out into town. I still couldn't believe how perfect this morning had been. He'd fed me breakfast, kissed my forehead again, and then went and took his own shower.

All my life, I'd always taken care of other people, but who had taken care of me? Barrett had asked me that last night, and the answer had stared back at me in the face.

No one had ever taken care of me like he was now.

This was what I'd been missing.

Companionship.

Barrett's fingers were interlaced through mine as we took the long route from my house into town, like both of us knew this little bubble of just the two of us would pop as soon as we went back to reality.

Could I let myself fall into this, to feel comfortable with him, when I knew he would leave eventually? No matter what he said, this was just another job for him. Maybe a no-strings-attached fling while he was here would be okay, though. If the sex was anything like last night... I bit my lip. Yeah, I wanted more of that.

"What's going through your head, Eryne?" Barrett asked, squeezing my hand.

I wasn't sure I was ready to confess everything I was thinking. We barely knew each other. If I told him I was getting upset thinking he was going to leave, I'd scare him off. "Nothing." I gave him a small smile, like I was trying to reassure him as much as I was myself. "Should we stop and get coffee on the way to the newspaper office?"

He nodded. "Sure." His lips dipped low, pressing against my ear. "But only if you'll make me one."

I blushed, and then nodded, not sure why he liked *my* coffee so much. Still, it made me a little giddy, like a schoolgirl, that he liked my drinks. That he seemed to like *me*.

The bats were back in my stomach, and I couldn't deny the flutters every time I looked at him. Yeah, I might have had a tiny, okay, giant crush on Barrett Lockwood.

"Alright, Sugar. Lead the way." He kissed my forehead again, and I fluffed my bangs after he pulled away, hiding the flush to my cheeks with my hand, not sure why such a small action made me so flustered.

The Witches' Brew was busy—like it was every morning—and I slid behind the counter, saying hi to my employees as I busied myself making two cups of coffee, just the way I liked it. Barrett hadn't complained yesterday when I'd given him one loaded with sugar, so I figured he didn't mind. We'd already eaten breakfast, but I also stashed a muffin and scone in my bag for later, in case we got hungry while we were sleuthing around.

Two coffees in hand, I walked back around the counter, only to come face to face with Willow and her mate. They looked like they were sharing a moment, his hand curving over her pregnant belly, both of their eyes locked on each other.

Damien had stopped glamouring himself to look more human a few months into living in Pleasant Grove, and his blood red eyes hardly blinked as he looked down at my boss. Her light brown hair was pulled back into a braid, and she was wearing a dark purple dress that hugged her belly, while he—as usual—wore all black.

Much like Barrett, her mate was massive, standing over a foot taller than her.

I cleared my throat, not wanting to interrupt their moment.

"Oh." Willow looked over at me, blinking. "Hi, Eryne. Sorry, I didn't see you there."

I shifted awkwardly with both cups of coffee in my hands. "You're fine."

Barrett slipped in behind me, taking one of the cups from my hand and looking at me expectantly. His hand rested on the small of my back, and I relaxed into his touch.

"Who's this?" Willow asked, her bright green eyes darting between us.

Damien narrowed his, like he was evaluating another apex predator and taking him on for size.

"This is..." I looked up at Barrett, who tilted his head at me, reminding me of his wolf. "Barrett." I smiled at him, and wondered how to explain the rest of how we'd met. "I... you remember those healing potions I asked you for?" I asked Willow.

She nodded, and Damien frowned, like this was the first time he'd heard of it. With how overprotective he was of Willow, and knowing how he tried to keep her off her feet as much as possible, it didn't surprise me.

"They were for him," I offered. "He got attacked by some sort of..." I lowered my voice, not wanting everyone in the cafe to hear. "*Monster* outside of town a few weeks ago. We're just lucky I found him when I did." Sure, I'd left out a few small details, but that was the gist of it.

He chuckled, and I wondered if he was thinking the same thing that I was.

"Barrett, this is my boss, Willow. Her and her sister own the Witches' Brew. And this is her..." I looked at Damien, wondering what to call him. Mate seemed too personal, like that wasn't my right to call him that. I supposed husband sufficed. Her ring sparkled on her left hand. They'd had the ceremony last month, before Luna had given birth to her twins.

"This is my mate," Willow jumped in. "Damien."

He stuck out his hand towards Barrett. "Good to meet you," he said, in something that was almost a grunt.

The wolf shifter at my back reached out and shook his hand.

"You're a shifter," Damien said, a look of surprise crossing his face as they pulled apart.

Barrett nodded. "Yes."

Willow's eyes widened. "A shifter? I've never met another one."

"Wolf," he clarified. "I'm from a small town up in Vermont. Everyone in Walnut Ridge is a wolf shifter, though."

She looked at her mate. "He can turn into a wolf, and all you can turn into is a *cat*?"

Damien's eyes darkened, and he leaned down, brushing his lips over Willow's ear, and she blushed. "*Damien,*" she scolded. He looked satisfied with himself, and I could almost picture a cat licking his paw after killing a mouse, and I held back a giggle at watching them interact.

Willow turned back to me. "So... what are you two up to? Headed anywhere exciting?"

"We're actually going to the tribune," I said, looking up at Barrett. I wasn't sure how much I should say about what we were trying to do, but if anyone would understand—and be trustworthy—it was Willow. "There's something... strange going on."

"Strange how?" Damien asked, his deep voice somehow filling all of the space around us. As much as Willow teased him, he definitely wasn't a being I wanted to be on the bad side of.

I looked around us, keeping my voice lowered. "We think the town wards are failing. That's why the demons have been able to get through. And now... Barrett."

Willow bit her lip, looking at Damien. "I always figured that you were just able to get through because you were my mate."

He smoothed her hair with his hand. "I'm sure it's nothing."

Barrett shook his head. "The... *thing* that attacked me, it felt wrong. Unnatural. And whatever is affecting the barrier has the same smell—like a rot." His nose twitched, like he was remembering the scent. "Something is wrong with the town."

"And you think the town records will help you figure out what it is?"

I shrugged. There was no guarantee, but I had to have hope. "There has to be some reason the elders made the wards this way when they first created the town. Why they kept us isolated from the rest of the paranormal community. I mean, none of us even knew that demons were real until last year when Damien showed up. Who knows what else is out there?" A shiver ran down my spine thinking of whatever had attacked the wolf at my side, to cause those gashes and teeth marks. I definitely did not want to find myself face to face with a creature like that. I indicated to Barrett. "Until he showed up, I had no idea anything was even amiss. We're all in the dark."

Damien nodded his head, scratching his chin. "I should check in with Zain, too. Maybe he'll know something. "

Willow's eyes lit up. "You know I'll never turn down an excuse to see my sister and the twins." They were both so close, that I could only imagine being apart was hard on both of them.

He kissed the top of her head. "We'll go tonight." Damien turned back to both of us. "Are you okay here? I don't know what's out there."

Barrett tugged me tight against his body. "I'll keep her safe."

I could feel the truth in his words, and even though I should have been scared, I couldn't help but feel exhilarated. Like for the first time in my life, I was going to do something that really mattered. Something that would help every single witch in this town.

And I'd do it all with this wolf by my side.

CHAPTER FOURTEEN

barrett

P art of me didn't believe it till I saw it, but the mate bond between Willow and Damien was undeniable. The way she smelled like him, wore his mark—they were just like Eryne and I.

Fated, and yet, it didn't make sense. Before, I'd believed all mates couldn't exist outside our own species. Now... the entire world looked different.

We watched them walk away outside the coffee shop, and I couldn't get the thought out of my mind. "How many beings do you think never found their mate because they belong to a different species?"

Eryne froze. "Where is this coming from?"

I tilted my head in the direction they had gone. "Those two are mates, and yet she's a witch, and he's a demon."

"Right."

"You've all been isolated from the outside world for years. How many people here found their mate before that?"

She shrugged. "It wasn't very common."

Because they lived outside the wards. And now...

"You think there's truly a chance that outside this town... that there's actually a soulmate for everyone?" Her eyes filled with hope.

Fuck, I wanted to tell her, *you're mine*. It would be so easy. But if I told her now, would all this progress between us fall apart? It was so tender, so new. Especially after last night.

"I do," I responded. "I have to believe there is, just like I believe that good things exist in this world." I smiled down my redheaded witch. "You'll see, sugar. We're going to solve this, and then we're going to help your town all find their mates."

A flash of what felt like disappointment flickered through her eyes, but it was gone as quickly as it came. "You're right." She slipped her hand back in mine. "Let's go solve a mystery, huh?"

I dipped my head, unable to look away from her sparkling eyes, full of optimism, of hope. There wasn't a doubt in my mind that she could do anything she put her mind to.

After all, just look at me. She'd brought me back from the dead with grit, determination, and her own two hands.

I couldn't wait to find out what else she could do.

"It looks like no one's been down here in decades," Eryne said, coughing as she brushed more dust off the boxes of files in the archives.

I wrinkled my nose. "They probably haven't." The air was stale, musty, and the scents down in the storage archives were all faint enough that I doubted anyone regularly came to check on the files. Considering the amount of dust, they really needed to take better care of the place.

Her friend had so graciously allowed us down here when Eryne had explained what was going on—though she'd left a few details out, including the monster that had attacked me. I understood that she didn't want to create a panic through the town—it was the same reason my family had no idea about my real job. There was a fine line of information, and this was definitely *need to know.*

"How are we ever going to find anything down here?" She said, sounding defeated as she scoured the boxes. They didn't seem to be in any sort of date order, just haphazardly stored on the shelves around the room. After my inability to find anything concrete at the library, I wasn't really sure what I was expecting to find here, but I was just hoping for some sort of clue that could give us a lead.

I frowned. "Look for the earliest dates, and we'll go from there."

Eryne nodded, tucking a strand of hair behind her ear. "Okay. I can do that."

I did the same on the opposite side of the room, both of us working in tandem.

It was the most comfortable I'd ever been working with another person. Even with Ezra, I always kept my guard up. With her... I felt like I could relax. Like I could be *me.*

I was beginning to think this was hopeless, opening boxes and finding articles about nothing particularly useful, when Eryne made a noise, dropping a box onto the floor suddenly.

"Are you okay?" I asked, turning to look at her.

"I found something." Eryne said, gasping, clutching a paper between her hands.

"What?" I moved to stand behind her.

"It was behind a box, wedged in between the wall and the back of the shelf." She handed me a newspaper clipping. It was yellow and slightly faded, but the headline stood out to me. **PLEASANT GROVE CELEBRATES FIRST FOUNDERS DAY.**

There was a photo of a coven of witches—thirteen of them, to be exact—and a list of names underneath it.

"If they created the town, then they would have been the ones to lay the first wards. Each moon cycle, we give our magic to the barrier, to renew and replenish the spells, but they created them. Whatever magic they weaved inside of them..."

"That's what we need to find out," I finished.

"Right." Eryne nodded. "But this was three hundred years ago, B. There's no way we can find any of these women now. Witches live longer than humans, but not *that* long."

"What about their children? Someone might have passed down the knowledge to their descendants. We have to at least try, don't we?"

She bit her lip, staring down at the photo and looking at the names before pointing at two of the women in the middle. "Cromwell and Hallow.... Those are Wendy and Rina's last names. I think I remember something about Wendy's ancestor being the town founder. That's pretty far back, though. Maybe ten generations?"

"Do you think she knows anything?"

Eryne shook her head. "I doubt it. But maybe her mom or grandma does. Or..." She trailed off. "I can ask." She looked up at me, some of the hope from earlier restored. "Either way, it's a step closer, right?"

"We're going to figure this out," I promised. "It's all going to be fine." I pulled her in close, breathing in her sweet scent.

"I know it is," she whispered, those gorgeous blue eyes holding mine.

I looked around us. "Come on, let's get out of here. I think we've found all we're going to in this mess."

She nodded. "Probably a good idea." Eryne stuck the newspaper article into her bag, then gave me a sheepish look. "They won't even miss it," she insisted. She was probably right. It had been shoved into the back, and the likelihood anyone would come looking for it was low.

"In this age of technology, you'd think all of this would have been scanned and digitized by now."

Eryne laughed. "Don't let the town elders hear that. They treat computers like humans treat magic."

I snorted. "Sounds pretty familiar." I couldn't help but think about the push back Walnut Ridge had gotten.

We headed back upstairs, thanking her friend at the front desk for giving us access, and went back outside. The sun was out, and I tipped my head up towards it, enjoying the warmth on my face.

"I should talk to Rina and Wendy," she said, looking at her phone. "I can see if they know anything, or if their families do."

"I'll call my friend, too." I needed to loop Ezra in.

She worried her lower lip between her teeth. "Is he also a..."

"Hunter?" I supplied.

She nodded.

"Yes. He's the closest thing I have to a partner, though he prefers to work alone most of the time." I chuckled.

Eryne frowned. "Is that... common? To be so solitary?"

"For him?" I scratched my head. "As long as I've known him, yeah, I suppose."

"Huh." Her phone buzzed, and she looked up at me. "That's Rina and Wendy. We're meeting at the diner." She typed a message back, and I shoved my hands in my pockets. It was getting harder and harder to keep myself from touching her, especially after last night.

My wolf was possessive, but I had to control myself. I'd seen her wince in pain a few times when she didn't think I was watching her, and I felt like a goddamn bastard for hurting her.

Not knotting her last night had been smart—I could only imagine how sore she'd be if I had.

But damn if I didn't still want her, no matter what a selfish asshole that made me.

"Okay." I tucked a strand of hair behind her ear. Fuck it, I didn't care. "If anything happens, call me." I pressed a kiss to her forehead. "I won't be too far away."

She nodded. "Okay." The word was hardly more than a whisper. Eryne stood up on her tiptoes to press a soft kiss to my lips.

Reluctantly, I pulled away, knowing that she needed the time alone with her friends as much as she wanted to ask them about the photo. I understood that perfectly. If I was home, I'd want to tell my sister about Eryne, too.

One day soon, I'd tell her about the redheaded girl who had brought me back to life in every since of the word—but not yet. Not when it was still this *new*.

I shot off a text to her anyway as I watched Eryne cross the sidewalk and disappear into the diner, knowing I'd barely be able to keep my eyes off of her while she wasn't by my side. It was something I desperately needed to get control of.

BARRETT

Hope everyone's doing well back home.
Miss you.

FREYA

Miss you too, B. How's the road treating you?

It's good. Currently staying in a small town that reminds me a lot of home. Makes me miss everyone back in Walnut Ridge.

Come home soon. We'd all love to see you.

I will, I promise.

I'm holding you to that.

Good. Love you, sis.

Love you too.

With that weight off my chest, I dialed another number. To no one's surprise, Ezra answered his phone on the first ring.

"It's me," I announced—my usual greeting.

My eyes were still glued to the diner as I settled onto a bench across the street, at Eryne, sitting at a booth by the window. In perfect sight of me, like she knew I'd be keeping an eye on her. *That's my girl.* Her two friends came in a moment later, squishing in across from my mate.

"Glad you're still alive," he said, monotone.

"You too, asshole," I laughed. "It's only been two days."

"I'm assuming if you're calling me, that you found out something more?"

Rubbing my fingers over my jaw, I watched as Eryne slid over the newspaper article to her friends. "Yeah. It's not much, but... It's a start." I quickly summarized what we'd learned so far—and what I suspected. My visit to the library, everything I'd learned from Willow and Damien, plus our trip to the tribune this afternoon.

"They've been closed off from the rest of the world all this time. Sure, some of them went away to college, but... They had no clue we even *existed*, Ezra. None."

"And have you told her yet?"

I looked down at my hands. "No."

He clicked his tongue. "Why not?"

"It's too soon. She's not ready."

"Barrett..." Ezra warned. "You know what will happen if you don't complete the bond."

I groaned. "Don't remind me. Last night..."

He paused. "What happened last night?"

"Never mind." I cleared my throat. I didn't want to talk about it with him. The overwhelming need, the way my body had burned as I held myself back.

I didn't want to explain how right it had felt being with her. How enthusiastic she'd been about being with *me*. If I'd have expected her to be scared or apprehensive, I'd been dead wrong. I adjusted myself in my jeans, trying to change my line of thoughts so I didn't react in public. But fuck, it was hard, thinking about the way she'd moaned under my touch.

"Barrett," Ezra warned. "You're playing with fire. Be careful."

I knew I was. "It's going to be fine," I promised, though it felt more hollow than the same promise I'd made Eryne.

"I'll be there in a few days," he said. "I'm just finishing up a job, and then I'll help you sniff out whatever this is." He paused. "Not *literally*, though. Your nose is better than mine."

I grumbled. "Thanks." But I couldn't complain—I could use his help, and despite being an unusual pair, we worked well together. Plus, Ezra had his own unique skillset. "See you soon. Don't do anything I wouldn't do."

"Right. So everything's still on the table." His words were dry, but I chuckled anyway.

"Bye, asshole."

"Bye, Lockwood."

I hung up the phone, looking up to the sky.

There was one thing I knew for sure: Pleasant Grove would never be the same again.

And after last night, neither would I.

CHAPTER FIFTEEN

eryne

Wendy and Rina were crowded into the booth across from me at the diner after ordering drinks and appetizers.

It was strange to think it had only been a few days ago that I'd brought Barrett here, and now we were... *what?* Sleeping together felt like we were more, but I still had to remind myself that we barely knew each other. That he was a stranger. Even if the way he kissed me made me feel like I'd known him *forever.*

"Eryne." Rina's voice snapped me out of my thoughts. "You're blushing."

"Am not," I protested, shifting in my seat and wincing from the soreness between my thighs.

"Oh my gods," Wendy gasped. "Did you..."

I hid my face in my hands. "This is so not what I called you guys here for."

"Okay, but was it good?"

"*So* good," I admitted. "The best. Like... *wow.*" My voice sounded a little dreamy, even to my ears.

Rina's jaw dropped. "You know, when we told you to get that wolf man D, I didn't expect you to actually do it,"

"I didn't expect it either. One thing led to another and it just kind of... happened."

Wendy's brows furrowed. "But you... *wanted* it to, right? He didn't force you?"

"Gods, no." I shook my head. I'd wanted it—practically begged for him. And I'd do it all over again in a heartbeat if I had the opportunity. "He's the perfect gentleman, I promise. A little growly, sure, but... I honestly really like that. He's protective of me, and I think it's sweet." I looked out the window, where Barrett sat across the street, watching me. Like he had to keep an eye on me, or else something would happen. Instead of being creepy, it made me feel warm inside. Like he cared about me.

"Wow." Rina rested her head on her hands. "Do you think he has any brothers? I need a man like that."

"Ditto," Wendy agreed. "The dating scene in town is *not* it. The idea of kissing someone I've known my whole life? Ugh. As if." She made a face as she spun her fingers around, stirring her spoon in her tea without actually touching it.

After breaking up with my ex, I agreed with Wendy.

But this was the reminder I needed—that I had no idea about who he was—not really. "I'm not sure," I admitted. "I know he's from a town in Vermont, but..." I shrugged.

Our waitress dropped off our drinks, and I pulled the ancient newspaper clipping out of my bag. It was a miracle it hadn't turned to dust, honestly. "Anyway. About why I called you here." *Time to get back on track.* I slid the photo I'd found earlier across the table. "These are your great-grandmothers, right?"

Wendy and Rina both studied the photo, before setting it back down and looking at me.

"Yes..." Wendy finally answered. "How'd you get this?"

"The tribune's archives. It's a long story." One I probably owed them, if I was being honest.

They looked at each other, and Rina said, "We have time."

I took a deep breath before starting. "There's something strange going on, and I think it all connects back to why Barrett is here in Pleasant Grove. Maybe it's fate, but it just feels like we're supposed to figure all of this out." I bit my lip, knowing that they would be behind me no matter what happened. And so I told them everything I knew so far.

"Basically," I summarized at the end, "I need to find out about the ward that was placed on Pleasant Grove when it was founded. And seeing this photo made me realize that we might not know anything, but maybe our grandparents do. Anything they know about that time might be helpful. Or any old papers and books you can find."

"Well..." Rina looked at our blonde friend. "Grandma's still on the town council. There's a chance her mom told her something."

"I can ask my family," Wendy said. "I'm sure all that junk is still somewhere in our house. They're all incapable of getting rid of anything. My sketches from second grade are still hanging on the fridge in our house. And... I think the old Cromwell grimoire is still in the attic. I can poke around and see if I can find the original spell they cast. Maybe if there's any old spirits still lingering about, I can ask them about it as well." It was a big ask of her to even try, since I knew she hated using her ability.

"That would be amazing." I had a good feeling about this.

Wendy looked at Rina, then at me. "We should tell the rest of the coven. Especially since you're part of us now." She reached over, squeezing my hand.

Rina nodded, rolling her straw between her fingers. "I'm

sure they'd all help. It feels like we've been kept in the dark all our lives, and whether or not our ancestors did this to protect us, we deserve to know the truth."

"This all started with Willow and Luna, but it's so much bigger than any one of us," I said. "The whole town deserves to know the truth. All of us deserve better."

It was time for change to come to Pleasant Grove. Somehow, I knew it was up to all of us to fix whatever had been broken. We'd been sealed off from the world for so long, unaware that people like Barrett were even real.

What else was out there?

A shiver ran down my spine at the thought. I couldn't wait to find out.

Three nights later, the entire coven was all gathered around Willow's kitchen table—sans Luna, of course, who couldn't make the trip. Damien and Willow had just returned in the morning from their trip to the Demon Realm. She was snuggled up to him, wearing a dress covered in black cats and pumpkins, while he was wearing his usual outfit—all black.

When I'd first found out he was a demon, let alone the son of the demon king, it had been hard to wrap my mind around it. He seemed so normal. But slowly, he peeled that facade away, letting us get to know the real him. Honestly, until Barrett shifted before my eyes, I had struggled with understanding it. Now... I guess I understood, at least a little, why Willow had fallen in love with him.

Not that I was even *close* to falling in love with Barrett. It was way too soon for anything like that, especially considering I'd only known him for a few days. But I couldn't help but feel his presence in every room, like somehow my body recognized whenever he was around.

We hadn't had sex again since that night after the bar, but he still wrapped his body around mine every night, like an unspoken agreement between the two of us. Though I was pretty sure he just didn't want to hurt me again, considering how pained he looked when he realized how sore I'd been after the first time.

Now, I was *dying* for him to touch me.

Every time he looked over at me, his eyes flicked to my lips, and then back up. I ran my teeth over my bottom lip, wondering if he'd give me what I wanted if I begged for it.

"This is the first time we've ever had men at our coven meeting," Wendy observed in a low voice at my side.

"True," I murmured.

Damien and Barrett looked dangerously out of place in a house full of witches, but both of them had been bound and determined to be here. Since it was obvious we weren't going to be able to leave them out of it, we hadn't really tried. Two overprotective alpha-males tended to get their way in the end. Maybe I should have been worried about the rest of the girls finding out about Barrett, but none of them had batted an eye.

There were fifteen of us, all witches of different shapes and sizes, plus a demon and a wolf shifter, crowded at the old, ornate table, trying to understand what had happened hundreds of years ago so we could figure out what was happening *now*.

Cait and Willow were studying the grimoire that Wendy had found in her grandma's attic. Luckily, the woman was a hoarder, and had kept everything that she thought might be of use one day. It was truly a treasure trove of information.

"The spirits helped me find it," Wendy had told us.

We all knew the general history of the town—after the

Salem witch trials in the seventeenth century, witches had gone into hiding for fear of further persecution. That was why the wards had been created in the first place—to keep us safe from humans. Only, they'd spelled them to *only* allow witches in.

"I just can't wrap my head around why they would have shut the rest of the paranormal world out and pretended like they didn't exist," Willow said again. "It's just unbelievable to me."

Damien chuckled, his arm wrapping around her chair. "You have to remember, little witch, when we first met, you were convinced that all demons were evil. You kept going on and on about not making a deal with me."

"I mean, your brother *did* kidnap my sister. So maybe I had something to be worried about."

"Semantics." He looked over at Barrett, like he needed to defend himself. The rest of us all knew the story well. "She went willingly. And they're very happily married."

Barrett's eyes caught mine and I rolled my eyes. He laughed. It felt like we were sharing our own secret, like we had our own language that was comprised of no words at all.

"Sure, it kept us safe," Cait added, going back to the topic of conversation. She ran her fingers through her long, bright orange hair. "But at what cost? What have we lost by being so isolated from the outside world?" I'd always loved her style— she dressed like she didn't care what the world thought of her. Tonight, she was wearing a t-shirt for the band *HEX*—a girl band of witches from the eighties—with a turtleneck underneath and a pair of black, ripped jeans.

Damien cleared his throat. "Zain and I were actually talking about that last night. Because *we* always knew there were small communities of witches—it was why I came here, after all." He looked over at Willow, running his fingers through her brown hair. "If I hadn't been looking for Luna, I never would have found my mate." Everyone let out a soft *aww* as he pulled her tight, pressing a kiss to the top of her head.

It was the craziest story—and yet, so romantic how they'd found each other in a bizarre twist of fate. It reminded me a little of how Barrett had come into my life, actually—Damien had been stuck in cat form, cursed by a witch from outside Pleasant Grove—and Willow had adopted him from the cat shelter. She'd certainly had the surprise of her life when he'd revealed he was actually a *demon,* asked her to help break his curse.

Much like I'd been shocked to wake up in bed next to the redheaded man who was stuck to my side.

Not that I was complaining. I liked the companionship. I liked coming home to him in my house. He spent his days searching for clues—both in wolf form, and around town as a human—while I worked at the coffee shop, keeping everything running smoothly. And since I'd noticed he seemed more at ease when I wasn't working the front counter, I tended to spend most of my time in my office these days, working on my administrative work. Payroll, ordering and schedules took up most of my time, anyway. And it was what I enjoyed, what I really felt like I was good at. Sure, I didn't mind being in the front as a barista, but I'd forever be grateful for the Clarke sisters for the promotion to manager.

The last two nights, I'd come home to him cooking us dinner, and my heart had almost burst at how easy this felt. How... domestic.

I liked it too much. And that was a problem.

Barrett squeezed my shoulder, and I looked back at him, into those eyes that I'd stared at for all those days when I'd been nursing him back to health in wolf form, and my racing pulse calmed instantly.

Like he knew just what I needed.

It felt like there was some unspoken connection between us that I couldn't describe.

The girls at the other end of the table were sorting through the ancient boxes that Rina and Wendy had pulled out of their attics at the behest of their grandparents, who didn't know our true purpose in our investigation. If they had, I was pretty sure they wouldn't have been helping us.

Instead, they thought we were working on a project for preserving the town's history.

For now, it was better to keep it that way.

"This seems like a pretty standard spell," Cait was saying to Wendy, flipping through the old grimoire. She was our resident expert on spells and hexes, along with being Willow and Luna's cousin. "It's close to what the elders perform each month on the full moon to revive the magic. But there's something... missing." She frowned, running her fingers along the page. "Something different. I don't know how to describe it, other than that it feels *old.*"

"There is?" I perked up, tugging at the hem of my dark green dress as I walked over to her.

She nodded, pointing at the margins. "It looks like something's written here, but it's been hidden with magic."

I leaned in closer, almost able to make out an iridescent shimmer of writing. That wasn't uncommon with old spell books—hiding family secrets inside, covering up dark magic that shouldn't be used anymore. But with this, it felt strange.

Wendy frowned, adjusting her headband. "Why would someone do that?"

"To cover up whatever they did," Rina said, bending over to look at the book. "Obviously."

"What do you think we need to reveal it?" Willow asked.

"*Please*, please, please tell me we don't need blood."

Wendy's skin paled. She'd never liked the sight of it, which I knew troubled her particularly when she had *recently departed* spirits appear in front of her. Definitely not fun.

Cait furrowed her brow. "No. But I've read in old times, they used ink that would dry clear and only appear when exposed to fire, and I think that... Maybe..." She grabbed a candle from the center of the table, the wick flickering to life, and she ran it across the surface of the page, careful not to spill wax or burn the thick paper and it's magical text.

All of our grimoires were infused with magic, and while they were resistant to all the elements, you could never be too careful.

Shimmering gold text appeared on the page—notes from witches of the past, hidden for centuries.

"Wow." A shiver ran down my spine. "This is..." *Old* magic. It was incredible.

"Anyone else have goosebumps?" Rina held out her arm. "I feel like we've uncovered something that we were never meant to know." We probably weren't. I could just imagine our elders rolling in their graves as we uncovered the secrets they tried to hide.

Everyone quieted as Cait studied the words in the margins, and then flipped to the next page and repeated the process again.

Finally, Wendy asked, "Well?" We were all dying with anticipation.

"I'd have to see if Agatha left any notes behind," Cait said. "Then I can truly figure out the *why*. But I might have an idea of the *how*. And if I'm right, on the eve of the next full moon, we should be able to break it."

"But we don't want to *destroy* the wards, right?" I frowned, looking back at Barrett. "We just need to fix them."

Cait shook her head, twirling a long strand of bright orange hair between her fingers. "No. Whatever's been done—especially if your wolf is right, and it's been tampered with—needs to be undone." I blushed at the implication that he was *my* wolf, but I couldn't deny how much I liked it, too. "But maybe it's time to stop hiding from the rest of the paranormal world. The thirteen of us here are the strongest witches in Pleasant Grove. We can create a new barrier. A better one." She looked up at Barrett. "If he's right, then there might be beings out there that are our soulmates, our other halves. We owe it to all of us to find out."

My heart leapt in my chest. After seeing Willow and Luna so happy with their mates, it was hard not to imagine what it would be like to find mine.

But then my eyes connected with Barrett's, and I felt my stomach drop. I *liked* him. A lot. It was getting harder to deny that. What would happen if he found his mate, and then I had to say goodbye? I hated even thinking it.

Trying to shake the thought away, I turned back to the conversation.

"But the full moon is only a few days away. Can we even get everything ready by then? Breaking the wards will require a lot of precise magic," Willow said. Damien crossed his arms over his chest, giving her a look that said, *over my dead body.* "... And I'm not exactly sure I can participate in this condition." She waved a hand to her growing belly. I could only imagine how much strain it was on your body to grow a child, let alone to use that much magic as well. And she was seven months along now, with an adorable little waddle and a bump that couldn't be hidden.

"I'm sure we can find someone to fill in for you," Cait said, closing the grimoire and turning her attention to me. Or, rather... the man behind me.

"Why is she looking at me?" He mumbled in my ear, and I looked back at him.

Cait nodded to herself. "Yeah. You'll do. Maybe even better than one of us."

Barrett shoved his hands in his pockets. "Well... We were always taught that witches gave us our wolves," he shared with all of them. He'd told me this before, and I still thought the idea was incredible. "That they unlocked this ability within us. I don't have magic like you all do, but I'll do whatever I can to help. In a way, we're all linked. Whatever the reason your ancestors had for sealing the town off, I suspect it was much bigger than just humans persecuting witches."

"You think whatever is attacking the wards now was after us back then?"

My wolf man just shrugged. "It's plausible, though I doubt it. If it's been living nearby, feeding off the magic of the wards... We would have known sooner if it had been here for centuries." He looked between all of us. "The barriers between worlds are growing thinner. I think this one isn't from ours at all."

A shiver ran down my spine. *Death,* he'd said once. Gods, I didn't even want to think like that.

"Do you know of a creature that can do that?" Willow asked. "Feed off of magic?"

His eyes met mine. "Only one." The words were ominous, and I hated the way a trickle of fear ran down my spine. That didn't sound good. And I wasn't sure I wanted to know. "I've been going through every bestiary I can find in town and..." The room quieted as the candles flickered more intensely, the smell of the sage we were burning filling the room. He shook his head. "It's not good. I'm going to keep looking, though. I hope I'm wrong."

I breathed deep, trying to push the negative thoughts out

of my mind. Too many what if's plagued me. What if we did this, and something terrible happened to the town? What if the monster attacked when the barrier came down?

"Don't we need to make a plan for putting new wards back up? We can't just leave the town open to attacks." If this thing was whatever Barrett feared, then we were in trouble.

Cait scooped up the book. "Leave that to me. I'm going to spend the next few days studying these and then figure out a spell that will keep all the beings that wish to do us harm *out*. Barrett, do you think you can find whatever is out there, infecting the barrier?"

He dipped his head. "I have a pretty good idea where to start looking. And my partner is coming to town for backup. Between the two of us, well should be able to take care of it. There's not much that can stand a chance against both of us." I was pretty sure he was talking about his hunter friend, though he hadn't given me specifics.

"Anything you need," Damien said to the ginger haired man at my side. "I'm here, too. And my brother is just a call away."

"I'll keep that in mind," Barrett said, though he was staring directly at me. "Anything to keep the town safe."

Though I had a feeling *the town*, in this case, really meant me.

I couldn't decide how I felt about that.

"Mmm." I cozied up next to Barrett on the couch a few hours later, after our little coven meeting had been disbanded and everyone had gone home.

Cait had the spell book—along with a few more things Rina and Wendy had found in their grandma's attics that she thought would help her figure out the magic behind it, and I felt better, just knowing we had a plan. Roping the rest of the coven in was the right move, even though I felt anxious over the idea of anyone getting hurt because we'd involved them in this mess.

Right now, I didn't want to think about any of that. Not when my entire body was practically buzzing with awareness, begging for his touch. Right now, I didn't need words. I just wanted *him*. Every look, every small touch this evening, had just made me want him even more.

I ran my hand down his front, popping open the buttons on his shirt as I went.

"What are you doing?" He whispered as I kissed one of his pecs, and then the other.

"I want you," I said, knowing I wasn't above begging. "You haven't touched me. Not since that night."

His eyes softened, like he knew exactly what I was talking about. "But I hurt you." He slid his hand into my hair, cupping my cheek. Barrett's thumb stroked my skin, and it was almost like I could feel the turmoil within him.

I shook my head. "You didn't." I took his hand in mine, kissing his palm. "Please. I don't regret it. Not one bit. And I don't want you to, either."

His hand slid around the back of my neck as he kissed me softly, tenderly. Like I was something precious. Something he wanted to keep.

"Eryne..." Barrett murmured, fingers trailing from my hair to my collarbone, pushing my dress off my shoulder until it exposed the black strap of the garment I was wearing underneath. "Gods, you smell..." He took a deep inhale, his nose brushing down my skin.

I hummed as he snapped the strap against my skin, his fingers tracing the freckles that dotted my shoulders.

Pressing my lips to his bare chest, I tugged his shirt out of his pants.

"Like what?" I asked him, even though I sensed I already knew what he was going to say.

Barrett groaned, and the sound—goddess. My panties were completely soaked. "I can smell how wet you are," he told me, his voice rasping over my skin, making my nipples harden. "Like you *need* me." If he could smell my arousal, he'd know just how turned on I was. "*Fuuuck*, baby."

He pulled me tight against his body, neither one of us in a rush to move. I buried my face in his neck as he held my hips, both of us just soaking in the moment. I ran my fingers through his hair, languidly appreciating his body as he drank in my scent. I didn't know what it was about it that he seemed to find so intoxicating, but in this moment, I didn't care.

"*Eryne*," he said again, pressing his lips to swells of my breasts. "So sweet. Like sugar." His tongue dragged up my skin, and I let out a ragged breath.

When we pulled apart, his eyes were dark, roving over my body. I dug my front teeth into my lower lip and fluttered my eyelashes at him.

He slid his hand up my knee. "What are you wearing underneath this?"

I fluttered my eyelashes as I spread my legs for him. "Why don't you find out?"

Barrett's hands gripped the hem of my dark green dress, and he pulled it off my body, exposing the black scrappy mesh bodysuit I'd been wearing underneath. My nipples were already hard, pressed against the fabric, and I cupped my breasts, knowing it would make my cleavage spill out over the fabric.

I stood in front of him, knowing my body was on full display. "Do you like it?" I let out a breath.

"Fuck," he groaned, running his teeth along the bare skin of my neck. "You're so beautiful." His eyes traced over every inch of my body—every bit of skin exposed, where the straps and the mesh hugged my body, showing off every curve. "Like every dream I've ever had, come to life."

Was this why women liked wearing lingerie? If it was, I'd buy a million more sets, just to see him look at me like *this.*

"I'm not a dream, Barrett," I said, taking his hand and guiding his fingers right where I wanted them. "You can touch me. Have me. *Take me.*"

He groaned as I pressed a finger inside my core. I let out a moan as I felt him stretch me, knowing he'd find out just how wet I actually was. *Dripping.* I was a mess, and he'd barely even touched me yet.

"You're fucking soaked, aren't you, baby?" I whimpered as he pushed my thighs apart enough to add a second finger. "You need me to take care of you, don't you?" I nodded, biting my lip to hold back another moan as he pumped them inside of me.

"*Yes,*" I finally agreed, riding his fingers, rocking my hips as he worked me higher and higher.

But right before I could climax, he stopped. Pulled them out, and licked them clean as he kept eye contact.

"Then be a good girl and get on your knees." His voice was all command—deep and growly. It did something to me, the way I wanted to obey him. I *loved* it.

I let out a sharp exhale—and then I did exactly what he said, dropping to my knees in front of him. He looked every bit the alpha male, lounging on his throne on my couch, shirt open and exposing the chest I wanted to trace every ridge of with my tongue. Goddess, he was fit. And handsome. It should have been illegal to have a body that toned and still be the soft, caring man that I knew he was.

I rested my hands on his thighs as he pushed the straps off

my shoulder, exposing my nipples to the air. He made an appreciative noise as he slid his hand underneath my chin.

"You look so pretty on your knees for me." Barrett ran his finger over my lip, the rest of his hand supporting my jaw, keeping my eyes locked on his amber ones as I knelt between his spread legs.

I let out a soft moan as he pressed his thumb inside, closing my lips around it and sucking lightly. He groaned.

Sliding my hands up his thighs, I slowly dragged the zipper down his pants, freeing his hardened cock. My tongue swept across my lips, moistening them, before I dipped my head down, running my tongue over the head.

"*Yes,*" he grunted as I wrapped my hand around his shaft, sliding my fingers down till I hit his knot. It was incredible, thinking about taking it. He was already so big, filling me up until all I could feel was *him,* that I couldn't even imagine what it would be like to have his knot inside me.

"This is really going to fit inside of me?" I asked, pressing soft kisses down his length and over his knot. It wasn't even swelled yet, but I imagined it did its job—keeping everything inside of me—well. He hadn't come inside of me last time, and even though I knew it was irresponsible, I wanted him to.

I'd never gone without condoms with my previous partners, but now that I'd felt him bare inside of me, I wasn't sure I could go back.

"We'll work up to it," he promised, rubbing his thumb— still coated in my saliva—all over my bottom lip.

I let my eyelashes flutter shut once again. "Okay," I whispered. "I want to make you feel good." Dipping my head back down, I ran my tongue around the crown, tracing the rim before taking the tip into my mouth, all while massaging his knot.

He groaned. "Baby. Oh, fuck, *Eryne.*"

Somehow, even though he had all the power, with me on my knees in front of him, I liked that he seemed content to let me explore at my own pace. He wasn't forcing me to take him in deep—though I doubted I could, since he was massive—rather, just encouraging me as I figured out what drove him crazy.

Reaching my free hand between my thighs, I rubbed my clit before slipping a finger inside, moaning around his dick as I sucked him off.

Fuck, this was *liberating*. I'd never been so turned on going down on a guy before.

Though I'd never felt this same connection to anyone I'd dated before. Not like I did with Barrett. And even though I didn't know how this thing would end, where it would take us, I wanted to explore this.

I kept up my pace, letting Barrett show me what he liked, soaking up every grunt and groan of his, knowing I was the one that was going to make him come. He was hard as steel, and each pump of my hand down his shaft had him groaning. I could tell he was holding back, his hips jerking every few seconds like he wanted to thrust into my throat, but he was letting me stay in control.

Barrett buried his fingers into my hair, gripping it as I alternated between sucking and running my tongue over the crown, coating his cock with my saliva as I kept pumping him with my hand. I lapped up each drop of salty pre-cum as I thrust my fingers into my entrance, so wet I was coating my hand in my release.

I moaned around his cock as I got closer, knowing he was just as affected as I was.

He tightened his grip on me, breaths turning to pants. "I'm so close," he moaned. "Please, baby. I don't want to come down your throat." Barrett let out a whimper as I doubled down my efforts, not stopping. Not yet. Not until he came. I wanted him to feel as good as he'd made me feel.

Without warning, he pulled me off a fraction of an inch before he came, coating my mouth and lips with his release.

"Holy fuck," he groaned, dropping his head back against the couch as I swallowed, licking my lips, admiring the way the sticky liquid painted my chest.

"You can say that again," I murmured, sitting back on my ankles and then climbing back onto the couch next to him. He cupped my jaw, roughly bringing our lips together, like he didn't even care that I tasted like him.

He let out a grunt, scooping me up before carrying me towards my room.

"What are we doing?" I asked, tracing my finger through his chest hair.

"Now it's my turn to taste *you*."

And oh, how I liked the sound of that.

barrett

W as there ever a more beautiful sight in the world than my mate, kneeling before me in lingerie, sucking my cock like it was her sole mission in life?

Yes. It was this.

Eryne, legs spread open on her bed, that short ginger hair unfurled around her, circling her like an copper halo. Her pretty pink cunt, exposed just for me, looking like a feast.

I ran a fingernail down her sternum, watching as she shuddered under my touch. As soon as I'd gotten her into the bedroom, I'd shred that black mesh bodysuit off her body, turning one of my fingertips into a claw. The open heat on her face had made it worth it, as did the wave of arousal I could scent from her.

I'd buy her another one, if she wanted. I'd buy her a hundred, just to make her happy. As long as I was the only one who got to see her like this.

She'd been touching herself while she sucked me off, and it had been one of the hottest things I'd ever seen. And while I hadn't meant to come in her mouth, I couldn't deny how much my wolf liked our mate covered in our scent.

For the last few days, I'd held back. I couldn't explain why —maybe it was that I felt guilty being with her when she didn't know the truth, but she made it clear tonight exactly what she wanted. *Me*. Us. It gave me hope that maybe, when I told her that she was my mate, that we were meant to be together, that she'd actually give us a real shot.

"B," she whimpered as I rubbed my thumbs over her nipples, pressing soft kisses to her neck and chest. "I need—" Eryne squirmed underneath my body, and I shushed her with a kiss to her lips.

"I know," I said. "I'll give you what you need, I promise." I lavished her with kisses as I moved down her body, positioning myself between her spread legs, trailing my fingers up her thigh and stopping right where I knew she wanted me.

Pressing a kiss to each of her inner thighs, I finally gave her what she needed. My cock twitched with the first swipe of my tongue over her entrance, her sugary sweet taste flooding into my mouth. Gods, she tasted... *perfect*. Like mine. I closed my eyes, letting out a moan as I lapped up her juices, savoring my first taste of my mate on my tongue.

Eryne's fingers ran through my hair before she dug in, pulling at the longer strands on the top, but nothing could keep me from my relentless pursuit of her sweet pussy. I sucked at her clit, alternating between suction and burying my tongue inside of her cunt over and over.

Her fingernails raked across my scalp, and she cried out. I was sure she was close—especially since she'd been fingering herself and I didn't think she'd orgasmed yet.

I wanted her to come on my face. Wanted to feel her pussy squeezing my tongue, for her release to flood my mouth, covering me in her scent like I'd done to her.

"*Fuck,*" she cried. "That feels so good. You..." The words were hardly more than a pant. "How are you so good at this?"

I pulled back, keeping her legs apart and nuzzling against the soft skin of her thighs. "Can't help it when you taste so fucking delectable, babe." Like sugar. She was so sweet, I couldn't believe I hadn't been doing this to her every single day.

Her fluttered eyes drifted shut as I dropped my mouth to her again, applying pressure to her clit with my thumb as I continued to bury my tongue inside of her pussy.

She cried out as a flood of wetness coated my tongue, and I closed my eyes as I drank it up, knowing she'd probably soaked my face and not even caring.

I was half-hard again already, just from eating her out, but I didn't even care about me. I was on cloud fucking nine, and I could take care of myself again later.

Climbing up the bed, I pressed a soft kiss to her lips before shifting us so I could pull her body into mine, spooning her and draping one arm over her abdomen to keep her in place. I ran my hands down her body, tracing her curves, and Eryne relaxed into my hold, her head resting on my chest.

"Mmm." She hummed as I traced circles on her soft skin of her thighs.

I kissed her shoulder. "Good?"

"Better than good," she said, letting out a dreamy sigh. "Like, *wow*. That's never been like that for me before."

I wrapped my arms around her waist, pulling her in close to me, enjoying the feeling of her naked skin against mine. There was something extra special about holding her like this, something that soothed every jagged edge of mine when I had my mate in my arms.

"It's never been like this for me before, either," I admitted, pressing a kiss to her forehead.

I needed to tell her—and soon. But after tonight, I didn't know how she'd react. When Cait had brought up the potential for soulmates, she'd frozen. Did she not want to find her mate?

She hummed, resting her arms on my bare chest, draping her naked body over my torso. "Tell me more about you. I realized the other day that I don't actually know that much about you. You told me you were from Vermont, but..."

I chuckled. "What do you want to know?"

"Do you have any family?" Eryne asked me, running her fingers through my hair. It was getting too long, and in desperate need of a cut, but I hadn't wanted to spend too much time away from her. Luckily, I'd picked up a razor one of my first days in town, so I'd been able to keep my beard from growing in.

"I do." I pictured my sister, her long auburn hair and obsession with cardigans and books. "I have a younger sister, Freya. She's actually a librarian back home. Our town is a lot like Pleasant Grove. Humans don't know we exist, and we prefer it that way after we were hunted to almost extinction a few hundred years ago. Nowadays, wolves tend to keep to pack life." We were a social race, living in mated pairs and family units.

"So... you were safe." Her lips formed a soft smile.

I nodded. "It was the best place to grow up. Freya and I were always close, and we did everything together. I couldn't have asked for a better childhood. It's a great place to raise a family."

I wondered what life would look like if I took her home to Walnut Ridge. With two ginger haired kids, ones that could shift and use magic as easy as snapping their fingers. It was all so vivid in my mind. Almost like I could reach out and touch it.

With Eryne by my side, our life would be filled with warmth and laughter. Curling up by the fireplace together.

Keeping her warm during the winters. Letting her ride on my back as I ran through the woods in wolf form, so she could feel the wind whipping against her skin like I did. Watching her carry our children, bringing those sweet and innocent pups into the world.

But it wasn't real. I had to remember that. As much as I wanted her, she wasn't mine.

Not yet.

"How'd you get into this line of business?" She paused. "And what exactly does your family think you do?"

"Private security."

She bust out laughing. "What?"

"No, I'm serious. I used to be in training to be a cop, actually. Went through the whole academy and graduated, but then... it didn't feel right. I got recruited to be a part of the huntsman force, and the rest is history."

"Wow. That's crazy. Though I'm not sure what I really expected, honestly." Eryne ran her fingers across my freckles, like she was tracing constellations on my skin. "It's just strange to think there's a whole force of people whose job it is to catch monsters and keep the rest of us safe."

"Mmm. Well, someone has to do it. Might as well be me. It wasn't like I was attached to anyone back home." That was a topic we hadn't covered yet.

"No long term girlfriends or a wife I should know about then, huh?" The question sounded innocent, but I knew what she was really asking.

I tugged on a strand of her hair. "Why, were you concerned, sugar?"

She blushed. "That I was sleeping with a married man? Not really." Eryne furrowed her brows together. "You don't really seem like the type."

"I'm not. And I've never done that before." All of my

previous relationships, we'd gone on multiple dates before we'd ever taken the next step. Call me old-fashioned, but I liked to woo a girl first. Eryne deserved the wooing, even if I wanted nothing more than to curl my naked body around hers like this every night.

"*Sex?*" She blinked. "I don't believe that."

I laughed. "No. I wasn't a virgin. I don't normally make a habit out of begging a woman to have sex with me on the first date though, either." I took her hand in mine. "But when I'm all in with someone, I'm all in. And believe me when I say, I'm all in, Eryne."

She gave me a soft smile, leaning forward to press her lips against mine. "Good. Because I kinda like you a lot, Barrett Lockwood."

The words were music to my ears. "I like you too, Eryne Fowler."

Eryne smiled, curling against my chest.

"Now, I want to know more about *you*," I said, running my fingers down her bare back.

Her teeth raked over her lower lip. "Well, I'm an only child. I spent most of my childhood trying to blend in versus standing out. Not an easy feat with bright ginger hair."

I tugged on a lock. "I think it's beautiful."

She blushed. "Thank you." She pushed a few strands of hair off my forehead. "Yours is too."

"We match."

I grinned, once again thinking about those two redheaded toddlers running around one day. "Yeah. We do."

"What else?" She hummed. "I got Nutmeg—my hedgehog —when I was little. My parents thought I was crazy, picking her as my familiar, but we just clicked. But I was always taking care of injured animals. That was how I found out about my healing affinity." Eryne looked down at her palms. I thought about how she'd healed me, taking care of me. The warmth that had flooded my system from her touch, her magic mingling with mine, helping my own rapid-healing abilities come back online. "My parents joked about me becoming a vet or a nurse, actually, but I never saw myself doing it for a job. I guess I just wanted something that felt like it was for me. I thought about going to college in the human world, but I hated the idea of having to hide who I was for four years to blend in. So... I stayed."

We'd talked about that before—when I'd asked her if she'd ever left.

"And that's how you ended up working at the coffee shop?"

She paused for a moment. "It sort of landed in my lap when I was in between things. Willow posted a position for a barista, and I wanted to move out of my parents' house, and one thing led to another... I guess you could say it was a little bit of kismet." She gave me a warm smile. "Just like finding and saving you was."

"Thank the moon that you did." Pressing a kiss to her forehead, I cupped her cheek with my palm. *"You're* beautiful, Eryne. Inside and out."

"Stop," she said, though it was a weak protest. She looked away, a bashful smile on her face.

Dropping my lips to hers, I ran my tongue over her lips until she opened for me, and held her like that as we lost ourselves in each other's mouths, lips moving softly as our tongues explored, like a dance with no choreography.

My cock, already hard again, pressed against her hip, and I groaned as she ran her hand down my shaft, caressing my knot.

I pressed the tip of my finger in her entrance, feeling her tight, wet heat sucking me in. Eryne let out a breath, turning her head to look back at me.

"You're so responsive," I murmured, tightening the arm I had draped across her stomach as I slid another finger inside her. "It drives me fucking crazy." If I wasn't so afraid of taking her again, I'd slide home right here and knot her. But I was trying to hold back.

"Then why didn't you... touch me for the last few days?" she whispered, fiddling with her hair in front of her face.

"Fuck," I cursed, sitting up and pulling her into my lap. "Eryne." I brushed her bangs back, running my fingers through her soft waves. "It wasn't like that." I wanted her. I *always* wanted her. Didn't she know that?

"I don't know why I'm upset. I know this is just... casual." She shrugged her shoulders, looking away.

"Is it?" I asked, dragging my thumb under her chin to bring her face back to mine and looking her straight in the eye. "Because this doesn't feel casual to me, Eryne." And I didn't just mean the sex.

"I don't know what I'm feeling," she admitted. "But we haven't talked about it."

"No, we haven't," I agreed, rubbing my thumb across her jaw. "And that's my fault for not clarifying."

She let out a soft breath, eyes fluttering shut.

"I like you," I repeated, brushing my lips over hers. "No matter what else is happening out there, this, in here—this is us." It wasn't enough, but it was a start.

"Okay." She murmured, cuddling back against me. I ran my thumb over her shoulder blade as she interlaced our fingers, relaxing into my hold.

"I want you," I murmured. "I always want you. But I don't want to rush this, either."

Her eyelids grew heavy as I continued to hold her. We stayed like that, wrapped up in each other's arms, until we fell asleep. I wasn't sure I'd ever been so comfortable and content before.

Then again, I'd never felt this close to my mate before.

I was truly bewitched by her. By every single facet of her personality. She was soft and sweet, and yet there was a fire within her that couldn't be put out.

It gave me hope.

That maybe, just maybe... in the end, she'd pick me too.

My mind was still running a hundred miles a minute, especially after spending the evening with her coven. Last night with Eryne, I'd taken my mind off of the creature in the woods, whatever was feasting off the magic of the wards like a parasite, but I couldn't ignore it any longer.

I had a hunch, and I hoped like fuck that I was wrong.

> BARRETT
>
> Going for a run. Will be back soon.

> ERYNE
>
> Be safe.

> Aren't I always?

> I don't like the idea of that thing shredding you to pieces again.

> I'll be at the Witches Brew when you're back.

> You know, if you want some company.

I liked that she cared about me. That she didn't want me getting hurt.

For her sake, I didn't want to be right. Because if it wasn't just some paranormal being who was living off the magic of their barrier, slowly eroding the magic and turning it into something else... then I wasn't sure Ezra and I alone were enough to take it down.

Damien had offered, but could I trust the man? Sure, he seemed pretty smitten with his pregnant mate, and even though I could practically feel the power coming off of him in waves, he was still a demon. For a long time, wolves hadn't trusted demons. Though anymore, I didn't know what was real, and what had been fabricated by the elders all those moons ago to keep us apart.

It was clear we all had a purpose now. To bring our communities back together. To keep the people of this town safe.

For me, to keep my mate safe. To prove to her that this was real.

I shifted in a flash, leaving my clothes behind as I darted towards the woods. I needed answers. Needed to know exactly what we were up against.

And this time, I wasn't leaving until I found the monster behind this.

Before he doomed every single witch in this town to a slow, painful death.

CHAPTER SEVENTEEN

eryne

Watching the sun rise on Pleasant Grove in the mornings was a sensation I didn't often experience. Mostly because I was a night owl who preferred to watch the sun *set* instead. Still, I couldn't deny that it felt good to get out of the house, to use some time alone to think.

Barrett was out for a run. He'd texted me this morning, which had instantly made me feel better considering I'd woken up to an empty bed.

It was the first time in days that I hadn't had his arms around me, sharing a good morning kiss before we started the day, and I couldn't help but feel a little disappointed in waking up to cold sheets.

I also couldn't help but feel like this was all too good to be true. I didn't want to let myself hope, to even dare to wish for more. After all, everything could change in the blink of an eye. Still, his words last night felt so sincere. Like he meant every single one of them.

This doesn't feel casual to me.

I like you.

No matter what else is happening out there, this, in here—this is us.

But that didn't change the fact that this was only tempo-rary. That eventually, he would leave. With his job, how could he not? Plus, his home base was back in Walnut Ridge—with his family. Could I sacrifice myself, the town I loved, if he asked?

I wasn't sure I could.

Which was the real problem. I wanted to ask him to stay, but how could I, when I wasn't even willing to go?

I leaned on my broom, surveying the empty shop. Soon, everyone would be pouring in for their morning coffee and pastry. Then, I'd be busy enough that I wouldn't have time to think about Barrett Lockwood or the way he'd come into my life like a tornado, dismantling the walls I had built before I'd even known it.

"What am I going to do?" I asked the silence.

I'd always done my best thinking alone. Maybe it was because I'd been an only child, because my parents had raised me to be so independent, or because I'd never truly felt like I fit in growing up. Even in a town of witches, there'd always been something different about me.

Maybe because some part of me had always been waiting for *him.*

I shook my head, storing my broom and fidgeting with my dress.

"Get your head on straight, Eryne," I muttered to myself. I had more important things to do today. I needed to order inventory for the rest of the month, including the delivery that would take place Halloween week. I had our numbers from last year, but forecasting was always tricky. Still, I knew what our best sellers were, and the last few weeks of October would require double the amount of pumpkin extract and canned pumpkin.

Even though I wasn't our baker, I couldn't help but miss Luna during moments like these. She had a way around the kitchen, and everyone was obsessed with her baked goods. But I couldn't fault her when she was so happy, raising twins with her husband and mate, not to mention living in a palace and being a literal queen.

I'd always imagined being a mom one day, having a big family full of love and laughter. That dream had always felt so far out of reach, until suddenly... it didn't. My mother was constantly hounding me, asking when I was going to settle down. Was it too early to hope that maybe Barrett might be the one?

My phone buzzed, and I grabbed it, reading the texts from my coven.

CAIT

Tomorrow's the full moon. Everyone ready?

WILLOW

Yes.

CAIT

Not you.

WILLOW

I might not be able to help, but I'll still be there if you need me.

Besides, a baby isn't going to keep me away from my girls.

WENDY

All ready here. Grandma got wind of what we're doing, and she found another old box of journals. Bringing it over now, Cait.

RINA

Does anyone feel this like... crazy rush whenever they think about what we're about to do?

Because this is exhilarating. It's like we're breaking the rules. Takes me back to high school...

I snorted, typing out a reply.

ERYNE

What would you know about breaking the rules, Rina?

CAIT

She's got a point, Reens. You graduated with a 4.0 and ran the school newspaper.

RINA

I can be a bad girl, thank you very much.

WENDY

...

WILLOW

No comment. Now, does anyone know where I can find a piece of candy corn pie? I have a craving.

CAIT

That sounds disgusting.

WILLOW

Don't knock it till you try it. Besides, the baby loves it.

CAIT

I'm still trying to get used to the idea of my baby cousin having a baby, Wil. Don't make it weird.

ERYNE

I don't have any pie, but if you come down to the bakery, I think I can find something for you.

WILLOW

Sold.

I could almost imagine them bickering. The Clarke girls were all close, and I'd often longed for that growing up. I couldn't count how many nights I'd wished on the full moon to bring me a sibling. But it was always just me and my animals.

I don't want to be alone again. The thought hit me like a pang to my chest. I'd gotten so used to Barrett being around the last few weeks. First, as a wolf—like a giant puppy, following me around—and then in the last week, as a human. I meant it when I told him I liked him. Not just because he was the most handsome man I'd ever met, but because he was maybe the most caring person I'd ever met. He acted like a giant puppy half the time himself. Before meeting him, I used to laugh when girls called their boyfriends golden retriever types. Now, I was pretty sure I understood.

Though Barrett was all *wolf.*

Biting my lip, I finished tidying up as my opening girls came in, heading behind the counter and pulling their aprons on.

An awareness prickled at the back of my neck—like I was being watched.

It was different than the awareness I felt when Barrett was around. That was comfortable, like cozying up under a warm blanket. I shivered, turning my head to look out the big windows.

There was a tall blond man across the street outside, unmoving, standing next to one of the black lampposts. A chill ran down my spine. He was dressed in all black, in a three piece suit that didn't *quite* seem like it was from this century.

I couldn't help but feel like he was watching me. How long had he been there? I'd been so lost in my own thoughts all morning that I hadn't even paid attention, but something about this didn't feel right.

And then I blinked, and the man was gone. Just like that— *poof*—into thin air. For a split second, I almost thought I saw a bat flying away, but that couldn't be possible.

I picked up my phone, dialing the number without a second thought. "Barrett?" I breathed out, trying to ignore the way my body was shaking as I walked into my office and sank down onto the couch.

"Baby." His voice was soft. "What's wrong?"

"I don't know," I whispered. "Something weird just happened."

The street was empty—had I imagined it?

The rustling of branches filled the phone, and then his voice was much clearer. "Do you want me to come over there?"

I shook my head, even though I knew he couldn't see me. "No. I'm probably just seeing things that aren't even there." I forced out a laugh. "It's okay. It's fine. Maybe I just didn't get enough sleep last night."

He sounded concerned. "Are you sure? I can be there in a few minutes and check it out."

"I'm sure," I reassured him. "Don't worry about me. We're opening the doors now, so I'm just gonna go back to my office and work on some paperwork."

"Promise you'll call me if anything else happens?"

Just hearing those words from him already made me feel better. Knowing that he'd drop anything, within a moment's notice? That was something I couldn't take for granted. "I promise."

We hung up, agreeing to meet later at the bar after I finished work for the day.

Sitting in my chair, I took a few deep breaths, trying to collect myself. Why had that freaked me out so much? It wasn't like strange things didn't happen in this town all the time. It was a town of witches after all. I'd grown up used to the unexplained and eerie things.

But that felt... different. More menacing. I could barely focus on my work, the anxiety plaguing me. Was he connected to the wards, somehow? Maybe I did need Barrett to come down here. He could sniff around and see if there was any trace of the blond man...

My office door opened, and Willow walked in, munching on a pumpkin muffin.

"Hi," she said, her mouth full of food. "Sorry. S' good." She sat in the chair in front of my desk, a to go cup in one hand, and her treat in the other. She balanced her muffin on her belly. "Two months to go, and I feel like I'm going to be as big as a house before I deliver."

I laughed. "It's your shop. You don't have to apologize to me." She looked around the office, and I wondered if she was thinking about all of the memories she'd had here.

"You made it yours," she said, a soft smile on her face. "This place... It was Luna's dream, and I loved it because of her. But now, it feels like a part of my past versus a piece of my future. And I'm so proud of everything you're doing."

"Thank you for saying that," I said, feeling the warmth in my chest. "For everything, really. For the longest time, I didn't really know who I was."

"And now?"

"And now..." I gave a hesitant smile. "I think I'm starting to."

"He's good for you, you know," Willow said, reaching over and squeezing my hand. "Barrett."

I bit my lip. "I don't know... It's still so new. And he's going to leave, eventually."

"Unless you ask him to stay." She popped the last piece of muffin in her mouth and chewed.

I shook my head. "I couldn't ask him to do that. His job... It's important, you know?"

She nodded. "But that doesn't mean *you're* any less important, babe."

Warmth spread to my cheeks. "I just..." I just *what?* "It scares me, you know. How fast it feels. How much I like him."

"You don't have to explain it to me," Willow started, looking down at her bump, like that said everything. In a way, I guess it did. They met last October, and a year later, they were expecting their first kid. "It was fast for us, too. But after a month together, I knew. He's my soulmate, so sure, that played into it, but also... I couldn't deny that I loved him." She gave me a bashful smile. "Damien showed me how much he cared for me every day. There was no way *not* to fall in love with him, demon and all."

I looked away. "I don't know if I *love* him," I whispered. It was too soon for that. Sure, I liked him, but liking him and *loving* him were two different things. Liking him and being willing to upheave my entire life for him was another. "Maybe I just don't know what I want."

"I think you do know. And I think it terrifies you."

I thought about how Barrett answered the phone earlier. About how every time he called me *baby,* and I wanted to melt. Or the way he clung to me like I was his lifeline sometimes. About how much joy he derived from feeding me. All of it was more than I'd ever experienced in any of my other relationships growing up.

I thought I knew what love was. But now that I was thinking about it, I wasn't sure I'd ever really known at all.

Not until Barrett came crashing into my life, a wolf who needed me to nurse him back to life, and started showing me what I deserved, each and every day. I meant what I told Willow—it was too soon to love him.

That didn't mean I wasn't starting to.

CHAPTER EIGHTEEN

barrett

The Witches' Brew was abuzz with customers, almost every single table full of witches chatting to each other, enjoying coffee and sweet treats. The place smelled like vanilla and coffee beans, a scent had me wishing for cozy mornings spent together on the back porch, curled up under a blanket.

Maybe after we saved the town we'd have time for that.

Without waiting for one of the baristas working out front to show me back to the office, I walked through the shop, following the pull to my mate. It was never very hard to find her thanks to that thread that tied us together—and the way I could pick her scent out of any crowd. Right now, the scent was slightly sour, and I hated the way her fear and anxiety changed it. I wanted her to be happy, always.

Opening the office, I found her sitting at the desk, chewing on her otherwise perfectly manicured nail, staring at the computer screen. She'd pulled on a dark green sweater dress, a color that I was absolutely obsessed with on her, and I imme-diately wanted to march over there and pull her into my arms.

Last night had been *amazing,* but I wanted more. It was getting painful holding back. And I knew what that meant for us, but I was still trying to keep myself under control. To wait to bond to her until I was sure that she wanted that too. But it was painful, fighting the need. And soon, I knew I wouldn't be able to.

Eryne looked up, and it was like her mask melted away, every trace of the business woman fading, turning her into the woman I *knew* I was developing feelings for.

"Come here," I said, opening up my arms.

She didn't even hesitate, standing from her desk and practically launching herself into them. I nuzzled my face into her neck, rubbing my scent into her skin. There was a deep, primal need inside of me to make her smell like me, and it was even harder to ignore after her phone call this morning.

"It's okay," I murmured as I rubbed her back. "I'm here."

"I don't know why I'm so freaked out," she said, dropping her forehead against my chest as I stroked her hair. "It could have just been nothing. But it felt like he was *watching* me."

"I'm here," I repeated.

My mate relaxed, wrapping her arms around my back and hugging me tight before pulling back a fraction of an inch to look up at me. It was when we stood like this that I could really appreciate how much smaller than me she was, how I wanted to tuck her against me, to keep her safe. If I could always protect her from anything in the world that could possibly hurt her, I would.

"You're so good at that," she murmured as I brushed my thumb across her cheek.

"Good at what?" I whispered.

Eryne's lips tilted up, and it felt like the sun was shining again after a week of rain. My heart beat faster in my chest. "Calming me down. Making sure I'm okay."

"I always will," I promised.

She nuzzled her face into my chest again. "I might hold you to that."

I chuckled. "Good—I expect you to, sugar. You're always keeping me in line, after all."

Cupping her jaw with my hand, I bent down to kiss her, feeling her rise to her tiptoes as she threw her arms around my neck.

"Thank you," she said, those beautiful blue eyes looking up at me through her lashes. Gods, she was beautiful.

I brushed her hair back behind her ear. "Anything." Her eyes traced my face, like she was trying to memorize it, and I couldn't help my smirk as they landed on my lips, her teeth burying themselves in her lower lip. Every time she did it, it made me want to bite her lip instead.

"You got a haircut," she finally said, reaching up and running her fingers through my hair.

I nodded. "This morning. Needed it." My wolf hadn't liked it, but he wasn't the one who needed a trim to his coat, so I told him to suck it up.

She hummed. "I like it." I'd left it longer on the top, since she seemed to love running her fingers through the strands and tugging on it.

"Good. Now, what do you say I help you take your mind off of the man from earlier?" I asked, dropping my lips to her ear and tugging on her earlobe with my teeth. I could smell her arousal almost instantly—the sweet flowery smell practically filling up her office, making me even more desperate for her.

She bit her lip. "Here?" Eryne looked around the office, cluttered with boxes and paperwork.

"Do you have a better idea?" I asked, tracing a finger down her collarbone, underneath the neck of the sweater. "You smell so sweet, baby."

Without a word, she interlaced my fingers with hers and tugged me towards the door, peeking out of it before leading me into the kitchen.

"What are we doing?" I whispered.

She shushed me, pulling me in to the spotless kitchen. The stainless steel appliances practically gleaming, and it still smelled faintly of sugar and pumpkin, like whatever had been baking in here this morning. Eryne traced her fingers over the countertop in the middle of the room, like she was deep in thought.

"Coffee?" she asked, looking away from me.

I shook my head, wrapping my arms around her middle from behind. "I'm only thirsty for one thing, sugar."

After last night, I was desperate to have her taste on my tongue again. I'd always been told there was nothing better than the taste of your mate, and now I knew it was true.

Next time, I wanted her to ride my face—but that would have to wait.

She let out a small moan as I scraped my teeth down her neck, desperate to sink my canines into her pulse point. *Bite her,* my wolf said. *Mark her.*

"Is anyone going to come back here?" I asked, running my hand slowly down her leg, towards the hem of her dress. She was wearing a black pair of tights underneath it, along with her favorite pair of combat boots, and I wanted to rip them off of her.

Eryne shook her head. "Not likely... but there's always a chance." Her voice was breathy, her scent growing even stronger. *She liked this,* I realized. She was turned on by the idea of someone catching us in the act, and fuck if that didn't make my cock twitch.

"Fuck," I groaned. "You're a little vixen, do you know that?" I dipped my hand underneath her underwear and tights, rubbing two fingers over her clit before dipping them inside. She was soaked and *needy*, and there was no way I was going to leave my mate wanting.

Slow enough to torture her, I tugged her sweater dress off her body, every inch revealing her skin to me, before dropping it on the floor. Her lacy bra and underwear set made my mouth go dry as I took all of her in.

"How attached are you to these tights?" I asked, shifting one of my fingers into a claw and lightly pressing it against the thin black material.

She shook her head, letting out a few rough breaths. "I'm n-not."

"Good." I tore them off of her, letting them fall to the ground, exposing the thin layer of lace that concealed her perfect pussy from me. Picking her up, I set her on the counter, placing a hand on either side of her. "Look at you," I praised. "So beautiful. And all mine."

She nodded, eyelids fluttering. "Yes, Barrett. I'm all yours."

Her hand traveled down, exploring until she cupped my length, squeezing it lightly through my pants.

"Sugar..." My voice was low. "You're driving me crazy." I cupped the back of her neck, kissing her roughly, swirling my tongue with hers. She let out a moan into my mouth, and it was all the encouragement I needed to keep going, kissing her hard as I cupped her breasts, running my thumbs over her nipples in circles.

She squeezed my erection harder, and I let out a curse, pulling away. "I'm not going to last if you do that, baby," I said, nipping at her neck before sliding my fingers underneath the waistband of her panties. "Up," I ordered, helping her lift her hips so I could tug them down her legs.

Kneeling on the cold floor, I looked up at her, running my

nose over her inner thigh. She let out a sharp inhale when my hot breath ghosted over her cunt.

"Now... I need that sweetness on my tongue," I said, running my flat tongue up her entrance.

Eryne whimpered, her fingers digging into the wooden counter as I lapped up her juices, savoring every last drop. I could feel her getting closer, her breaths turning to cries, and I stopped right before she could come.

"Mmm," I said as I stood up, running my hands up her bare thighs.

She shivered, and I grabbed my discarded flannel shirt, draping it over her shoulders so she'd be surrounded by my scent. Covered in it.

"What do you want?" I asked, leaning down to suck her nipple through the lace of her bra.

"I want you to fuck me," she said, her words in such stark contrast to her sweet voice. "*Please.*"

With a groan, I unzipped my pants, pulling out my cock and running the head through her entrance, coating the tip in her juices. "I can't knot you," I reminded her. We'd be stuck together while my knot deflated, and I had no interest in being caught while buried deep inside of her.

"Right." Was it me or did she seem almost... disappointed?

I dropped my forehead against hers. "Next time," I promised, kissing her softly.

She nodded, letting out a small gasp as I pushed inside of her. It felt so fucking right, being inside of her again, feeling her warmth surrounding my cock. I let her adjust to my size for a moment, waiting until she squirmed underneath me before moving again.

"I want to knot you so fucking bad," I admitted, voice low against her ear. "Want to fill you up till you're dripping with my seed."

Eryne moaned, digging her fingers into my shoulder. "Please, I want that." She whimpered as I pulled out a few inches before thrusting inside of her again. Each motion was shallow, but I avoided being too rough with her.

"I'll be locked so tightly inside of you that you won't be able to get away. But you wouldn't want to, would you? Because you're my good girl, and you're going to take every-thing I give you." My voice was rough—more alpha wolf than human.

She framed my face with her hands, kissing me in response as I tightened my grip on her hips, burying myself deep inside her pussy, both of us groaning into each other's mouths as I filled her completely. I explored her mouth with my tongue, her taste of coffee and sweet caramel exploding on my tongue.

"Mmm," I groaned. "Almost as sweet as your pussy."

Her cheeks flushed pink. "Barrett..."

Pulling back, I slammed in again, bottoming out inside of her. I was careful not to let my knot pop in place, holding back out of fear of accidentally joining us together.

"Harder," she begged, raking her nails across my scalp. "*More*." Her voice was like sin when she asked me like that, all breathy and needy.

I groaned out a, "*Fuuuck*," as she clenched around me, her pussy tightening around my cock like she was milking me for everything I was worth.

Eryne cried out as her orgasm hit her a few pumps later, and the feeling of her cunt spasming around me set off my own release. With a grunt, I wrapped my hand around the base of my cock as I came, squeezing around my knot to prevent it from going inside of her. She threw her head back as I groaned, still pouring every drop into her warmth.

Finally, when we were both panting and spent, I pulled

back, kissing her softly before pulling out. She gave a tiny whimper, and I cursed myself internally. "Did I hurt you?"

She shook her head, a dreamy smile spreading over her face. "No. I just..." Eryne bit her lip.

I leaned forward, nipping at it when she let out a gasp of surprise. "Stay there," I said, watching as my release dripped out of her onto the countertop.

Yeah, that was... *hot.* My wolf was more than satisfied, knowing we'd filled her up.

"Oops," she giggled. "Guess that's not exactly sanitary." Her cheeks turned red. "Luna would *so* kill me if she knew about this."

"Good thing she's not here then," I said. Turning to the sink, I looked for a washcloth, and a second later, one drifted over to me.

I looked over at Eryne, and she looked coy. She did it often around her own kitchen, levitating bowls and ingredients over to her, but I'd never been on the other side like this.

Dampening the cloth with warm water, I walked back over to her, softly cleaning her up before helping her back into her panties. She shrugged my flannel shirt off and lifted her arms up over her head as I guided her sweater back on before putting my shirt back on, buttoning it up.

As much as she'd smell like me for the rest of the day, I also liked that her scent clung to my shirt, letting me smell like *her*, too.

"Mmm." She leaned against me, wrapping her arms around my back. "Thank you."

"I should be thanking you," I said, brushing her hair back behind her ear and fluffing her bangs.

We finished cleaning up the kitchen together, including bleaching the counter. It was the least I could do, really, after defiling the bakery like that.

"Sorry about your tights," I said, looking down at the shredded nylon.

She laughed. "It's fine. I'll just go home and change before the bar later."

I hummed, rubbing my face into the crook of her neck, making sure she was drenched in my scent even more. "You sure you still want to go?"

Eryne leaned forward, hands gripping the collar of my shirt to bring my ear down to her level, her voice dropping low as she murmured, "Yes. And before you go getting all territorial and possessive of me, remember whose cum I'm filled with, baby." She winked, pressing a kiss to my cheeks before slipping out of my hold.

Baby. Fuck me, there was no way I was going to be able to hold back tonight. Even if she was completely covered in my scent.

Eryne looked considerably more calm now than she had this morning—especially after this afternoon's orgasm and finishing her first drink of the night at the Enchanted Cauldron. Rina, Wendy, and her were dancing together on the floor, and she looked less stressed than she had in days.

I was content to just nurse my drink at the bar as I watched her, letting out a small growl of warning when any men approached her group. Three beautiful women all dancing together in a bar? I wasn't an idiot—but I wasn't letting some fucker hit on my mate, either.

It helped when she reminded me that my cum was still dripping out of her when she walked in, wearing the sexiest fucking dress I'd ever seen. I wanted to wrap her up, to keep anyone else from seeing her like that, but I loved how happy she looked—effortlessly confident and gorgeous. Her hair was curled into waves, and she'd clipped a piece of hair back, showing off her broomstick earrings. The dress dipped low on her back, and she had a new pair of heeled boots on, ones that I couldn't *wait* to take off her later.

Goddamn, I was the luckiest wolf alive to have her as my mate. This tiny witch who had no idea how much she'd already changed my world.

The song changed, and she came back over to the table, swaying her hips as she grabbed her beer, drinking it as she watched me. She stepped between my thighs, free hand running up my leg—and then she stopped. Froze, like she'd just seen a ghost.

"Eryne, baby," I murmured, squeezing her thigh. "What's wrong."

"That's him," she said, letting out a little gasp as her hand found my wrist, tugging on the sleeve of my jacket. "B. That's the man I saw earlier." Following her line of vision, I saw who she was talking about and let out a low growl.

Eryne's eyes widened as I stood from the chair. "Stay here," I barked.

"But—" I didn't listen to the rest of her sentence as I marched over to the blond man who was currently leaning against the bar, sipping on his glass of whiskey casually. Like he knew exactly what he was doing, the fucker.

"What the fuck do you think you're doing, asshole?" I asked, pinning him against the wall in barely the blink of an eye. "You scared my girl."

A fang popped out from his top lip as he snarled back at me. "Good to see you too, Lockwood."

I growled again. "Don't you fucking touch her," I said, poking at his chest. "Don't even *look* at her."

She's mine, my wolf growled. *My mate.* Mine.

182

He rolled his eyes. "I wouldn't dream of it."

I let him go, still baring my canine teeth at him in a warning.

"Barrett?" Eryne's soft voice popped up behind me. "Who is this? How do you know him?"

I cleared my throat, shoving him back, not caring that everyone else in the bar was staring at us. "Eryne, this is my... partner, Ezra Darkmire." Though that still wouldn't stop me from tearing his throat out if he went near my mate.

"But he's..." She trailed off, no doubt taking him in fully. "You're not a wolf, are you?"

"Perceptive, little one," Ezra said, in that perfect north-eastern accent that he could never quite shake, even after all these years. "A shifter, I am not." His red eyes were curious as he gazed between me and my mate.

Eryne swallowed, and *fuck*, I should have told her about him sooner. But I'd thought I would have more time. With his blond hair, blood red eyes, and pale skin, I couldn't imagine what she thought of him.

"You're early," I said, keeping an arm around my mate to keep him away from her. I could see her studying him curiously, wondering what, exactly, my partner was.

"Am I?"

I glared at him. He picked underneath his nails before taking another sip of his drink.

"A vampire," he said, turning to my mate. "That's what I am."

She turned to me, hurt on her face. "You brought a vampire to my town? I thought you told me they were dangerous, and I should stay away from them."

Ezra chuckled. "Well, there's certainly one reason he wants to keep you away from me."

A deep rumble came from my chest, a warning.

My girl frowned, clearly needing more of an explanation.

"We've been partners for a long time," I explained. "Other vampires aren't like Ezra."

He smirked, leaning in closer to both of us. "Or maybe that's just what he wants you to believe." Two fang s popped from his upper lip.

I narrowed my eyes at him. "Are you here to help or not?"

Ezra stood up straight, composing himself. "Of course I am. I've never let you down before, have I?"

"No, you haven't," I agreed, albeit begrudgingly.

My girl interlaced her fingers through mine, and wrapping her other arm around mine, leaning her full body weight against me. I dropped a kiss to her forehead. Her scent flooded into me, and I let out a breath, feeling the rage, the need to go full alpha, receding.

"Eryne, are you coming back? Wendy and I were just—Oh." Rina's eyes widened as they met Ezra's, and she froze for a moment, staring at the vampire in front of her. "Hello."

His eyes flashed golden for a brief second, and he swallowed. I wasn't sure what was going on inside his head— though she paled in comparison to Eryne in my eyes, I couldn't deny that she was a lovely witch, with her long brown hair pulled back in a high ponytail, exposing her neck, and that purple dress showing off her figure.

Ezra, the fucker, said nothing. His red eyes were alert, searching—like he was still processing something his body already knew.

"Okaayyy, well..." She turned back to Eryne. "You coming?"

My girl turned to me, and I nodded. "Ezra and I need to talk. Have fun with your friends, baby." I squeezed her hand. "I'll come find you after."

"Okay." She stood up on her tiptoes and kissed my cheek.

"Don't take too long. And then you can take me home, and we can have a repeat of this afternoon." Eryne ran her fingers up my fly.

Fuck. "That's mean."

She looped her arm through Rina's. "I like to call it motivation." She blew me a kiss.

"Vixen."

Eryne winked. "Have a fun chat, babe."

When I turned back to Ezra, he raised an eyebrow at me. "You still haven't told her, have you?"

I crossed my arms over my chest. "Why do you say that?"

"Because, if you had, she'd be wearing your mark on her neck. Though she does reek of you, so I suppose you're halfway there."

I growled again.

He lifted his hands up. "Sorry. I'll stop."

"Please," I gritted out. "My wolf is a little possessive of her." And I had no desire to shift in the bar to protect her honor.

"A little?" He laughed.

"We should talk somewhere a little... quieter," I said, looking around the room. Sure, it didn't look like anyone was listening to our conversation, but I didn't want to take any chances when most of the witches in this town had no idea what was happening.

We walked outside, the cool night air surrounding us like a blanket.

"Ezra," I started, making sure I could keep my eyes on the girls through the window.

"You found something," he announced, knowing me well enough after so many years of working together.

I kept my voice low. "I found the lair."

He gave me a pointed look, those icy eyes piercing through me. "I thought I told you not to do anything without me. It could have been dangerous."

"Relax. It wasn't there." Though my wolf hadn't wanted to get close to it regardless. He was being a pain, only wanting to be around our mate.

"But you know *what* it is."

"Yeah." I nodded. "And it's worse than I originally feared."

"Well, don't leave me hanging," Ezra said, sarcasm bleeding through his tone.

"Wraith." It was hard to deny, when I laid out all the information in front of me. I'd been flipping through books at the library, trying to find another answer, but it was the only explanation that made sense.

"*Fuck*," he cursed.

I agreed with the sentiment wholeheartedly. Wraiths were undead creatures born of evil and darkness. They despised the light—living in dark, damp spaces—and fed off of energy, infecting the land slowly with their own unique brand of poison.

It was a creature that should never have been let out of the depths of the underworld, and yet, there was one *here*. Here, in my mate's idyllic small town, feeding from its magical barrier.

"At least I understand how so many beings have been able to break through the wards now," I said, tossing back my drink. "While it might be keeping humans out, it's hopeless against the rest of our kinds."

"Do you think they know?"

I shook my head. "At least, not yet. But their coven... They want to destroy the wards."

He frowned. "We can't let them do that. At least, not yet."

"What other choice do we have?"

"Call *them*."

I shook my head. "No way. Anything but that."

"You know what we have to do, B."

Unfortunately... I did.

CHAPTER NINETEEN

eryne

Barrett walked outside with Ezra, and I turned back to Rina. "What was that?"

She frowned. "What?"

I didn't think I was mistaken—something had happened between them. Some connection as soon as their eyes had met. "When you saw Barrett's friend, you totally froze. What happened?"

Rina looked down at her deep purple fingernails, inspecting them like she was worried she'd cracked her manicure. "Nothing."

Wendy gave her a pointed look. "Sabrina."

She groaned, crumbling under the weight of her best friend's stare. "Ugh. I don't even know where to begin." Rina looked outside, where the two guys were now chatting. "Look, I know I don't talk a lot about my gift. But I can see auras. On *everyone*. His aura is..." She shivered. "I've never seen a color like that before. So... deep and *angry*."

My eyes widened. "You can? What does mine look like?"

"Green." She turned to Wendy. "And yours is pink, before

you ask. I'll tell you more about it later. I just..." Rina looped her arms through both of ours. "Come on. Let's get another drink. I need something to wash that feeling away."

"Fine," I started, "but I'm not finished with this conversation. We're coming back to this eventually."

She waived me off, ordering a round of shots when she got to the bar. After we all threw them back, we headed back to the dance floor.

The flood of alcohol running through my veins made everything brighter, more bubbly, and *lighter*. I let loose, swaying my hips back and forth to the beat of the music, only coming back to myself when I felt a warm body slide in behind me, wrapping an arm around my waist.

"There's my girl," Barrett's deep voice murmured against my ear. I instantly relaxed against him, leaning my head on his chest so I could look up at him.

My girl. Yeah, I was. I smiled.

"Hi," I said, feeling cozy and content in his arms as he rocked me in time with the music.

"Hi." His free hand cradled my shoulder, his thumb rubbing back and forth over my skin.

I pressed my ass back against his jeans, feeling his cock hardening as I moved my hips. My nipples pebbled in my dress, and I was *very* aware how much I wanted this man. Ever since this afternoon, I'd wanted more. And I really wanted him to take me home and finally let me feel his knot inside of me.

I reached up, running my hand down the side of his face. "Take me home, Barrett."

He didn't waste any time. As soon as the door closed behind us, Barrett had me up against the wall, his lips on mine as his hands wandered, pushing my dress up and revealing the black lace panties that barely left anything to the imagination.

"Fuck me," he groaned, snapping the waistband against my skin before pulling them down my legs. "It was so hard holding back." Barrett buried his face in my neck, inhaling deeply. "So hard when you smell so fucking good all the time. So sweet."

He pushed his thigh in between mine as he leaned forward to take my mouth with his. I rocked my hips against him, already feeling the ache building inside of me—the need to have him inside of me.

"Bedroom," I gasped as he kissed and sucked at my neck.

His eyes darkened as he pulled me into his arms, carrying me into my room and set me on the edge of my bed. Barrett dropped to his knees, unzipping my heeled boots and letting them drop to the floor, before pulling my dress off over my head. I wasn't wearing a bra underneath, since the fabric would have shown, and I ran my fingers over my nipples, cupping my breasts as he looked down at me.

Standing up and stepping towards him with the sway of my hips, I returned the favor, unbuttoning his shirt, and unbuckling his belt, and then flicking open the top button of his pants. He kicked them off eagerly, and then was back on me, kissing me hard as his hands explored my bare skin. Barrett's cock came to life between us as our tongues explored, pressing into my stomach, and I moaned as I reached down, stroking his length with my hand, feeling his knot at the base.

I spun us around, pushing him down until he laid back on the bed, lounging across it like he *belonged* there. He watched me as I took him in—all of him. Every last inch. Barrett was all muscle, six-foot-three and *delicious*, like he was sculpted from granite and chiseled by the goddess herself just for me.

There was no taking my eyes off of him—not that I even

wanted to. It was such a stark contrast to weeks ago, when I'd been taking care of him when he was hurt. Now, besides a few healed scars, there was nothing to show it had ever happened.

But through it all, he was still my wolf. Still the man I was falling in love with. It was hard to deny, especially when he did things like show up at the bakery just to make sure I was okay. My heart melted a little more every time he showed how much he cared—how much he valued me. It was more than just whatever physical connection was between us, whatever made us so explosive in the bedroom.

It was like there was an invisible string, tied between him and me. Pulling us together, even when we didn't know it. That thread had brought him here, to *me*.

And for now, I didn't even care if this would end someday. If he'd go home and find his mate and leave me behind. Because right now, he was mine.

My girl, he'd called me. I wanted to be his. Wanted this— his knot, his everything.

"Come here, baby," he murmured, fisting his cock. I bit my lip as I watched him jerk himself off, running my fingers down my thighs and pressing two of them inside my slit. It was hard to deny I was wet—especially when I knew he could scent my arousal now.

Unable to resist any longer, I lifted myself into the bed, climbing on top of him, dropping my knees to either side of his hips. I trapped his erection between our bodies, planting my hands on his chest as I leaned forward to press my lips to his.

Barrett ran his hands up my thighs, his gaze taking me in, like he was trying to memorize this moment. Or maybe that was just how I felt, because I didn't want to forget one single moment.

We'd had sex before, but this felt different. Like something *more*.

Maybe because he'd promised to give me his knot tonight. I'd been hesitant at first, but now I wanted to know what it felt like inside of me.

"You're so hard," I observed, my words breathy. Was that really what I sounded like? Pure sex?

"I feel like I could explode just from you rubbing your pussy all over my cock," he groaned as I rocked back and forth over his length, feeling my wetness coating his length. He squeezed my hip. "I want to be inside of you," he said with a groan as I ground my pussy down on the tip, needing more friction. "No—I need it." His forehead was dotted with sweat, like he'd been fighting his urges, and I wanted him to let go. To not hold back anymore.

"Yes," I agreed.

Lifting my hips, we both guided his length inside me, and I let out a sigh of pleasure as I took every last inch.

Barrett groaned as his cock speared me, hips thrusting up involuntarily, like he was just as desperate for this as I was. He filled me completely, and I'd never known this feeling of fullness before him. It was like I could feel him *everywhere*.

His knot sat at the base, and I squirmed, trying to fit it in too.

Barrett chuckled, lightly slapping my ass before gripping my hips. "Not yet, Sugar. You're not ready for that."

I pouted, clenching my insides around him. "But you told me I could feel it."

"So needy." He reached up, cupping my breasts and massaging them, thumbs flicking over my nipples. "You will, baby. But first, we have to get you nice and relaxed." He leaned forward, taking one into his mouth and sucking lightly. "I need you to come first."

I threw my head back, arching my back into him as I started to move my hips back and forth, each forward movement causing his knot to press against my clit, proving me delicious stimulation that was going to make me come faster than I ever had before.

He grunted, as I started moving faster, combining the rocking motion with raising and lowering myself on his cock, riding it with abandon. I was lost in the pleasure, in all of the feelings that were taking over my body, desire and lust flooding through my veins and begging for *more, more, more.*

"I'll give you more," he promised.

I cried out as he timed his hip thrusts in time with mine, helping bounce me on his length. "Holy fuck," I gasped, my orgasm already starting to crest inside of me. "*Barrett.*"

Every single time I dropped back down on him, his knot pushed against my entrance. I was so wet, my juices were dripping down his shaft. His eyes were glued to the spot where his cock disappeared inside of me, fingers gripping my hips so hard I was pretty sure that I'd have marks tomorrow, and the entire scene was so erotic that I couldn't hold my voice back.

"Ohmygods," I sobbed as my climax hit me, wave after wave of pleasure bursting through my body as Barrett kept thrusting up into me and guiding my hips in a rocking motion.

"Knot me," I begged him. "Please."

He let out a guttural sound, his hand closing over the back of my neck and bringing my lips down to his. "Fuck," he said against my lips. "Are you sure?"

I nodded, running my fingers up his chest as I kissed his neck, on the same spot he was obsessed with on me. "I want to feel all of you."

Plus, after earlier, I was pretty sure there was no going back for either of us. I was quickly growing addicted to the feeling of him filling me up, of knowing what it felt like to have his knot swelling inside of me. He was as hard as steel, his tip pressed against the entrance to my womb, and each shallow hip thrust only seemed to nudge him in deeper. "Come inside me," I encouraged, tightening my muscles around his length. "Please."

"Tell me you're mine," he demanded.

"I'm yours," I promised. It surprised me how easily the words slipped out. How I didn't even have to think about it. "I'm yours, Barrett."

Barrett let out a grunt as he gave one last punishing thrust, and my eyes widened as I felt his knot pop into place, stretching me even further.

"*Oh,*" I managed to squeak, feeling his warmth spill inside of me as he came. "Fuck. That feels—" I shut my eyes, letting all of the sensations crash over me. I was still overly sensitive from my orgasm earlier, but I couldn't hold back, my body shaking as another one hit me.

"Eryne," he moaned, clearly feeling the effects as my pussy spasmed around him. "You're so fucking perfect. So perfectly made for me. Gods, you feel so good." His hands cupped my ass, fingers digging into my soft skin, and I cried out again. It felt like every part of my body was a nerve ending, coming to life with his exploratory touch as he filled me with his cum.

I cupped his face with my hands, pressing soft kisses to his neck, his face, the sides of his lips until he took control, capturing my mouth with his in a lazy kiss. The stretch from this position and his knot were almost too much for my body to handle, but I couldn't stop now.

"Fuck," Barrett said, letting out one last groan as he slumped back against the pillow. "You were..."

"Not bad yourself, Wolf-Man."

He wrapped his arms around me, rolling us so we were both on our sides and stroked my face, pushing my hair off my damp forehead. We'd worked up quite a sweat. I hummed, nuzzling my face into the crook of his neck, enjoying the feeling of his strong body wrapped around mine. He'd always been like my personal space heater, but I definitely preferred cuddling with him like this, skin to skin, versus when he was a wolf.

"So, how long will we be..." I looked down between us, wiggling my hips with him still buried inside of me. "You know."

He chuckled, kissing my forehead. "Maybe thirty minutes."

"Mmm." I laid my head on his chest, letting my eyes drift shut as he rubbed my back in soothing circles.

I must have fallen asleep, all warm and content, because I didn't stir again until Barrett was tugging on his knot, like he was testing our connection. He rolled me over onto my back, letting my head rest on the pillow.

A rush of cum spilled out of me as he pulled his knot out, and his eyes darkened. Barrett scooped up his release and pushed it back inside of me, like he needed to make sure not a single drop escaped.

"B," I groaned.

"That's so hot," he muttered, kissing my inner thigh.

Thank the gods I was on birth control, because I was pretty sure with that amount, I'd get pregnant no matter where I was in my cycle. Before I could blink, Barrett scooped me into his arms, carrying me into my bathroom and turning on the shower, making sure it was warm before setting me down on the tile floor. He carefully washed my body and hair, taking care to make sure he'd cleaned every spot before turning to the clean himself, letting the water rush over his face and chest. I watched, mesmerized as he ran his hands through his damp auburn hair, soap dripping off his chest hair.

"You're so beautiful," I murmured, unable to keep my eyes off of him.

"I think that's my line, sugar," he said, his lip curling up in a smirk. He dropped a kiss to my lips before pulling me back under the shower spray, devouring my mouth.

We got out after the water ran cold, and he wrapped me up in one of my fluffy bath towels, insisting on drying me off before carrying me back to bed.

And then, curled up in his arms, our fingers interlaced, I could feel the drowsiness hitting me after he pressed his lips to my forehead. In his arms, because there was no place I'd rather be. A smile curled over my face, and I thought about what Willow had told me this morning.

I knew what I needed to do.

To figure out how to ask him to stay.

Because I didn't want to give him up. Didn't want to live in a world where he found a different mate, where I had to live with the idea of knowing he wasn't mine.

After tonight, I sure as hell felt like I was *his*.

CHAPTER TWENTY

barrett

"So nice of you two to join us," Cait said, looking between the two of us as we walked into Willow's house the next day, fingers interlaced.

Eryne blushed at my side. "Sorry."

Willow, Damien, Cait, Rina, and Wendy were all already here, with Ezra in the corner, leaning against a wall. I wasn't sure how he'd gotten himself invited, but figuring that out wasn't my highest priority right now.

We'd slept in this morning—she was worn out, even though I knew she didn't want to admit it. No matter how ready she'd been, I could tell she was moving a little slower this morning. I'd fully intended on making it up to her, waking her up with my mouth, but we'd been sidetracked with a barrage of texts from her coven, so my plans had been put on pause. For now.

At the moment, it felt like we were two teenagers who'd been caught doing something bad, and I hated that. We were two consenting adults—what we did in our free time was no one's business but ours. My wolf was restless, wanting me to claim her.

I planned to tell her everything—after the wards were fixed. After this situation was under control. Once I knew there was nothing else standing in between her and I being together. Besides, I didn't want to add any more stress to her plate.

Later, I promised myself.

"So, what's going on?" I asked as we settled into the two open chairs at the table. It was storming outside, and it added to the general gloominess that had settled over the gathering. Everyone's mood felt sour, and I had an unpleasant feeling settle in my gut. My wolf whimpered, wanting *out.*

Damien crossed his arms over his chest. "When were you going to tell us that you knew what was living outside the wards, feasting on the town's magic?"

I cursed. Dammit, Ezra. "I only found out yesterday."

"But you suspected," Willow stated, frowning.

Nodding, I looked at Eryne. There was hurt in her eyes—hurt that I'd kept this from her. "I didn't want anyone to worry until I was sure." I went on to explain everything we knew about wraiths. Ezra and I had never faced one ourselves, but we'd been trained with how to deal with them.

"Knowing that, we're not sure it's still a good idea for us to destroy the wards. This being, this *wraith?*" Cait practically spat out the word. "Whatever is keeping it out there is the only thing keeping us safe. We have to put the protection of the town first."

Eryne slammed her fist on the table. "No. The wards need to go. We can recreate them, right? They're keeping us isolated and not in a good way. We've been kept in the dark for hundreds of years, and for what? To keep us safe from the others like us?" She shook her head. "I don't want to live like this any longer. We need to know the truth." She looked to

Damien, and then Ezra, though she avoided my eyes. "Last year, we all thought demons and vampires were bedtime stories told to keep us from acting out. None of us had any idea until Damien came into town that there was even anything we were missing. But now we know. And I can't go back to that." She looked at me. "It might have taken one injured wolf shifter for me to find out, but I know we deserve better than this."

My mate had a point. It was time to change that—for us to stop being hidden and secluded from each other. After all, witches and wolves weren't so different. I could imagine wolves living here, frolicking through the woods and finding their own places in the community. It would be their choice, but I knew what I would choose.

I'd choose Eryne every time.

Though my job as a huntsman could put her at risk. I knew it, and yet I couldn't stop from wanting to be around her. From wanting to keep her. I knew what could happen if we didn't complete the bond soon, but was she ready for that? Was *I* ready for it?

I wanted her to want me. To care about me. Not because I was her mate, but because she loved me.

Love. I shut my eyes. It was too soon for something like that. Too soon, and yet... I'd loved her from the first moment I set eyes on her. As soon as we bonded, she'd know exactly how I felt. All of our thoughts and feelings would be shared, and it would be impossible to keep anything from her.

Willow nodded. "You're right. And it's not just us who deserves better. Pleasant Grove could be a haven for all of us— shifters and vampires and witches alike. Locking ourselves away from the paranormal community may have been our ancestors choice, but it doesn't have to be ours."

"Should we put it to a vote?" Rina asked. I noticed she was sitting on the opposite side of the table as Ezra, and she'd been glaring daggers at him or pretending to ignore him most of the time we'd been here. I was intrigued to know if something had happened between them, why she seemed so disgusted by his presence.

Wendy looked between all of us. "I agree with Eryne. And I want to unwrite the wrongs of my ancestors. I think we owe it to everyone in town."

Everyone murmured their agreement.

"So, we're still doing it then?" Cait asked.

Ezra brushed a piece of imaginary lint off his suit coat. "Great. Now that we've gotten that out of the way, we need to strategize. We have to be smart about this, or else."

Damien rapped his fingers against the table. "That's the smartest thing you've said all day, Vampire." His eyes seemed to flash a deeper red.

My partner's lips curled, revealing his fangs. The wolf inside of me was instantly on edge, sensing danger and ready to leap to action at any second. Demon and vampire—I wasn't sure if I wanted to find out who would win.

"No fighting, both of you," Willow said, reaching out and putting a hand on her mate. "We're all working together towards the same goal."

"Fine," Damien huffed.

Ezra didn't say anything, just looked away.

It was going to be a long afternoon.

Hours later, I found Eryne outside on Willow's back porch, slowly rocking on the porch swing. The girls had mostly moved on to what they needed to do to rebuild a magical barrier that would keep humans out without keeping Pleasant Grove shrouded from all those who weren't witches.

There was a chance, of course, that they were opening up their home to more evil creatures, the likes of which Ezra and I had tracked and hunted all over the country, but it was a trade off they were willing to make in order to restore balance, the way nature intended.

"Oh." She blinked up at me. Draped over her lap was a knitted blanket, and she was running her fingers over the fibers while staring out across the street. "Hi."

Willow had gone all out decorating the house for Halloween—one I'd learned used to be her parents house before they'd passed away many moons ago. Carved pumpkins decorated the porch, including multiple featuring cats. The entire neighborhood was decorated, just like Main Street, and it truly felt like it could have been a stock photo or something featured in a magazine. It was cozy and homey in every way, and though I'd never had strong feelings about the holiday one way or the other, I had to admit that I found it charming here.

I leaned against one of the poles of the porch railing, watching her and studying her face. Last night had been amazing, but she was quiet today,

"I'm sorry I didn't tell you sooner," I said, shoving my hands in my pockets. "Last night was..." I sighed. "I didn't want to ruin that."

"We can't keep secrets from each other," she whispered. "This will never work if we do. Whatever this is."

"We're whatever you want us to be," I answered, though the words felt like cracks in my heart. I wanted more—of course I did.

Sitting down next to her, I took her hand in mine, pressing a kiss to her soft skin. "What's wrong, sugar?"

She shook her head. "It's stupid."

I rubbed my thumb over her hand. "Whatever you're thinking, it's not stupid," I promised. "I can't do anything if I don't know what's going on inside that pretty head of yours." I tapped the middle of her forehead, between her bangs

Eryne leaned her head on my shoulder, letting out a small sigh. "I trust you." My mate looked up at me, those big blue eyes full of so much emotion that my heart clenched in my chest. "You know that, right?"

I brushed her hair back from her face. "I do. And I'll do everything I can to be worthy of that trust. I owe you my life, Eryne. There's nothing I wouldn't do for you. I couldn't repay that debt in a million lifetimes."

"It's not a debt, Barrett. You don't owe me anything. If I had to do it all over again, nothing would stop me from saving you that night." She pressed a kiss to my lips. "I'd never regret this. You."

I cupped her cheek, running my thumb back and forth over her skin. "Eryne. From the very first moment, I've never regretted anything. And I know it's fast, but—" Here was my perfect opening. The chance to tell her. *You're my mate.* When I opened my mouth, however, I couldn't form the words. "But I want to be with you. No matter what that looks like."

"After this is all over, are you going to go home?" Eryne asked, wrapping her arms around her torso like she was hugging herself.

Home. What would that even look like now? Was home a place, or was it just a person? And if it was, then home was wherever *she was.* Home was Eryne.

But that wasn't what she was asking, and I knew it.

"Probably, yeah. I haven't seen my family in... awhile." I shrugged. "It's overdue." But I wanted to bring her home with me. To introduce her to Walnut Ridge as my mate—as the witch who had saved my life and showed me a completely different one.

"Right." She nodded her head, biting her lip. "It's just..."

Eryne looked up at the sky. "Fuck, I didn't think this would be so hard."

"Sugar, are you breaking up with me?"

She laughed. "No. The opposite, actually."

"Thank fuck, because I'm not letting you go." I pulled her into my lap, cradling her body. "You're stuck with me, Eryne. No matter what happens, you can't get rid of me."

"So, you'll stay?"

"Yes." I brushed a strand of hair off her face.

"What about your job?"

"I'm perfectly happy being your twenty-four/seven space heater, baby." I winked. "Besides, I can still do my job and stick around town. I can keep Pleasant Grove safe." That was better than any job I'd ever accepted. More important, too. Because keeping Pleasant Grove safe meant keeping Eryne safe. Keeping my mate safe.

She let out a sigh of relief, throwing her arms around my neck and holding me tight. I did the same, wrapping mine around her waist, breathing in her sweet scent and letting it steady me. Appreciating the fact that no matter what happened today, at least I had my mate in my arms.

And she was mine.

"It's time." Cait's voice was ominous, like a prophecy we couldn't escape from, and we all followed her into the back-yard. The sun was setting, and we still had to prep for their spell circle before the moon was in the perfect position over the sky.

"We'll perform the ceremony in the spot where the barrier is the weakest," Willow explained, like we hadn't all been there when we made our plan. She turned to Ezra and Damien. "You two are on standby in case that... *thing*—" A visible shiver ran through her body. "—decides to make an appearance. And Barrett will stand in for me."

"I'd feel better if you stayed in the house," Damien was saying, not for the first time.

She stood on her tiptoes and pressed a kiss to his jaw. "And I'm not leaving my girls to do this alone."

He sighed, like he knew that would be her answer, kissing her lightly as he rubbed his hand over her bump. "I just want to keep my girls both safe."

I turned away, feeling like I was intruding on an intimate moment between them.

Eryne walked towards me, wearing a velvet cloak over her dress. The rest of the coven all wore identical ones, with pointy witch hats on their heads, and the energy was completely different than it had been hours before. Maybe it was because of the full moon, but it felt like I could feel magic buzzing through the air, pulsing all around me. I could even feel it in my veins—maybe because we'd been created by witches. I didn't have magic, but I'd be acting as a conduit, and I was just glad to be able to help.

My mate extended out her hand to me, and I took it, interlacing our fingers.

"We'll do it together," I promised her.

She nodded. "Whatever happens, I'll never regret any of it," she reminded me.

They were words I'd keep reminding myself of, over and over. Especially because I didn't know how much longer I'd have them.

How much longer she'd truly be mine.

CHAPTER TWENTY-ONE

eryne

The spot we'd chosen to create our magic circle was deep in the woods. For anyone watching us, it might have seemed a little strange, this group of thirteen witches—plus a vampire, a wolf shifter, and a demon—walking through the forest with candles and other supplies levitating behind them in the air, but for Pleasant Grove, this was a normal Thursday. Mostly.

Of course, nothing felt normal. There was a gravity in the air, an importance I couldn't shake off. This felt so much bigger than any of us. So much bigger than Barrett and I, so much more than just fixing a wrong from the past.

Maybe we'd never truly find out what the witches who founded this town were trying to keep out, or if they'd just been prejudiced against other paranormal races, but at least we could fix it now.

We wouldn't tell our children that demons would come and grab them if they were bad, that making deals with one meant giving up your soul, or that vampires were nothing but bloodthirsty creatures who would feast, happily, off our blood.

Though the latter was still out for debate, really, considering I knew nothing about Ezra, not really. Sure, he was Barrett's friend, and they'd worked together long enough that he trusted him, but was that enough for me?

It still stung that he'd told Ezra about the creature attacking the wards and not *me*. The girl he was... what? We were more than just fucking—he'd made that apparent with our conversation earlier. That word felt crass. It wasn't just sex, and both of us knew it.

We'll do it together. He didn't try to tell me not to, to warn me away because he was worried about me. Like he knew that I was too stubborn not to see it through. That after all we'd done, all we uncovered together, he knew that I couldn't leave it alone until we'd made a change.

That was what I loved about him.

And I did. Dammit, it was early, but I felt the love swelling in my heart, wanting to burst out. But it wasn't the right time. I wanted to tell him cozied up on my couch, or standing in the middle of the gazebo in town square, surrounded by lights and pumpkins. Not in the middle of the dark, damp woods, about to perform a spell we weren't even one hundred percent sure worked.

But the girls surrounding me weren't just my coven, or my friends... they were my family. And as much as I'd kept myself closed off for so many years, they'd all always been there, waiting for me to take that step. I held my head higher, squaring my shoulders, feeling the magic bursting through my body. There was no feeling quite like this, like unifying with your sisters, knowing your actions weren't just going to change your life but everyone's lives. For the better.

"I'm so proud of you," Barrett murmured into my ear, squeezing my palm.

I smiled up at him, wishing I could tell him everything I was feeling.

He said he'd stay. That was all I could ask for. The rest of it, well—we'd figure it out. But he wasn't going to leave.

That was the reassurance I'd needed to really let myself fall, wasn't it? To accept the feelings that had been growing from that first night.

"We're ready to begin," Cait said, looking up at the moon high in the sky. Sure enough, the circle was complete, thirteen candles levitating and the other ingredients for the spell in the middle. Each member of the coven was evenly spread around the clearing—Cait, Gretchen, Tammy, Tally, Sophie, Olive, Iris, Constance, Celeste, Rina, Wendy, and me.

We each took a step forward in front of one of the candles, reaching our hands out to the witch next to us. Barrett took my hand, taking Willow's spot, though she remained close by, and I knew she'd still be filtering her magic into him and the spell.

Cait began chanting the spell we'd all memorized, a mixture of latin and the old language that had long ago lost its meaning. I closed my eyes as I poured all of my energy into our purpose, visualizing breaking the magical barrier, allowing the wards to come down so we could build them anew.

Barrett was right—the magic we were tearing down felt like poison, and a slimy feeling crept down my spine. The candles flickered out, and then we were plunged into darkness, only lit by the light of the moon.

"This would be a great time for Luna to show up with her weird moon powers," I heard Willow murmur to Damien behind us.

The air grew cold, and I shivered, feeling the magic cracking and scattering.

A bolt of lightning hit the direct center of where our circle had been, and we all stepped back, dropping our hands and breaking the circle.

"Did it work?" I asked, unable to detect that faint buzz of magic where it had been before.

Cait's face was pale. "I think so. But I..."

Something shrieked in the woods, a noise that sounded like nails on a chalkboard, and everyone froze.

"What was that?" Wendy's eyes were wide.

"The wraith," Ezra answered. "We've angered it. You stole it's energy source." He inspected his nails, like he couldn't be bothered.

Barrett let out a snarl—a noise I'd never heard from him before, more wolf-like than anything else, and leapt forward, changing in an instant from man to beast. He took off in a flash, disappearing into the trees in a blur of paws and red fur.

"What's happening?" I asked the vampire next to me.

He flashed his fangs. "Now, we hunt."

I shivered again—I didn't like the sound of that.

Not one bit.

After escorting us back to my house and making sure all of us were okay—plus that Willow was tucked onto my couch and off her feet—Damien disappeared back into the darkness, his eyes flashing a deeper red than I'd ever seen him.

He seemed even bigger than normal, if that was possible, like his powers were about to burst out of him.

"I should be out there," I said, staring out the sliding glass door. I had Nutmeg cuddled into my shoulder, and even with her cuddling against me, I still couldn't help my anxiety.

My heart hadn't stopped beating rapidly since Barrett had shifted and lunged after whatever had been in the woods.

"You know he wouldn't want you to risk yourself, babe," Wendy said, coming behind me and wrapping her arms around me.

Rina squeezed my free shoulder. "Wendy's right. You could get hurt."

"Don't you remember what that thing did to Barrett? How I found him?" My eyes welled with tears. "I can't lose him again, you guys. I just can't. And I hate that we're here just... *hopeless*. We didn't even get a new barrier up."

The fact that we were so vulnerable right now, that any human could walk into a town full of witches and discover the secret we'd been guarding for more than three hundred years was terrifying, but not as terrifying as the idea that something would happen to Barrett.

I'd never even gotten to tell him how I felt.

"You love him, don't you?" Wendy whispered.

I nodded, tears dripping from my eyes. "I don't want to lose him."

"You won't," Rina promised.

Unfortunately, it was one she couldn't keep.

Wrapping a blanket around myself, I stepped onto my back porch, the morning light already leaking through the trees.

The rest of the girls were asleep inside, though I knew they were mostly there for moral support for me, and Willow, who had fretted over all of us until Cait had finally made her a cup of tea and took charge of the rest of us.

I had a cup of coffee in my hands, the warmth spreading through my body making me feel a little bit more like a person again, but I hadn't drank a single sip yet. All I'd managed to do this morning was take a shower and pull on a fresh set of clothes.

Barrett hadn't returned.

I felt sick. Like this monumental, life altering thing had happened, only I had no control anymore.

The trees rustled, and I perked up.

"Barrett?" I called, holding my breath.

Instead, it was Ezra. He held his side, blood leaking down his shirt. His skin had lost some of it's usual pallor, and his eyes were closer to black than their usual red.

"Oh gods." I rushed over to him. "What happened to you?"

He groaned. "Ambush."

"Is Barrett okay?" I asked him as I guided him into a chair on my porch, pulling his hand away to find a similar wound to what Barrett had been covered in weeks ago.

He jerked away when I tried to touch him to pull his shirt back. "*Don't.*"

I frowned. "I can heal you." I let my magic run into my hands, glowing warm light coming from them. "It's my ability, and I—"

Ezra shook his head, cutting me off. "You shouldn't touch me. Barrett... He'll be feral."

I didn't understand. "Why? You're hurt. I want to help. Barrett would want me to help his friend, too."

"No. I need to feed. But... *Fuck.*" He ran his fingers through his blond hair, blood from his hands coating the strands. "I can't feed from you." The vampire rubbed at his forehead. "Besides, your scents are all over each other."

My cheeks burned. That was mortifying. "You can... smell that?" I knew Barrett could scent me, but I hadn't realized that anyone else could. For some reason, I'd just thought it was a wolf thing.

"Your mate didn't tell you?"

I frowned. "My *mate*? I don't..."

Everything hit me all at once. *Barrett*. How possessive he was over me. How right it felt to be with him. The connection I'd had with him, since the very first night. He was my...

How was this possible?

Ezra went deathly still. "You really didn't know."

I shook my head, a sinking feeling settling in my gut. I couldn't believe it. How could he not tell me? How long had he known and kept it from me? "No," I whispered.

Letting my blanket fall to the floor, I looked out into the forest.

My mate.

Barrett was my mate.

And he was... what? Hurt? Missing? A sob escaped my throat.

Whatever reason he hadn't told me, I couldn't let it end like this. Couldn't live in a world without him, a world where I never told him how I felt. Just yesterday, he'd told me he would stay. And today, it felt like that could all be slipping away from me.

"I need to find him," I said, worry filling me to the pit of my stomach. I turned back to the injured vampire. "Where is Barrett, Ezra?"

"You can't go out there," he said, clutching his side. "You'll be in danger. A wraith is no joke, Eryne. He can't—"

"I can take care of myself," I said, narrowing my eyes and heading into the forest.

There was nothing that was going to keep me away from Barrett.

From my mate.

From the man I loved.

Nothing.

I tried to imagine his face, letting whatever connection was between us guide me to him. Following the path back to the clearing, I found where we'd broken the spell last night. The candles laid discarded on the ground, the spot where lightning hit the middle of the circle scorched. Barrett's pile of shredded clothes still sat where he'd shifted, a reminder that he was in wolf form. It was eerily quiet, and I could only hope that I was going in the right direction when I followed a path of broken branches and trampled bushes.

A branch cracked behind me.

"Barrett?" I whispered, cold fear trickling down my spine.

But I didn't feel his presence, the way I always could. I felt... fear.

There was a sound, almost a snarl, and then my vision went black, and everything ceased to exist.

Barrett, I tried to cry out. To scream for him. But I was drowning, lost in an endless abyss, and I couldn't seem to figure out how to find my way out of the darkness. I was growing weaker, my legs tiring, and I couldn't breathe.

So instead, I succumbed to it, no longer having the energy to fight.

CHAPTER TWENTY-TWO

barrett

S omething was wrong.

I was wrong. Something I didn't like to admit often, but in this case, we were vastly unprepared for the scene that had unfolded as soon as the girls brought the barrier down.

It hadn't been one wraith, but a whole nest hiding out, like they were in wait for us. Even with the three of us, we were outnumbered by their horde. It seemed like they were planning for exactly this scenario, trying to feast on our energy. They weren't easy to kill as it was, considering they were undead and could reanimate unless their heads had been completely severed from their skeletal bodies.

Ezra was right. I should have called them. Something I'd begrudgingly agreed upon after he'd gotten hurt, the wraith sending him slamming into a tree, those poisonous nails scraping through his flesh. How long did he have? I hoped he made it back.

Lightning cracked in front of us, and I darted back, jumping to the side to keep it from scorching my fur. The electricity crackled through the wraith who swiped his bony hand, nails sharpened into points, towards Damien. It exploded upon contact, though another quickly replaced it.

"What the hell are these things?" Damien's brother—Zain —growled. He'd arrived last night, stepping through a portal of darkness after Damien had gotten the girls to safety.

It was the only reason I could breathe easier, knowing Eryne was safe. It was the only reason I could even focus.

I bared my teeth against another wraith, watching the demon princes out of the corner of my eye. I'd never seen anyone move like they did, effortlessly darting through the shadows and portals they created in an instant. Snapping my teeth, I lunged for the creature, sinking into rotting flesh and old fabric.

The two looked so similar to each other—dark hair, both massive, maybe six and a half feet tall—and seemed to share similar powers. The main way I could tell them apart was their eyes—Damien's were blood red, and Zain's were bright gold.

How many had we killed? I'd lost count. Black blood dripped from my maw, and I couldn't get the taste of rot out of my mouth.

"They're like no demons I've ever faced," Damien said, wiping his forehead before using his shadows to create a sword, slicing another's head clean off it's body.

"That's because they're not demons," came a voice like gravel, grating against my skin. "They're something worse." Black eyes met mine, and my wolf whimpered.

Death.

I hated interacting with the ghouls, because they felt all wrong. He was pale, wearing a black shrouded cape, with hair as white as snow. He waived his hand, and it felt like every wraith in the clearing was frozen in place.

"Heard someone called for me?" The ghoul smirked. His

eyes glowed white as he prowled toward the wraiths, like the grim reaper coming to collect their souls. In a way, I assumed he was.

I shifted back, thankful when Damien threw a pair of clothes at me. I wasn't sure where he'd gotten them from, but I didn't really care. Quickly pulling on the jeans and shoving my feet into the boots, I dressed quickly, knowing I couldn't do anything else in wolf form.

We'd pushed them back into a circle, but now, they all were suspended, frozen in air—in *time*.

"What's he doing?" Zain asked as we watched the ghoul's eyes flare each time he approached a wraith, before it disappeared in a cloud of dust.

"Eating their souls," I deadpanned, pulling on the jacket. He was absorbing them, and I didn't want to think about the process any more than that.

"Jesus. And I thought things were bleak in the demon realm," Damien said, crossing his arms over his chest. "Blood demons seem like walk in the park now, eh, brother?"

Zain elbowed Damien. The two seemed close, though it was obvious Damien loved to get a rise out of his older brother.

A scream pierced through the forest, and I whipped around, trying to identify the source. Even the ghoul's head turned, glow fading from his eyes from absorbing the last wraith.

"I thought we got them all," I said, frowning. We'd spent most of the night driving them all together into the clearing and picking them all off, one by one. It was really a miracle they hadn't eaten right through the barrier with the amount we'd found.

It would have only taken another day or two, by my calculations, before Pleasant Grove would have been swarming with them.

"There must be another close by." The ghoul's eyes shifted back to their normal shade of unsettling black. "I'm Cassius, by the way," the ghoul said, extending his hand towards us. "I'm sorry I wasn't here sooner. We're a little short-staffed right now." I didn't know quite how ghouls were born—or made—but I could only assume their job was one most mortals wouldn't want to sign up for.

"I thought we had it handled," I said, shaking my head.

A piercing pain hit my skull, and I winced, pressing my hand to my head.

Barrett. Her voice called out to me in panic, and I felt my heart lurch in my chest. "Where's Eryne?" I asked them all, eyes wide. "Something's happened."

"Last I saw her, she was at the house," Damien said. "All the girls promised to stay together."

I shook my head. "She's not there." The mate bond confirmed that.

Damien looked away for a moment. "Willow confirmed that she left this morning after Ezra showed up. None of them realized she was gone until after."

"Fuck," I cursed.

"Your mate?" Zain asked.

I nodded my head. "We haven't even completed the bond yet. I can feel her, but it's faint. Foggy." If only I had told her yesterday. If only I'd finished the mating already. I groaned. "This is all my fault."

"It's not," Damien reassured me.

Zain ran his hands through his jet black hair. "Something similar happened with my wife—my mate—not long after we'd been together. My father kidnapped her." He shook his head, like he was trying to rid himself of the memory. "Use the bond—whatever is there—to find her."

Shutting my eyes, I focused on her. Wherever she was felt

cold and damp, and though I couldn't reach her on the other end of the bond, I could feel that she was still breathing. "She's still alive," I said, rubbing at the spot above my heart. We all knew what the end of that statement was. No one seemed willing to say it out loud, however. "And she's shivering." There was only one place I could think of where she could have been.

"The cave," we concluded, all at once.

There must have been one that stayed behind to guard the nest.

One that had somehow found my mate.

And from the pit at the bottom of my stomach, I had a bad feeling I knew what we'd find there.

"Let's go," I said, ready to shift back into wolf form to run there.

Zain shook his head, and a portal opened in a patch of darkness. "Come on. This is quicker. And she'll need you in that form."

The woods were unusually quiet, and a layer of damp moisture clung everywhere around us. Fog had rolled in, and a shiver ran down my skin. It felt wrong.

Zain wrinkled his nose. "It reeks."

The ghoul pushed away a layer of bushes. "They're foul beings. They never should have been able to escape." He turned to me. "They're being sent back where they belong."

I nodded. That was all we—and the witches of this town—could ask for.

That was what I tried to remind myself of as we all stepped through the portal.

Not the idea that my mate was alone and hurting, and I hadn't been there to protect her.

The darkness dissipated around us, and my eyes adjusted to the low lighting of the cave.

Zain's hands came to life, electricity—lightning—sparking between them, giving us a better view of what we were looking at.

"They were definitely here," Cassius confirmed. "Follow the bond," he told me. "It's the strongest magic there is. That's probably why they snagged her after they lost their food source."

I let out a growl, darting forward in the cave, my supernatural speed allowing me to almost fly through the dark rock. Though I didn't have teleportation powers like the two demons or ghoul at my back, I wasn't going to back down from this fight.

Deeper and deeper we went into the cave system, as I followed the thread that tied Eryne to me. It was faint, but I could practically smell her scent, the sweet sugary scent like apples and cinnamon filling the area, pulling me to her. Always, always pulling me towards her.

There was a figure ahead of us, laying in a heap at the back of the cave.

I took a step towards my mate, unable to keep away from her for even a moment longer.

"Wait—"

The sound of nails scraping on stone echoed through the cavern, and then a wail filled the space as the undead being appeared in front of us. It was larger than any of the ones we'd fought, likely the source of all of the attacks on the town barrier. They weren't capable of speech or rational thought, opening its ghostly mouth to reveal a line of sharpened teeth.

I shuddered, thinking of what it had felt like when I'd been attacked all those weeks ago. *This* was the creature that had attacked me. I could feel it. Whatever we'd fought before had merely been mirages compared to this abomination.

"Return to the place you belong," Cassius's eerie, ominous voice shook the ground. The wraith shrieked, letting out a sound that felt like nails scraping against a chalkboard. In his hands, a glowing white scythe appeared. It looked like it was made out of bone, the blade of the sharpest metal I'd ever seen.

The thing lunged, and before I could shift again to attack it, a lasso of darkness reached out from both sides of the room, circling it's hands and wrapping around it's neck, keeping it in place.

"Finish it," the demon brothers said, grunting under the weight of holding the creature back.

Cassius nodded, stepping forward and launching his weapon at the head of the wraith.

It let out another sound, though this one was worse.

"Be gone from this earth," Cassius said. **"You are not permitted here."** His eyes glowed as the entity let out one last shriek before the black raggedy cloak it seemed to be wearing collapsed to the ground, empty.

"So, what are you," Damien asked, turning to the ghoul at our side. "Like, the grim reaper?"

Cassius's eyes met his. "*Worse.*"

Ignoring the conversation, I darted forward towards my girl.

Her eyes opened, that beautiful shade of blue blinking back at me, groggy and disoriented. "Barrett?" Her voice was weak, body shaking. I scooped her up into my arms. My mate looked so small, so fragile.

"You're okay," I promised her, carrying her out of the caves and towards the morning light. "You're safe now. And I'll never let anything happen to you ever again."

She grabbed at the collar of my jacket with each hand as I walked outside into the sunshine. Whatever darkness and cold had been clinging to the earth this morning, it was gone now. "I was looking for you."

"I'm here, baby," I said, setting her down on her feet outside of the cave.

I inspected her everywhere, like I could find proof of her physical wounds. My wolf couldn't rest until he knew that she was okay. That she hadn't been hurt. A little bruised, maybe, but still whole.

"You came," she whispered, her hand cupping my cheek.

Of course I had. "You called," I responded, placing my hand over hers and feeling her warmth returning. Somehow, through the bond, she'd called for me. Through our bond. The bond I'd been putting off completing. I shut my eyes, dropping my forehead to hers. "My mate."

She sucked in a breath. "Yes. I am, aren't I?"

I nodded. "You are."

Her eyes grew glassy. "Why didn't you tell me?"

"I didn't want to pressure you," I said, running my thumb over her cheekbone. "I wanted you to be able to make the decision. If you felt like you were forced to be with me because of this bond, I would have hated that."

"I still would have chosen you," she said, voice soft. "You're every dream I've ever had, Barrett Lockwood."

"In every lifetime, in every moment, I'd choose you, Eryne Fowler." I kissed her softly. "I'm sorry I didn't tell you sooner. I wish I had. We could have completed the bond, and then this never would have happened. You never would have been put in harms way. If something had happened to you, sugar..." I shuddered. "I don't even want to imagine what would happen if I had lost you."

"I feel the same way. When Ezra told me... I didn't want to risk never having told you how I felt. What if you'd been attacked again? What if I was too late this time?" She shook her head. "I couldn't have lived with myself."

"It's okay," I promised her. "We're here. We're alive. We're together."

And for now—that was all that mattered.

The rest of it—the barrier, the wraiths, dealing with the repercussions of our actions—those were all a problem for another day.

Right now, I just wanted to hold my mate.

CHAPTER TWENTY-THREE

eryne

H e'd come for me. Of course he had. I'd never doubted he would, not for a single second. He was mine, and I was his, and we were *alive*.

"Barrett," I whimpered, feeling the tears pooling in my eyes. The emotions rushed through me, making me realize how close I'd come to losing everything I'd come to hold so dear. How close I'd come to becoming some terrifying monster's next snack as it slowly drained my magic from my body.

"My mate," Barrett said, wrapping me in his arms. "I thought I'd lost you."

I snuggled against his chest, feeling like everything was righting itself as he held me tight. "You could never lose me, Wolf-Man. It's like you said. You're stuck with me." Warmth flooded through my chest as I pushed my healing magic into him, feeling his body knit itself back together. He'd had a cut over his eyebrow that was trickling blood, and I didn't even want to imagine the other injuries under his clothing.

"Fuck, but I love you." Barrett kissed me, desperately, showing me just how terrified he'd been of losing me.

"Say it again," I said, eyes fluttering as he pressed a kiss to my neck, over that spot he loved.

He rubbed his nose against mine. "I love you, Eryne. My sweet mate. My little healer. My everything."

I took a deep breath, telling him what I knew to be true. "I love *you*, Barrett. Thank you for finding me." I shut my eyes, savoring the feeling of his hands rubbing my back, his woodsy, spicy scent in my nose. For a brief moment, I'd thought I might never feel this again.

"I should be the one thanking *you* for finding me. Saving me." He pressed his lips to my forehead. "For bringing me back to life, literally and figuratively."

From that very first moment when his wolf's eyes had connected with mine, we'd both been changed forever. And I didn't want to wait any longer.

"Make me yours," I said.

His eyes flared with desire. "*Here?*"

I nodded, wanting to complete the bond like he'd mentioned. Whatever that entailed. "I want you."

Barrett looked around, crowding me against a tree and letting my back rest against it.

He tugged my sweater to the side, exposing more of my neck and shoulder, and I watched as his canine teeth grew out of his mouth, elongating into the teeth of a predator. Of a *wolf*. His lips pressed against my bare skin, so soft, like he was worried he'd hurt me.

"Do it," I begged, craning my head to the side. "Please, B. Bite me."

He groaned, scraping his teeth over my skin. I let out a moan, surprised at how turned on I already was. Barrett pushed a knee in between my thighs, his hands running up my sides. "My saliva has healing properties," he told me. "But it shouldn't hurt. I'll make you feel good."

I nodded. "I trust you."

"Fuck," he cursed, holding my neck with one hand, and my waist with the other. I shut my eyes, letting my head fall back against the tree as I reached out, gripping his jacket tight before he finally sank his teeth into the spot between my shoulder and neck.

I let out a gasp as his teeth sank into my skin, because he was right. There was a small prick, but it didn't hurt at all. Not when emotions came rushing into me—*his* emotions. *His* love. The feelings he'd been holding back all this time. They swirled with mine, every feeling in my body heightened to the max, and I cried out at the bliss, the pleasure of it all.

Barrett, I whined, rubbing myself against his leg, every brush of denim hitting my clit.

I know, baby, he said back, the words popping into my mind instead of either of us saying them out loud. I could feel all of my emotions flowing back into him, and I knew he felt the desire in my veins the same way I felt his.

"Your house?" he gasped, eyes wild as his nose flared, no doubt smelling my arousal. My need. I needed him to fuck me, and I needed it *now*.

I couldn't hold back my moan. "No. The girls are still there." He groaned as I pulled at his shirt blindly, untucking it, before running my fingers up his abs. "Here," I begged him, smoothing my hands over his chest. "Take me here."

His hands shook as he unbuttoned my jeans, pushing them into my underwear before his fingers found my slit, finding out what I already knew—I was soaked. My body's response to my mate.

"So needy," he muttered. "My little mate needs to get fucked, huh?" He ran his tongue over the bite mark on my neck, no doubt healing it. I hoped it left a mark. I wanted everyone to know I was his, to see how he'd claimed me for the entire world.

I nodded as he slid two fingers inside of me, hitting the spot inside that made me see stars. *"Yes,"* I cried. "Yes, I need you."

Barrett took his jacket off and laid it down on the dirt before guiding me down gently, pushing my sweater up to expose my breasts. He kissed the swell of each one before helping pull my jeans off, exposing me to the cool air of the forest.

We were both so lost in each other, in the moment, that I didn't even care that someone could see us right now. I just needed my mate inside of me, to know that I was completely, wholly *his.*

He didn't hold back, unzipping his pants and freeing his cock before sliding inside of me with one thrust, filling me completely. I let out a gasp at the fullness, my back arching as I shut my eyes, savoring the stretch of him inside of me. There were no words. We didn't need them. Not when we could feel each other's emotions, each other's thoughts and desires. It was a wordless communication I'd never experienced before, and I wanted *more.*

He was so big, and I wanted that knot in me once again. I wiggled my hips, trying to get him deeper inside of me, as he gave me another punishing thrust, hitting my cervix.

"Fuck," I cried, wrapping my arms around his back and digging my fingers into the soft material of his dark t-shirt. "More."

His eyes were dark as he looked down at me. "Are you sure?"

"I can take it," I begged, wrapping my legs around his back and forcing him deeper. "Give me your knot, *mate.*"

Barrett groaned, like he knew there was no way he could deny his mate. After another few shallow thrusts, he pushed it inside of me. I came as his knot locked inside, my cunt clenching around him, and then he was spilling inside of me, filling me up, and his teeth found my neck again, plunging in to the spot where he'd just marked me, and oh, *Gods.*

Another orgasm burst through me before the first had even subsided. I was crying, pleasure like I'd never known torrenting through my body as we both came, liquid already seeping out around his knot and trickling down my thigh because there was so *much.*

Was this what it was like with your mate? If so, I never wanted it to end.

Finally, when we both collapsed, breath rough and completely spent, Barrett adjusted us, sitting back against the tree as he cradled me to his body.

We were still connected together until his knot deflated, and there was nowhere I wanted to be except right here—with him. I wrapped my arms around his neck, burying my face into his shirt, taking deep pulls of his scent.

He chuckled. "A bed might have been better, my mate." Barrett picked a leaf out of my hair, and I blushed.

"Say it again," I repeated from earlier.

"My mate." He kissed my forehead, then my cheeks, then my lips. "I love you, my mate."

My lips widened into a blinding smile. "I didn't think I'd ever get to hear you say that," I admitted, a blush warming my cheeks.

He frowned. "Why not?"

"Well... look at you. I just didn't think you'd be mine." There was no universe where I thought that I'd be mated to this sensitive, yet sexy, shifter.

Barrett smiled, his fingers roving over my face like he

couldn't decide what to focus on. "I've always been yours, Eryne. From the very first moment when you saved me, your touch kept me going. Knowing my mate—" His voice cracked, full of emotion. "Knowing you were mine, that was how I fought to come back to you. Even when I couldn't shift to tell you what you meant to me."

"Oh." I looked up at him through my eyelashes. "And here I'd thought I had a new pet wolf."

He laughed. "I'll be your good boy whenever you want, sugar." Barrett winked at me, and I blushed harder. His knot was still firmly inside of me, hard and keeping all of the cum inside of me.

I clenched around him, and he groaned. "Don't do that."

"Why not?" I gave him a coy smile.

He swatted my ass. "How long do you want to be stuck like this?"

I pouted. "Fine." I'd be good—even though I didn't want to be.

"So... what now?" I asked, looking down between us.

His hand pushed my hair back behind my ear. "Now, we wait for my knot to go back down, and then I'm going to take you home and we're going to clean ourselves up—" He pulled another leaf out of my hair. "—and then we'll reconvene with the rest of the group."

Even though I knew it was the right thing to do, the idea of having to go see everyone after this was mildly mortifying. Especially since Ezra—and probably Damien, too—could *smell* him on me.

I groaned. "Everyone's going to know what we were doing out here."

"So?" He gave me a mischievous grin. "I like them all knowing that you're mine." Barrett nuzzled his face against my neck. "That we smell like each other."

"Mmm."

I guess that wasn't so bad.

We decided it wasn't worth the risk of humans finding Pleasant Grove if we left the barrier down any longer, and so we'd decided to perform the spell to recreate the wards that night. Only these wards were stronger—interlaced with magic from all of our species: demons, witches, and wolf shifters.

I slumped on the couch in between Rina and Wendy, exhausted and drained. After everything, it would take a few days for my magic to replenish itself in my body, though ordinary things like levitation were still doable in small bursts.

Leaning my head on Rina's shoulder, I watched my mate across the room. Barrett was in Willow's living room, talking with Damien and Zain, though I could barely keep my eyes open enough to listen to them.

It had been a long day. Honestly, the last two days felt like two lifetimes. I'd been kidnapped by some sort of evil un-dead being, almost drained of my magic and life, and then Barrett had rescued me. And we'd had the most insane sex of my *life*.

He looked over at me, eyes heating, like he knew exactly what I was thinking about. And then I realized that he probably *did*, now that we were bonded. I ran my fingers over his mark.

Earlier, in the bathroom, I'd stared at it for a long time, appreciating the spot where he'd marked me. It was still red, but he'd been right when he said his saliva would heal it.

I liked the way it showed off his possessiveness. And he seemed to like it too, if how he acted after was any indication.

He'd almost ripped Ezra's head off when he'd found out the reason I'd come after him—and subsequently been taken. That

Ezra had revealed we were mates before Barrett could tell me. It had required all of us to pull the two apart, panting and bleeding from both teeth and nails. Ezra had been telling me the truth when he'd told me that Barrett would go feral if I touched him, barely letting me out of his sight when I tried to heal the vampire. In the end, I'd just taken care of my mate, knowing someone else from the coven could help Ezra.

Barrett felt like shit, but I knew it was just the alpha wolf in him, trying to protect his mate. An instinct that he couldn't control. Though he was better now that we were mated. I could tell, because every time he looked over at me, his eyes caught on my mark, and his heart slowed.

I rested my hand over mine, knowing they were beating in tandem.

The door opened and closed, and a white haired man dressed in black slipped inside. I faintly recognized him from the cave when Barrett had come to find me, though everything had happened so fast that I hadn't had a chance to say anything to the men who had helped my mate. He hadn't been there when we'd re-cast the barrier tonight, which I hadn't even thought about till now.

I felt Wendy sit up straight next to me, the blanket that had been draped over us falling to her lap. Looking over at her, I saw her eyes grow wide as she stood. *"Cassius?"* The word was barely above a whisper, as she reached out towards the white haired man, then seemed to think better of it.

He looked like he'd seen a ghost. "Wendy?"

I looked between the two of them, wondering what was going on.

"What are you doing here?" She snapped, the words were cold—so unlike my friend.

"I—"

Barrett looked over, noticing the man standing inside the

door, and interrupting before I could find out what was happening. "Cassius," he said, coming over to shake his hand. "Thank you again for the help."

Cassius gave a curt nod. "I was just doing my job." He looked over at Wendy, and then back at my mate. "They are taken care of, and shouldn't bother the town again."

"We owe you one." Barrett shoved his hands in his pocket.

Willow stood up from the table slowly, Damien instantly at her side as she curved a hand over her belly, almost waddling across the floor towards Cassius. "Thank you," she repeated Barrett's sentiment. "For keeping my mate safe."

Cassius shook her hand, nodding again, and she nuzzled back against Damien's chest.

I smiled, imagining Barrett and I like that one day, when we decided to start our own family. For so long, the idea of having a husband and kids had seemed so far off, but now it was within my grasp, and the idea made bats flutter in my stomach.

Yes, I wanted that. I wanted everything with Barrett.

One day at a time, I reminded myself. After all, we had an entire lifetime together.

CHAPTER TWENTY-FOUR

barrett

Now that the imminent danger had passed, I just wanted to spend time with my mate, to curl my body around her and wring orgasm after orgasm out of her body until she was crying for me.

Unfortunately, that hadn't happened yet.

Ezra, Damien and I were all around the table, discussing how to keep the town safe now that it was open to any number of paranormal beings.

"I think I'll stick around," Ezra was saying, adjusting his sleeve.

Cassius's dark eyes seemed to wander over to the couch. "I will as well. There's a chance that there are still more nearby. It would be neglectful of me to ignore my duty again."

I frowned. "But didn't you just say—"

He glared at me. Shrugging, I gave up on that. If he wanted to stay, who was I to stop him?

The witches hadn't known what to make of Cassius's being, and it was clear there was still so much they needed to know about other paranormal beings and this world they'd just opened themselves up to. *Baby steps.*

I wasn't going anywhere. My job, being a hunter, meant I normally traveled, but I had more important things to keep safe here. My mate, and her family. This town that she loved.

And from Ezra and Cassius's expressions, it was clear they felt the same. I didn't pry, but I wondered if it had something to do with the two witches in the other room.

Maybe I'd been right, posturing that there were witches here who had never found their fated mate because the town was closed off. Maybe they'd find the same happiness Eryne and I had. Only time would tell.

Eryne's eyes drifted shut again, and I stood up. "I should take her home," I told the table. "It's been a long day." Most of the coven had already left, leaving Rina and Wendy curled up on the couch with Eryne, and Willow had gone to bed an hour ago after one too many yawns.

Even Zain had departed, saying he needed to return to his wife and their newborn twins. I understood—I couldn't imagine leaving my pups after becoming a new father. Eryne and I hadn't talked about having a family yet, but I hoped she wanted one. I already couldn't wait to get her pregnant, to see her grow round with our pups.

"That's an understatement," Damien said, gripping the back of his neck. "But I agree. My mate's exhausted, and I want to hold her as she sleeps."

I looked at all of them, feeling more grateful than I could ever put into words. "Thank you for helping me find my mate —for not hesitating to risk your own safety for hers. I'm forever in your debt."

With that, I went and scooped up my sleeping mate, letting her rest her head on my shoulder as I carried her back to my car, buckling her in and driving us back to her cozy house.

As I stepped onto the porch, I marveled at the thought that in such a short time, this felt like my home, too. That as long as she wished it, it would be our house, the place where we started our life together. And every step felt monumental. Like the world was changing, rearranging itself beneath my feet to fit this new life we'd created together.

Eryne stirred in my arms before I crossed over the threshold, sleepily blinking up at me before her eyes lit up, a soft smile curling over her face. "Hi."

"Hi, Sugar," I said, taking another step. "We're home."

"Mmm." She cuddled into my chest. "No place I'd rather be."

I couldn't agree more.

"Thank the moon," I said, wrapping my arms around my mate's waist from behind after she walked in the house, dropping her bag on the counter. "I finally have you all to myself again."

"Barrett," Eryne laughed. "I've only been gone for a few hours." She had her weekly coven meeting with the girls today, and I'd pouted all morning when she had told me *no boys allowed.*

I crossed my arms over my chest. "It was a long few hours." I'd never really appreciated the passage of time before, or how fast it seemed to move when all I wanted was to slow down and savor every moment.

It had been a week since we'd restored the town wards. A week since we'd officially been mated. A week since everything had settled for the better.

A week of officially being *together.* I was happy and content here, living with her, but I knew I had to have some serious conversations about the future before I could put down actual roots. Plus, I needed to go home—to stop living out of my car and feeling like I was just living off of my mate. Not that I minded her home, the bed that had become *ours.*

The promise of a lifetime together should have been enough, but I wanted more. Wanted a ring on her finger. Wanted *everything.*

Eryne hummed as I slowly swayed us back and forth in the kitchen, leaning her head back on my shoulder. She let her eyes drift shut.

"Come home with me," I whispered against her ear, pressing a kiss to the side of her head. "I want you to meet my family."

She looked up at me, a soft smile on her lips. "Are you sure?"

"That I want them to meet my mate?" I said. "Absolutely positive. I want them to know the woman I've fallen in love with." I kissed under her ear.

My mate blushed. "When?"

"Sometime next month, maybe?" It was only a week until Halloween, and I knew how excited she was for it. Plus, as much as I knew she would love fall in Walnut Ridge, winter was even more beautiful. Maybe I could take her to my family's cabin up in the mountains when we visited.

I knew she'd like it up there, and I couldn't wait to show her the place I'd grown up, just like she'd shown me around Pleasant Grove.

Her eyes fluttered. "Okay." The word was a whisper.

"Okay?"

Eryne nodded. "Okay. I'd love to come home with you."

"Good. Because I don't want to be apart from you." I nuzzled my face against her neck.

She giggled. "No one told me that becoming mated would make you a stage five clinger."

I playfully rolled my eyes, though she wasn't wrong. After almost losing her, it was hard to let her out of my sights. Part of me still couldn't believe I'd almost lost her before I'd had a chance to tell her how I felt.

Eryne wiggled out of my arms, going to check on Nutmeg. The hedgehog was just happy to be around our witch, and I knew it comforted her to have her familiar even just sitting on her shoulder.

"What do you want to do for dinner?" She asked, setting Nutmeg back in her enclosure.

I licked my lips. "I have some ideas."

"Oh?"

Nodding, I scooped her up into my arms and carried her into the bedroom. Our bedroom. "I want to eat *you*."

"Oh, the big bad wolf has me in his clutches, hm?" Eryne said, running her nails along my scalp.

I grinned. "That's right. And I'm never going to let you go." I set her down on the floor, slowly stripping every piece of clothing from her body before she did the same to me. Pressing a kiss to her mating bite, I let my hands wander down her body.

My mate climbed on the bed, scooting until her back rested against the pillows as she parted her thighs for me.

"Mmm." I licked my lips. "Look at that perfect pussy, all spread out for me."

She ran her fingers up her thighs, circling her clit. "Are you going to come have a taste, or just leave me to take care of myself?"

I groaned, watching her dip her fingers inside her entrance. "Fuck, baby. I want you to ride my face."

Her lips formed a small *o* as I laid down on my back,

helping guide her onto my mouth. Her thighs rested on either side of my head, but she was hovering above me, like she was hesitant to suffocate me. I didn't care about that, though—I'd do anything for this woman.

"Sit," I commanded her, gripping her thighs before pulling her down so all of her weight rested on me, every bit the alpha wolf who wanted to take care of my mate. "Let me taste that sweetness, sugar."

The first taste of her on my tongue was always like heaven, and I moaned as I lapped at her entrance before burying my tongue inside her warm cunt, thrusting it inside of her as she rocked her hips against my face. My fingers dug into her thighs, and each time she let out a cry, all it did was spur me on. She was moving frantically, and I knew she was close when she whined my name as I feasted on her pussy.

Fuck, she was perfect, and all mine. I hummed against her clit as a flood of release coated my face, flattening my tongue over her entrance and drinking it all up as she rode out her orgasm.

Without warning, I lifted her up, moving her down my body and lining up my cock with her entrance before sinking inside of her.

"*Oh*," she gasped, splaying her hand over her stomach, like she could feel where I was buried inside of her. "Fuck. Barrett." Eryne tightened around me. "You feel so good."

I pumped into her from below as she rocked her hips, bouncing on my cock as we both worked ourselves higher and higher. Sliding my hands up her thighs, I gripped them tight, helping her move up and down on my length before adjusting our positions and laying her on her back, allowing me to take over. Blinded by lust, I couldn't help but thrust with abandon, rutting inside of her.

"Baby, please," she cried, dropping her head back. "I'm so..." She let out another moan. "I'm so sensitive."

Reaching down to suck her nipple into my mouth, I circled it with my tongue, lavishing both sides with equal attention. My little vixen wrapped her arms around my back, digging into my skin with her freshly painted fingernails, and I cursed, feeling my knot inflating.

I pulled out before I could come, squeezing my dick as she practically panted watching me fisting my cock. "What do you want, mate?" I asked her as I slowly pumped my dick.

"Your knot." She fluttered her eyelashes as she cupped her tits, biting her lip as she looked up at me. "Please."

Humming, I positioned my head between her thighs and nipped at her skin. I wondered what it would be like to mark her here, too. To have my bite all over her body, some of them just for us.

Her eyes were heated as I looked up at her, licking and sucking everywhere except where she wanted it. Finally, when neither of us could take it any longer, I dragged my tongue through her entrance once more. "I need another one," I told her. "Let me feel you come on my fingers." I pushed one, then a second, finger in her entrance, her wet cunt clinging to me, sucking me in.

"I can't," she cried, shaking her head as I crooked them inside of her, massaging her insides gently. "I can't come again."

"You can," I said, circling her clit with my tongue as I pressed on top of her stomach with one hand, my fingers pumping inside of her. "You can give it to me."

She whimpered.

"Be a good girl and I'll give you my knot," I told her, blowing on her clit before sucking on it again. "I just need you to come for me one more time first. Get all messy for me, sugar."

I kept up my ministrations, fucking her with my fingers as I circled that sensitive bundle of nerves with my tongue over and over, keeping one hand pressed over her womb. With gentle pressure, I built her up higher and higher, her breathy noises turning into cries.

"*Ohmygods*," she let out. "Fuck. Barrett."

I just kept licking her through it, tasting her orgasm on my tongue, watching the expression on her face as she let go. She collapsed on the bed, chest heaving as she came down from the high. Sitting up, I pulled my fingers out of her, wrapping my hand around my dick to coat my skin in her release. I hoped sex between us would never stop being this explosive. That I'd never stop having this desperate need to be inside of her, this overwhelming desire to knot her, over and over.

"Roll over," I told her.

"Hm?" She asked, blinking up at me with those pretty blue eyes, .

I ran my fingers through my hair, pushing it back off my forehead. "I'm going to knot you now, just like I promised, baby."

Grabbing her ankle, I spun her around, giving me that perfect view of her backside.

Eryne laid her head against the bed, her ass high in the air, arching her back. I coated my cock in her slick before plunging into her again, slamming to the hilt.

She was so wet that every thrust inside of her I could hear it, her arousal dripping out of her pussy.

It was rough and messy and perfect.

"Going to fill you up, my mate," I promised, squeezing her ass as I snapped my hips against her. "Need to keep you so full of my cum that it keeps dripping out of you. To keep you bred until you're all round and carrying our child."

Eryne let out a moan.

"Do you want that, sugar?"

"*Yes,*" she cried. "Yes. Yes, I want that."

I let out a grunt. "Fuck." I pushed my knot into place, spilling my cum inside of her, feeling her come another time from the sudden intrusion of my hard knot as it continued to swell. We were connected so intimately, and I couldn't stop, not until I'd poured every last drop into her womb.

Yes, my wolf agreed. *Breed our pretty little mate.*

Leaning down, I pressed a kiss to her back.

When we finally collapsed against the bed, breathing rough and spent, I gathered her up into my arms, her back pressed against my front, my knot still buried deep inside of her. Splaying my fingers across her stomach, I imagined what it would be like to watch her swell with our child. The idea made me half feral, and yet I couldn't

"Did you really mean that?" Eryne whispered, interlacing the fingers of our free hands.

"Hm?" I kissed her neck, pressing my teeth over my mark.

"About getting me pregnant." She turned her head to look at me.

I could feel the warmth creeping up my neck and ears. "Well—yeah. But only if you want that."

She smiled, and the expression warmed my insides. "I love you, you know that, Wolf-Man."

I nodded. "Of course I do."

"Even if I hadn't been your mate, I would have wanted a future with you. A life. A family." She wiggled around my knot. "I'm on birth control, but whenever it happens... I want to have your babies."

I hummed, banding both of my arms around her abdomen

and holding her even tighter. "Maybe we should get married first."

Eryne laughed softly. "Maybe we start with meeting your family, and then we go from there."

"This doesn't count as a proposal, by the way," I told her.

"I'm already your mate," she murmured, eyelids growing heavy. I yawned, feeling sleep coming on. My knot was still firmly lodged inside of her, and showed no signs of softening any time soon. "Everything else is just a bonus."

"I love you, Eryne," I said against her ear. "My little healer. You're the best thing that ever could have happened to me, sugar. And I'll never take that for granted. Not for one single moment. You have me totally bewitched, and I wouldn't have it any other way."

We fell asleep just like that—wrapped up in each other, dreaming of a future that felt more in reach than ever.

"Where are we going?" I asked as Eryne pulled me along behind her. At least this way, I could appreciate the view. She'd pulled on a burnt orange sweater dress with thick black tights and my favorite heeled boots of hers, as well as a pair of pumpkin pie earrings.

She grinned back at me. "You'll see."

I knew how much she loved showing me around her town, so I didn't ask too many questions. Fall in Pleasant Grove was... intense. I knew that more than ever after being here for the last months.

When we finally arrived at our destination—the pumpkin patch—I had a hard time not laughing. There was a tan banner hanging up overhead painted with pumpkins that read *Pleasant Grove's 250th Annual Pumpkin Festival.*

"That's a lot of years of pumpkins, Sugar."

She hummed in response.

The pumpkin patch to my right was massive—housing thousands of pumpkins of all shapes, sizes and colors, and, I had to admit—was the perfect setting for a pumpkin themed event.

"The market has all sorts of different pumpkin foods to try. Anything you can think of, someone's made from pumpkin. There's a corn maze, too. And once it's dark, there's a dance in the barn." Her eyes sparkled. "They hang up all these lights and couples slow dance, and it's so romantic." Eryne let out a sigh.

I tugged her to my side. "I can't wait to see all of it, baby." I pressed a kiss to her forehead. "Where do you want to start?"

She bit her lip. "Well, honestly... This is my first year in a while enjoying the event. My ex didn't really enjoy it, and the Witches' Brew normally has a booth, so I've worked the last few. I decided that we'd take this year off, though. I couldn't imagine doing it without Willow and Luna, and with their pregnancies..." Eryne shrugged. "So, really, it's a first for both of us." She turned to look at me, and I tugged on a strand of copper hair.

"Well, we still need to get our pumpkins," I whispered in her ear. "We haven't carved any yet." They'd be our first of many, together. Just like today would be our first of many trips to the pumpkin festival. I didn't have to be a witch or a seer to know that.

She looked up at me, beaming, and I knew it was the right thing to say.

Hand in hand, we headed towards the patch, determined to find the perfect pumpkins.

And I knew later tonight, we'd slow dance in that barn until the moon was gone from the sky and the stars twinkled above us, until I took her home, carrying her sleeping form into bed. Then, I'd pull the love of my life into my body and whisper sweet nothings of love and adoration into her ears until we both fell asleep.

Eryne looked back at me, catching the sweetest smile on my face. "What?" She asked.

I grinned. "Nothing."

I love you, I told her through our bond. That thread between us was shimmering gold, brighter and thicker than ever.

Her answering feeling of love, warmth, and acceptance was all I needed.

For now—and the rest of our lives.

CHAPTER TWENTY-FIVE

eryne

It was my favorite day of the year, and somehow it was even better now. Though maybe that had something to do with the sleeping wolf shifter who was still in my bed.

The one who smelled like pine trees and mountains, like spice and musk. The one who wrapped his body around mine every night, holding me tight and letting me borrow his warmth like his life depended on it.

Goddess, I couldn't believe how lucky I was that he was mine. The last few weeks together had been amazing. I loved going to work and knowing he would be here when I came back. That no matter what happened, Barrett was mine.

I finished in the kitchen, padding back to our bedroom. This morning, all I'd pulled on when I woke up before him was his discarded t-shirt from yesterday, enjoying the way it smelled like him and how it hit me mid-thigh, further emphasizing how much bigger he was than me. I loved how tall he was—how safe and secure I felt in his arms.

Almost as much as I loved how rough and filthy he could be

with me, giving me his knot and pumping me full of his seed every night. I was still on birth control—and I had my fertility pendant, so while nothing would happen yet, I was already getting used to the idea of letting him get me pregnant. Maybe not yet, but... soon.

My parents had met him and were already obsessed with their future son-in-law, something I was very grateful for. He was a great guy, and I was lucky that fate had chosen us to be together. Barrett was a gift I'd never stop thanking our Goddess for—not for the rest of our lifetimes.

Pushing the tray onto my nightstand, I climbed onto the bed, sitting next to my mate. He stirred, no doubt from the smell of pumpkin and coffee.

"Happy Halloween," I said as Barrett blinked his eyes open. He was shirtless, only wearing a pair of boxers, and I pressed a kiss to a smattering of freckles on his shoulder blade.

"Mmm." He pulled me onto his body, kissing me languidly. "Good morning."

I bit my lip to stop from smiling so hard. "Morning. I made breakfast." I grabbed the tray and put it in front of us.

"What did I do to deserve you?" Barrett kissed the side of my head as he grabbed one of the mugs, blowing on the hot liquid before taking a sip.

Smiling, I did the same, savoring the warmth and sweet blend of flavors.

Looking up from my cup, I found him chuckling. "Hm?"

"You have a little something..." Barrett reached over, swiping over my upper lip and grabbing a dollop of whipped cream. His tongue darted out, licking it off his skin, and then he leaned forward to kiss me, tongue darting into my mouth. He moaned. "So sweet."

"B," I groaned. "The food's going to get cold." I'd made a

small spread of our favorites—including pumpkin pancakes decorated with chocolate chips to look like jack-o-lanterns.

He gave me a small pout. "Fine, I'll behave. For now." My wolf smirked at me as he cut a piece of pancake and fed it to me. "But no promises about after."

I chewed it, eating a few more bites before he finally took a few of his own. "We have the party with the coven this evening," I reminded him.

"So you're all mine until then?" His eyes heated, his arm banding around my waist until he tugged me on his lap. "I like the sound of that."

Smacking his chest, I rolled my eyes. "You're insatiable."

"Guess my mate just brings out the best in me," Barrett said, chomping on the bacon I'd made.

"Or the worst," I muttered, though I didn't really mean it. He knew I loved him like this—dirty talk and all.

He kept alternating between feeding me bites and eating himself—though I'd made the bulk of the food for him, knowing how fast his metabolism worked, so after I was full, I drank my coffee as he chowed down on the remaining food.

I let my eyes drift shut, full and blissfully happy, wondering if I'd ever enjoyed a Halloween this much. I didn't think so.

"Are you sure this doesn't look dumb?" Barrett asked, tugging on his tunic for the dozenth time this evening. He had a quiver full of arrows strapped to his back, and he looked every bit the hunter I knew he was—even if this was completely different than his normal uniform.

"I'm sure," I responded, swiping my red lipstick on and fidgeting with my hat in the mirror.

My outfit this year was mostly pieced together from my closet. With everything that had happened with him, the town wards, and the wraiths, I hadn't had time to actually go shopping. Still, I loved the way I looked. The dark green corset framed my curves, and my orange plaid skirt had pockets.

He wrapped his arms around my corset, tugging me against his chest.

"Barrett," I protested, wriggling in his grasp. "I have to finish getting ready, otherwise we'll be late to Cait's party." Knowing them, they'd never let me live it down if we were.

He leaned down, pressing a kiss to my cheek. "I just want to take a moment to admire my mate." His lips brushed over my ear. "You look amazing, Sugar."

I let out a ragged breath as his beard scraped over the sensitive skin of my throat. He'd been letting it grow out, and red scruff covered his chin. I was obsessed with it, and I definitely didn't want him to shave any time soon.

"Fuck," he groaned, inhaling deeply. "I just can't resist you when you smell so sweet." He pushed my black shirt to the side, exposing my mating bite so he could run his mouth over it. Barrett was obsessed with it, and I knew he hated when it was covered. "Like sugar, baby."

"Barrett." His name was a whimper, barely more than a weak mewl. He knew what he did to me.

My wolf-man stood up, fixing my top and pressing a soft kiss to the tip of my nose. "I'm sorry. I'll be good." His amber eyes were mischievous, though.

"What do you have planned for tonight?" I asked, quirking an eyebrow at him.

He just grinned. "Nothing. Now finish getting ready so I can get my witch to her party."

My witch. The words still sent a tingle down my spine. *Mine.* I'd never expected to be able to call him mine. At the end of this, I'd thought I would have to let him go. Who would have thought the man I'd fallen in love with would end up being my mate?

It was like the universe had known I needed this gruff, rugged wolf-shifter to come and completely change everything, to show me exactly what I had been missing. *Him.*

"I just need to put my shoes on," I answered, giving myself one last look-over in the mirror as I slipped my dangly pumpkin earrings in.

My black sparkly cape was attached to my shirt at the shoulders, and it brought the entire look together. I'd put black tights on before I got ready, but my heeled boots were sitting next to the bed.

He scooped me up, carrying me over to the bed and setting me gently on the edge, kneeling in front of me as he slipped my feet into each boot, one after the other. It was so tender, the way he laced up each one with such focus and precision, nothing like our usual bedtime activities. Normally, he was taking things *off* of me, not putting them on.

"Don't worry," he said, voice low as he finished the last knot. *I plan on stripping all of this off of you later and reminding you exactly whose you are.*

Excitement—and a bit of arousal—coursed through my veins as he sent the thought directly into my mind. I hadn't gotten used to him being able to know what was going on in my mind yet, but it had made a lot of things easier. Like anticipating each other's needs and moods.

Maybe it was just a wolf shifter thing, the fact that it didn't take much for him to turn me on, for my body to be ready to take him with barely a look or a suggestion. Or maybe it was just him—that handsome, sculpted jaw, his body that drove me wild, or the way he could make me weak in the knees from just a small smirk.

"Time to go?"

I pressed my thighs together, wondering how I was going to make it through the night. "Yes. Let's go get some treats."

Or, knowing Cait... a few tricks.

Almost everyone who lived in Pleasant Grove seemed like they were out and about, trick-or-treating and enjoying the festivities of All Hallow's Eve. I tugged on the hem of my skirt as we walked up to Cait's house. It was the first time I'd come to the Clarke Halloween party as a part of the coven, and it felt like I was truly a part of something bigger than myself.

Laughter and halloween music could be heard as we wandered into the house, looking at all of the decorations.

"She really outdid herself this year," Wendy said, stepping up at my side. Barrett kissed my forehead, before heading into the kitchen to grab us both a drink.

"Wendy the good witch?" I asked her, looking at her outfit. She was dressed in a red robe, complete with a hood and holding a broom.

She blushed. "Well, it felt fitting."

"And where's our Sabrina?" I asked, scanning the room.

"Probably bickering with Ezra again," she said, rolling her eyes.

Rina and Ezra seemed to be locked in some sort of weird mortal combat. I wondered when the two of them would break the tension. She'd joked about me and Barrett when we first met, but I was pretty sure there was something going on between her and the blond vampire.

"What about you and the ghoul?" I asked, nudging her side.

She blushed. "Cassius? It's not... We're not..." She looked away. "Remember the guy I dated in college?"

I frowned. "I thought he was human."

"Well, he was. Is. I think." Wendy ran her fingers through the side of her hair. "But his older brother..."

Oh. Now I understood her reaction. "He's your ex's *brother*? And you had no idea what he was?"

She shook her head. "You know how it is. Using our powers is forbidden outside of Pleasant Grove's barriers. I didn't..." Her eyes grew distant. "Whether it was a glamour, or something happened, I don't know. But I haven't seen him in years. Until I saw him at Willow's house, I thought he was *dead.*"

"Wends..." I squeezed her shoulder.

"It's fine," she insisted. "It's all in the past."

I gave her a small smile. "If you say so." Though it sounded like there was a lot of unresolved feelings there. Whether they had to do with her ex-boyfriend—or his brooding, white haired older brother, I wasn't sure.

Barrett came back to my side, sliding an orange mug into my hands. It smelled like one of Willow's brews of apple cider, topped with... I sniffed the cup. "Whiskey?"

He hummed against my hair as I took a sip, letting the liquid warm me from the inside out. It made me feel loose and bubbly, and I couldn't help the overwhelming feeling of happiness that came over me. I leaned my head against my mate's shoulder as we visited with some of the other witches at the party.

I noticed Willow across the room—she was dressed like a candy corn princess, her puffy tulle skirt almost distracting from her belly, and I almost giggled, seeing Damien looking so grumpy yet besotted with his pregnant wife. I could almost picture Barrett and I like that, and his answering grumble of satisfaction in his chest told me everything I needed to know.

Spinning around, I wrapped my arms around his neck, staring up at his amber eyes, knowing his gaze said everything and nothing at the same time. Standing on my tiptoes—and grateful for the extra few inches my heeled boots gave me—I gave him a soft kiss. He caught my lower lip with his teeth, letting them rake against my skin before dropping another peck on my lips.

I love you, I told him, resting my forehead against his.

Barrett rubbed his nose over mine, shutting his eyes. *I love you, mate.*

"Look who came for a visit," Willow announced excitedly as she waddled back into the room, distracting me from my mate.

Luna had a baby strapped to her chest—as did Zain, looking protective and yet smug with one hand resting on his wife's back. "We thought the twins might as well have their first outing," she said, rubbing slow circles on the baby's bottom. Her blonde hair was braided down her back, and she was wearing a light lavender dress, a crescent moon shaped circlet resting on her forehead. She looked every bit the queen I knew she was—ethereal and almost glowing.

"Against my better wishes," Zain muttered, looking down at the twin strapped to his chest. The blonde haired baby holding on to his finger, making cooing sounds.

"It's not fair that *you* got to come for a visit without me," Luna pouted. "And I was tired of being cooped up in the palace."

Damien chuckled as Zain whispered something in his wife's ear.

"That's about to be you, you know," Barrett said to Damien, who glared at my mate. "Wrapped around your wife's finger."

"I'm not sure you should be talking, B," Ezra said dryly. "Eryne practically has you on a leash."

I blushed, but Barrett sent me a heated glance. *He's not wrong,* he murmured into my mind. *You can gladly put a leash on me, Sugar.*

"This is Orion," Luna was saying, gesturing the dark haired baby she was wearing. "And that's Raelynn. Rion and Rae for short."

Zain wrapped his arm around his wife, and she leaned against him, like he was supporting her weight. Keeping them both afloat. Their little family made warmth burst through my chest.

"I have a surprise for you," Barrett whispered in my ear awhile later, after we'd all had a chance to meet the twins and fawn all over them.

"You do?" I spun around to look at him, raising an eyebrow.

He nodded, holding out his hand. "Outside."

I looked around us at the party. It was getting later, and while I loved spending time with the coven, I wanted some time alone with my mate, too. Wendy and Rina were on the couch, whispering conspiratorially. Willow and Damien were swaying slowly in the corner, his hands cupping her stomach as they shared their own soft moment. Everyone seemed like they were enjoying themselves—even Cait, who was holding Raelynn in her arms, whispering to Luna's baby girl.

"Yeah." I smiled at him. "Let's go."

We wandered outside, and Barrett interlaced our fingers, wordlessly bringing me along with him. I didn't know where we were heading, but I knew I'd follow him anywhere. Passing tons of trick-or-treating little witches in all sorts of different costumes, we turned towards town.

"Come on," Barrett said, tugging me down the path illuminated with glowing jack-o-lanterns and floating candles that led to the gazebo in the middle of Main Street. The entire scene was like something out of a dream. It was always beautiful, but right now it felt even more so. Like *magic*.

Halfway up the path, I tugged on his hand, bringing us to a halt. "What are you doing?" I whispered as he turned to face me. He didn't answer, cupping my cheeks, and I could *feel* the love in his chest. The desire. And the worry, too. The anxiety.

"You know there's nothing to be anxious about, right?" I asked him, frowning. Rubbing over my mating mark, I looked up at him. "I'm yours. And you're mine."

Barrett held my face so tenderly, gazing down at me with an expression that I couldn't quite describe. Love? Lust? Amazement? Maybe it was a mixture of all three. The need was clear, and my heart skipped a beat.

"Eryne," he started, his thumb brushing over my cheek. "There are no words to describe how utterly, wholly, and completely *bewitched* I am by you. Your soft heart. The way you care about others, putting them before yourself. How you brought me back to life, and show me every day why life is worth living. Why I want to live by your side. You're my mate and the woman I love, but you're more than that. You're my future. My destiny. You're the very thing I've been living my whole life for. Something I was working towards even without knowing it. Every step, every choice I made, led me to you."

My eyes were glassy, and I blinked, trying not to cry. "Barrett..." The word was hardly a murmur.

"I know this is all still so new. And we're just at the beginning of our story. But I have a question I really want to ask you, and it can't wait." He grinned, sliding down to one knee in front of me and pulling a small black box out of his pocket. "At least... I don't want to."

My eyes widened. Was this really happening now?

"Eryne Hazel Fowler, will you do me the honor of being my mate and my wife? Will you marry me?"

What else was there to say? "Yes," I nodded, tears spilling from my eyes as he slid the gorgeous ring on my finger. Happy tears. The band was detailed like a vine, complete with small leaves, and the diamond in the center was surrounded by an emerald stone on each side.

I wanted to marry him. Wanted to be his wife. Wanted everything with this man that had changed my life in so many ways. More tears streaked down my face, and I couldn't help it. "Yes," I repeated. "I want to marry you."

"Don't cry, baby," he said, standing up to kiss me softly.

"I'm just so happy," I told him honestly as he wrapped me up into a hug.

He grinned. "That's all I could ask for."

And then he kissed me again, in the middle of that magical, illuminated gazebo on Halloween, and everything else in the world faded away.

It was just him and I, and this night was just the beginning.

CHAPTER TWENTY-SIX

barrett

ONE MONTH LATER...

"Wake up, baby" I said, reaching over my center console and placing my hand on my mate's thigh, squeezing it lightly. She gave a grunt of annoyance, blinking her eyes open a few seconds later.

"We're almost there, sugar," I told her, knowing the sign for Walnut Ridge was coming up soon. An excitement filled me like I hadn't felt before—at least, not in a long time.

I couldn't wait to show her everything. It was my first time going home in so long, and I couldn't wait to show my *fiancée* the town I'd grown up in. To have my family meet her, to get to know the woman I loved. She'd taken off work from the café for the next two weeks, ensuring everything was ordered, schedules were made, and everything was prepped so the operation would still run without her. If anything else happened that my mate hadn't anticipated, they could always call her and she would troubleshoot from here.

But I was glad to be taking her away. To get her all to myself for awhile. No coven, no coffee shop, no best friends. Just the woman I was going to marry and me.

I squeezed her thigh again, not taking my hand off of it, simply running my thumb over her skin. That was how we'd spent most of the drive, because my wolf hated when I stopped touching her, even for a second.

He was damn possessive, but so was I, so it all worked out.

The pull-out for the overlook came up on the road, and I turned off, parking the car and going around to open her door. She placed her hand in mine and I guided her towards the railing.

"Welcome to Walnut Ridge, Eryne," I said, tugging her into my side. We stood at the overlook, the town expanding below us, nestled between the mountains. It was the perfect place to hide a community of shifters, to assure we'd never be discovered by the humans who once hunted us to near extinction.

"It's beautiful," she said, eyes wide as she took in the view.

There was a light layer of snow that had settled over the town—common for November in Vermont—and it looked every bit like a winter wonderland. My wolf ached to run, to jump and leap through the snow, but I wanted to capture every single one of Eryne's reactions, so I didn't dare shift.

"It's even better in the fall," I told her. "When all the leaves are orange and yellow, the landscape looks like a blanket."

Eryne let out a happy sigh. "I can't believe this place is real," she whispered, her fingers reaching out like she expected it to be a painting.

"I know what you mean," I said, tugging her to my side.

We were both wearing jeans, though Eryne had pulled on her favorite dark green sweater this morning and a pair of Doc Marten boots, while I'd grabbed a waffle knit thermal shirt and my favorite jacket. Pressing my nose to her head, I inhaled her sweet scent. Somehow, she always smelled like apples and cinnamon, though I'd determined part of that was her apple shampoo. Still, she was good enough to eat.

"Ready to meet my family?" I asked, turning to her.

She nodded, twisting her ring around her finger. "Are they going to think this is crazy? That we jumped into this so fast?"

I shook my head. "My mom's going to love you. And so is Freya. I just know it."

Besides, wolves moved notoriously fast. Once someone found their mate, it was hard to resist the pull of fate. I should know—I'd tried my hardest for so long to hold back. It had been impossible while being surrounded by her sweet scent and soft smile though.

My wolf let out a grumble of satisfaction as she reached up, running her fingers over my beard. She liked it, so I'd let it grow in, keeping it well-groomed but at the length Eryne seemed to love.

With a deep inhale of breath, she pushed her shoulders back, looking at me then the town nestled between the ridge. "Let's go."

***

We both got out, shutting the door behind us, and I interlaced our fingers as we walked up the path, pressing a kiss to the top of her hand. My mother's house was just the same as I remembered it—small, cozy and warm, but filled with so much love. It smelled like fresh-baked bread and *home*.

Though it wasn't home anymore—home was the witch beside me, the one who had captured my heart and soul.

"Remember that I love you," I said, holding her gaze.

"That bad?" She laughed.

It was the opposite. I was pretty sure they were going to

shower her with so much affection she wouldn't know what to do with it. I just smiled. "You'll see."

I knocked on the door, finding my mom at the other side, wearing an apron covered in flour, her hair pulled back into a tight braid. She had the same face as Freya and I, the same dark auburn hair we all shared and the same amber eyes as mine. Meanwhile, Freya had gotten my dad's blue eyes, and both of our parent's love of reading. She was a librarian, a year younger than Eryne, and my best friend growing up.

"Barrett," she said, wrapping me up in a bear hug before I could even protest. "My baby boy is finally home."

"*Mom*," I protested, trying not to roll my eyes because I was closer to thirty than ever, and she still treated me like I was the toddler who didn't know how to shift yet and was scared of the dark.

She let go of me, and her eyes drifted over to Eryne, who was standing on the porch awkwardly. "Oh, and you brought someone with you. Hello, sweetheart."

"Hi," Eryne murmured, looking bashful.

"Mom, I'd like you to meet someone important to me. Eryne. My mate." I grabbed her hand and squeezed it.

"After all these years, he finally brought home a nice girl." Mom gestured inside. "Come on. Let's get you both inside and then you can tell me the whole story. I'm sure you're both tired from the long drive."

I left our bags in the car and headed inside my childhood home.

"You look..." Eryne whispered as we followed my mom into the kitchen. "*Wow*."

I laughed, knowing exactly what she was thinking. "I know. We get that a lot."

"Mom," came my sister's voice. "Who was—" Her eyes widened as she saw me. "B." She grinned.

"Hi, Fey." I opened my arms for a hug.

When we pulled away, she peered at Eryne curiously.

I turned to my mate. "This is my sister," I said, gesturing to the dark auburn haired woman. "Freya. Freya, this is Eryne. My mate."

"Hey," Eryne said, sounding shy. "It's nice to meet you."

Freya's blue eyes lit up as she took in the woman at my side. "Well, I definitely didn't expect this when you said you were finally coming home for visit, but I can't say I'm upset." My mate stuck out her hand for a handshake, but my sister went in for a hug instead. "It's *so* nice to meet you." Freya turned her attention to me. "Wow. Mated. Look at you."

I puffed up my chest, wrapping an arm around my mate and pulling her into me. "It's a long story, but we're happy."

She rested her hand on my chest, nuzzling into me. "Yeah. We are."

Freya's eyes widened, and that was when I realized that it was her left hand—the one wearing my ring—that was in full view. "You're getting married?" She practically squealed. "Why didn't you lead with that? This is so exciting!"

Eryne blushed, her blue eyes catching mine. "It's still new."

The engagement still felt like a dream to both of us. After I'd proposed on Halloween—not wanting to wait any longer—we were taking our time with figuring out when we wanted to get married. After all, we'd only been together for a little over two months now. I didn't care if we got married tomorrow in the woods, but I wanted Eryne to have the wedding of her dreams. Whatever that looked like.

"I'm so happy for you. I can't believe my brother is getting married."

"What about you? Any boyfriends I should scare off?"

Freya wrinkled her nose. "You think I have time with how

busy I am working at the library? Besides, you know how small this town is. Who would I even date?"

"I keep telling you there's some nice boys down at the fire station, sweetie," my mom said, coming into the living room holding a plate of cookies. "You never know."

Freya groaned. "Mom, my mate is not some firefighter who is going to waltz out of the station and sweep me off my feet."

"You never know." My mom winked. "I have a good feeling."

My sister rolled her eyes. "You have a lot of feelings. Doesn't mean they come true."

Eryne looked at me and snorted. "I said that once, too. Turns out he sort of did."

I leaned down, pressing a kiss to her nose. "You saved me first."

"At least one of you is settling down. Come on. Tell me everything."

Hours later, we left my mom's house, our backset full of baked goods after we'd finished dinner. We'd told her our entire story —or at least the PG version of it—and she couldn't believe it was real.

They'd also only been a little pissed at me for keeping my job a secret all these years, but hey. You win some, you lose some.

And I'd won a lot with my mate.

"She's amazing," Eryne said, letting her eyes drift shut as she relaxed into the seat. "Your mom."

"And only a little intense," I joked.

I started driving towards our family's cabin in the mountains. Mom had asked us if we wanted to stay with them for the night, but we wanted our privacy.

After all, I had plans for my mate.

My girl hummed. "Thank you for bringing me here. It's beautiful."

I squeezed her thigh. "Just wait. It's only better up at the cabin."

She gave me a shy smile. "Do I get to see you run around in wolf form again?"

I barked out a laugh. "Maybe. Why do you ask?"

Eryne gnawed on her lower lip. "I think it's hot, watching you shift. Plus, I like your wolf. He keeps me warm, remember?"

"I keep you warm, too," I reminded her, thinking about exactly what I planned to do to her tonight once we got back to the cabin. After I stripped her bare, making her come on my tongue, I wanted to make her scream my name until her voice was hoarse.

And then, stuffed with my knot, I'd wrap her up in my arms and fall asleep with her full of my cock.

She blushed at the mental image, letting out a needy whine. The car filled with the sweet scent of her arousal, and I groaned. "*Sugar.*"

"I can't help it," she said, squirming in her seat. "That was..."

I grinned, knowing just how filthy it was. "Be a good girl, and I'll do it all to you once we get there."

Her eyes sparked with desire.

Thirty minutes later, when I'd pulled off the road onto the cabin, she crawled onto my lap, burying her fingers in my hair as she kissed me, her tongue meeting mine over and over, gasping into my mouth as she rocked against my erection.

"If I didn't know better, I'd think *you* were going into heat," I murmured, running my fingers down her spine.

"Shut up and keep kissing me," she groaned. There was no denying her, so I didn't try.

She sighed with relief as I unzipped her pants, plunging two fingers inside of her. She was so wet and needy, bucking her hips with each thrust of my fingers.

I pushed her jeans down her hips as she unzipped mine, her fingers wrapping around my cock as it sprang free.

"Oh, *fuck*," I said as she reached down, gathering her arousal and rubbing it over my length before guiding my tip onto her entrance.

She sunk down onto me, and we both groaned at the feeling of her warm, wet pussy wrapped around my cock, taking me in deep.

"Eryne," I groaned.

"Fill me up," she begged. "Knot me."

"Slow down, sweet girl," I begged her. Car sex was *hot,* but I wanted to lose myself inside of her, and this wasn't exactly the place for that. Plus, we needed more room.

She shook her head, nipping at my neck. Her little teeth buried against my skin, sucking hard. "Need your cum, baby."

I groaned. The little vixen knew exactly what she was doing to me. What my weak spots were.

Opening the car door, I wrapped my arms around her ass as I got out, each step towards the cabin causing my knot to rub against her entrance. Eryne wrapped her legs around me, keeping me buried deep. I'd have to get our stuff later, because I only had one thing in mind now.

Breed my mate. Give her exactly what she was begging for. To stuff her cunt full of so much cum, it would be dripping out of her for days.

We were a mess of limbs and clothes as I opened the door,

carrying us both inside of the house. I headed towards the master bedroom, driven only with need. I scraped my teeth against her skin, longing to bite her again.

The soft, plush bed was waiting for us, and I dropped her onto it, watching her tits bounce from the action.

She let out a whine as I pulled out, flipping her onto all fours and gripping her hips as I pushed into her from behind, each snap of my hips a punishing thrust.

"Told you I wanted to take my time with you," I told her, letting out a grunt. "But you couldn't wait, could you?" She moaned, her back arching as I gathered her hair into my fist, tugging it tight. "My needy mate just needed to get fucked, huh?"

"*Yes,*" she cried. "Fuck me, please."

"Gonna breed my pretty mate," I growled, the sound more animal than human, burying myself inside of her over and over and over again.

She screamed when I finally pushed my knot inside of her with no warning, her cunt spasming around me, milking my release from my body. I gave her everything she asked for, flooding her womb with my cum, guttural sounds of pleasure ripping from my chest as I bred her.

Eryne gripped the sheets hard as I arched her back further, sinking my teeth into her neck.

It was rough and messy but *fuck*, did it feel right.

After my body settled, I licked the mark on her neck, healing it with my saliva, picking up my mate and adjusting us on the bed so I could spoon her comfortably.

I ran my fingers up and down her side. "Is that what you wanted?"

She let out a hum of satisfaction.

I chuckled. "I wasn't too rough, was I?" She'd definitely

have bruises tomorrow. I could already see the purplish spots on her thighs.

"No." She looked up at me. "I liked it." She ran her fingers over my beard. "It was exactly what I needed."

I dropped my forehead against hers. "I don't know what came over me. I just had this burning need to be inside of you. To claim you."

Eryne shifted our positions so she was cradled in my arms, twisting on my knot until her front was pressed against mine. Her hardened nipples brushed over my chest, and my dick twitched inside of her. *Gods,* she was sexy. Especially when she'd been begging for my knot.

She rested her hand on my chest, drawing circles in my chest hair. "You know, about our wedding..."

"Hm?" I looked over at her, finding a heated look in her eyes.

"What do you think about the spring?"

I raised an eyebrow. "Any specific reason?"

She wiggled on my knot. "Maybe I want you to knock me up." Eryne leaned forward, her lips only inches from mine. "Hearing you talk about breeding me makes me want to go off birth control and let you try for real."

Maybe we both had a breeding kink. "Fuck," I groaned, already feeling myself getting hard again. "What about winter instead? Tomorrow," I insisted. Yeah, tomorrow was good.

She hummed as I grasped her chin with my fingers, taking her mouth with mine and kissing her languidly. We stayed like that until I was fully hard again—a feat, even for a wolf shifter—and I fucked my knot into her, each shallow thrust making me ram against her cervix, my tip pressed against the entrance to her womb.

I had half a mind to beg her to go off birth control right

then and there, to make a baby this weekend, but I also wanted to savor this time with just the two of us.

But if the goddess had given her to me, then I had no doubt in my mind that this was meant to be. Whatever had brought us together—fate or divine providence—it must have known what it was doing when it gave me this witch as my mate.

Of all the beings in the universe, she was mine, and I would never squander that opportunity. Would never stop being grateful that she was mine.

That I'd been bewitched by her, and I never wanted to stop being under her spell.

Because I was bewitchingly *hers*.

epilogue

BARRETT

SIX MONTHS LATER...

E ryne was snoring softly, her ginger hair spreading out around her. I ran my hands up her sides, savoring the feeling of her soft, bare skin. She made a little sighing sound in her sleep, and I nuzzled my head against her neck, kissing her mating mark.

My cock was hard, pressed against her back, desperate to bury itself in her. I let my fingers creep lower, between her thighs, and pressed one inside of her. She let out a small mewl, and it was all the encouragement I needed.

"Barrett," she whined in her sleep, and fuck, it was so sweet. *This* was how I wanted to wake up every morning, with my mate—my wife—in my arms, showing her how much I loved her.

I pressed another finger inside of her, crooking them to make sure she was wet enough to take me.

Eryne let out a moan, her head dipping back to press

against my shoulder, and her scent wafted up to me, the overwhelming sweetness hitting me in the face.

It had changed. It was even sweeter now, if that was possible. And maybe if I'd been paying attention, I would have realized what that meant sooner.

"Sugar," I murmured against her ear, feeling her pushing her ass against my cock.

"*Mmmm.*"

I wrapped one hand around her throat, the other over her flat stomach. *For now.*

It was summer, and we'd gotten married in early spring, just like we'd discussed when I'd first brought her home to Walnut Ridge. She'd gone off birth control after our ceremony, neither of us wanting to wait to start our family. It had been a few months since we started trying, and I knew there was a flicker of disappointment every month when she realized she wasn't pregnant yet. We were still young—only twenty-six and twenty-eight—but we both wanted it.

Wanted this little life I knew I cradled in my hand, growing inside of my wife.

It was early. Earlier than doctors would be able to detect it. I didn't think she'd even missed her period yet. And yet, I knew that she carried our pup inside of her.

"Barrett," she moaned, rubbing against my cock. "I need you." I couldn't deny her, especially not as she blinked up at me, her eyes drowsy with sleep yet so soft and full of love.

Leaning down, I kissed her softly before lifting her leg, sliding into her from behind. The first rays of dawn shined into our window, illuminating the room in a golden glow as I made love to her. It wasn't rough or frenzied, but slow and gentle. I cradled her to my body as I brought her to orgasm, making her fall over the edge before I came, careful not to knot her even when she whined and begged for it.

Soon enough, she'd know why.

But I wanted my mate to figure it out for herself. Wanted to see her face light up when she came to the realization that we'd succeed. The joy on her face would be worth it.

"Good morning," she murmured, a blissful smile curling over her face. "What a way to wake up." She let out a happy sound as she stretched.

"It is," I agreed. "Now, we should get up so I can feed you before you have to go to work."

Eryne pouted. "What if we just stay in bed all day? It's too nice to want to spend all day in the coffee shop."

I laughed. "You love your job, Sugar."

My girl huffed out a breath, blowing her bangs off her forehead. "I do," she finally agreed.

I scooped her into my arms, carrying her into the bathroom as I turned on the shower, waiting until it got to her ideal temperature before we both stepped inside. It was amazing how much hotter she liked it—but I'd mostly gotten used to it. Of course, sometimes I still thought it would scald my scalp, but I'd learned how to avoid that.

"What's on the agenda for you today?" Eryne asked as we sat at the island less than an hour later, eating the breakfast I'd made her as she pulled on her outfit and got ready for her day.

"Thought I'd go for a run," I said.

Her head perked up. "Oh?" Even after all these months together, she still loved watching me shift. Though part of me thought it was just so she could ogle my naked body.

Sometimes I mourned the fact that my mate wasn't a wolf —that we couldn't run together in the woods, but then I thought about all the other things I'd never have experienced if she wasn't a witch. I was grateful that I had her. That she could heal me with hardly more than the blink of an eye.

"That way I can check the wards and everything." It was

almost time for the monthly spell to power the town barrier, and I liked to check on it to make sure nothing else had decided to snack on their magic. So far, so good. There were jobs I could take, hunting monsters, but I'd happily stay here, close to my mate, using my skills to keep the town she loved safe.

She nodded. "Full moon is in a few days."

Once other covens in town had found out what happened, they'd suggested a rotating schedule to power them, instead of just the girls coven. It took a lot out of them every time they did the spell, so I appreciated that they weren't always in charge of it.

It had been months since the incident, and it seemed like the whole town had changed for the better. Sure, I couldn't seem to convince Ezra and Cassius that I had it under control and they could *go,* but as a whole, people were happier. There were new friends, new faces, and new relationships developing almost every day.

"Oh, Willow's supposed to bring the baby in to visit today," Eryne said, looking down at her phone.

Willow and Damien's daughter, Opal, was six months old and absolutely adorable, with a thick head of curly black hair like her dad and her mom's bright green eyes. And to think... next year, that would be us. A warm, fuzzy feeling unraveled in my chest.

I kissed the top of her head as I grabbed our now empty plates off the counter, carrying them to the sink. "That'll be fun," I offered, as I started washing the dishes.

Eryne hummed. "She really is so cute." Her eyes connected with mine, and I knew exactly what she was thinking. But I wasn't giving our little secret away yet. "Willow and I are discussing numbers for the fall." It was their busiest time at the coffee shop, and even though the Clarke sisters had more of a hands off approach now, they still owned the business.

Turning off the sink, I stood behind her, rubbing her shoulders. "Yeah?"

She let out a yawn, covering her mouth with her hand. "I feel like I've been more exhausted than usual lately. Maybe I'll come home early and we can watch that new show we've been talking about."

"Sounds good, Sugar." I'd gladly take more of her time. As much as she'd give me.

Some of the girls in Eryne's coven liked to make fun of me for being a house husband—whatever that meant—but I didn't care. This is where I belonged. This is where I wanted to be.

Because if I had her, everything else was just a happy bonus.

ERYNE

A little awareness flickered inside of me, waking me from my peaceful sleep.

I turned to look at Barrett, sleeping next to me in his wolf form. He shifted sometimes while he was asleep, and I had to admit I liked cuddling with his furry self.

It had been almost a year since we'd met. Almost a year since I'd found him, fur shredded and bleeding, and nursed him back to health, not knowing he was a man. That he was my mate, all along. These last few months since we'd officially tied the knot had been incredible. If it was possible, I knew, deep in my heart, that I loved him even more now. My *mate*.

My caring, compassionate mate, who had been so careful with me the last few days, like he'd known something I hadn't.

The other witches had told me there was a knowing, even though it should have been too soon.

Willow had sensed she was pregnant with Opal before a human pregnancy test would have even detected it. It had been a few days since she'd brought her baby girl to visit the cafe. I'd told her about how I was more tired than normal lately, how after a long day all I wanted was to go home to Barrett and curl up in his arms, and she'd just given me a knowing smile.

But I hadn't put two and two together until now.

There was, undoubtedly, a life growing inside of me.

My little witchling, or maybe a shifter pup. We didn't know what would come of a child who was half wolf, half witch. It was something Barrett and I had spent many nights discussing as I was curled into his body, waiting for his knot to deflate. Those soft, whispered conversations while we were connected somehow felt even more intimate than when he made love to me—or when he fucked me hard rough like I begged for.

I slid my hand over my abdomen, splaying my fingers over my flat stomach, though it wouldn't stay that way for long. Though I didn't know the specifics of shifter pregnancy, Willow and Luna were with demons, and their pregnancies hadn't been much different from a regular witch one.

Which meant in less than nine months, we'd have a baby of our own.

Barrett's wolf raised his head, a question in his eyes, and then he sniffed the air. Like he was scenting what I'd just discovered. I nodded. He shifted before I could open my mouth, wrapping his arms around my waist and pulling my body against his naked one.

"Barrett," I murmured, my eyes filling with tears.

Happy tears. Ones I couldn't hold back—not for the life of me. Because this was something I'd wanted for so long, and I'd worried it wouldn't happen. Barrett had told me how for wolves, it was harder to get pregnant if you weren't in a heat cycle, but since I didn't actually have one, we didn't know how long it would take.

"You're carrying our pup," he said, voice hoarse with emotion. It wasn't a question, but somehow, I knew he'd just been waiting for me to figure it out myself.

I bit my lip, looking down between us. "I am."

He picked up my hand, kissing my palm and then my wedding ring before nudging his head against my stomach, running his nose over my skin. "I don't think I've ever been this happy, Sugar."

"No?"

"No." Barrett gave me a wolfy grin. "To know I did this to you, the way your scent has changed from my pup... our baby... fuck, Eryne. It calms me in a way I could never explain. I don't deserve you, but I'll spend the rest of our lives making you happy."

I ran my hands through his hair as he kissed my stomach tenderly. So soft and sweet.

"What about where we live?" I whispered. I loved Pleasant Grove. This town, my job at the Witches' Brew, it was all I'd ever known. But I wasn't so naive to think he'd want to stay here. And part of me didn't want to deprive our child of growing up knowing other wolves, if they were a shifter. "Do you want to... should we move to Walnut Ridge? If they're a wolf?" I'd gotten close to Barrett's parents and his sister in our visits over the last few months, and I loved going and staying at the cabin in Walnut Ridge. Still, it was a big decision.

"There's nothing I'd love more than to take you back there with me. To build a house for us and them." He rested his hand over the tiny flicker of life inside of me. "But... "

"But?" I held my breath. It was a conversation we'd put off

having. Of course, he'd decided to stay here, but that didn't mean *forever.*

I loved him enough to know I'd follow him anywhere. Even if that meant leaving this place behind.

He grinned. "But I love our life here. Our friends..."

I thought about the community we'd built. My coven and their mates... It might not have been a community full of wolf-shifters, but they were our family. And my parents were here, too.

"They'll have plenty of kids to grow up with, that's for sure," I agreed. "And Pleasant Grove is a pretty great place to grow up." And it would only get better. Since opening the wards to other paranormal beings, we'd had a boom of new residents. It had taken some getting used to, but I loved it. "We can raise them the way we should have been raised."

In a world full of magic.

A world full of love.

A world where no one was kept out because of fear or prejudices. Where witches, vampires, demons, and shifters—and maybe even the occasional ghoul—could walk hand in hand down Main Street.

"Nothing sounds better." He wrapped his hand around my neck. "I love you, Sugar."

"I love *you,* Wolf-Man." I closed my eyes, letting my forehead rest against his. I slid a hand over my abdomen, not surprised when he placed his over it. "And our little pumpkin."

There was no doubt in my mind that this child would be a redhead, just like us.

He grinned. "I hope they look just like you." Barrett kissed the tip of my nose. "Your cute little nose and those big blue eyes."

I traced the freckles on his chest with my thumb. "They're doomed in the freckle department, that's for sure."

Barrett's laugh filled the room, and the feeling of love flowed through me, enough that I almost felt like bursting. His joy was so contagious, and it filled up every bit of me, the emotion so powerful through the bond.

"How long have you known?" I asked, thinking about the look of relief on his face earlier. Like he'd just been waiting for me to catch up."

"Only a few days." He ran his fingers through my hair, playing with the strands. I'd been letting it grow lately, and he was obsessed with it, like always. "Your scent changed. It's even sweeter now. Didn't think that was possible, but..." He placed both hands on either side of my stomach, like he was cradling our baby. "I was going to tell you, but... I wanted to see the look on your face when you realized it yourself."

"Is everyone going to know?" I asked, feeling my cheeks warm. "If you can... smell me, then can't everyone else?"

Barrett rubbed his thumb over my stomach. "I'm so finely attuned to it that it would be hard for me not to. The others... They probably won't notice right away. But we can ask the guys to keep it quiet until we're ready to tell everyone."

Key differences between our races—witches didn't have an overwhelmingly powerful sense of smell. Not like shifters and vampires seemed to. Even the demons had heightened senses, which just felt unfair.

I nodded. "I just don't want to get our hopes up in case..." I bit my lip. I didn't want to say it—to even think it—but what if I got used to this idea, and then it was ripped away from us? It was so early. Probably too early to know if it would take for sure. And yet, the happiness on my mate's face, the joy at the knowledge that I was growing our child inside of me, was impossible to ignore.

"Wolf pups are hearty," he told me. "*Strong*. We have a harder time conceiving, normally only managing successful fertilization during a heat cycle. For us..." He looked down at my stomach. "We don't really know. There's no records of any witches and wolves who have been mates before. But we'll take it one day at a time, okay, baby?"

I nodded, and he kissed my forehead. "One day at a time," I promised him.

And just like every other promise he'd ever made me, I knew this one would come true.

extended epilogue

BARRETT

NINE MONTHS LATER...

"Barrett," Eryne groaned from her desk. The Witches Brew was decorated with red and pink hearts, since Valentine's Day just a few days away, and I was dutifully sitting by her side, reading reports of various monster sightings from around the country.

I might not have been accepting new jobs right now, but that didn't mean I wasn't keeping tabs on what was going on in the world.

Perking up my head, I looked at my wife. "Is the baby okay?"

She was a week overdue, and I knew how stressed she was. At five-foot-two, she was *all* belly. I wasn't exactly small, and our pup was measuring in the ninety-ninth percentile of height and weight. He was all shifter, that was for sure.

"Fine," she answered, rubbing at her spine. "But my back is killing me."

"Willow keeps asking me when you're going on maternity leave," I said, giving her a stern glare.

She'd tried—for one singular day—and then went back to work, saying that she'd take time off when the baby was here.

"I feel so worthless sitting around. There's so much to do."

She'd been nesting like crazy over the last few weeks. The nursery in our new house was completed. We'd said goodbye to the small, cozy house where we'd fallen in love, needing more space now that we were adding another member to our family. It was bittersweet, but a necessity.

Thanks to all of the money I'd made over the years working as a hunter, I was able to chip in to help with the new house as well as buying us a cabin of our own up in Walnut Ridge, somewhere where we could go to visit often. We both agreed that staying in Pleasant Grove was what we wanted, but Eryne was firm in her decision that our children—plural, because she wanted this baby to grow up with a sibling—should grow up around other wolves, too.

It was still on the edge of town, backed up to the woods, giving me ample space to shift and run. Maybe one day, I'd teach our pups to run there too.

"You need to *relax*," I told her.

She pouted, placing both hands on her bump. "What I need, is this baby *out*."

"He'll come out when he wants to, sugar." I stood up, walking over to her and massaging her shoulders. "He's just comfy in there."

We'd tried everything to start her labor—curb walking, spicy food, and even sex. Thought I was willing to give the last one another shot.

"Comfy on my bladder," she muttered. "Help me up so I can go to the bathroom, will you?"

I reached down, helping pull her to her feet. She took a few steps towards the door, rubbing her back as she waddled. My wolf wouldn't let me take my eyes off of our pregnant mate, so I followed behind her closely, making sure I was there if she needed me.

Eryne gasped, clutching her belly. "*Oh.*" I rushed over to her, steadying her. She looked up at me, doing her best to look innocent. "It's fine," she reassured me. "I'm fine." Except... she *wasn't* fine, clearly. Her fingers dug into my arm where she held onto me, and she gritted her teeth as if in pain, baring down.

"Eryne." My voice was stern. "Are you in labor?"

Her teeth worked into her lower lip. "Maybe?"

"How long have you been like this?" I looked at my watch, trying to time the contraction.

She winced. "A few hours? It wasn't that bad at first. I didn't think it was anything to worry about." Eryne looked down at the wet spot spreading on her leggings. "And... I think my water just broke."

I picked her up, carrying her over to the couch. "I should call the doctor." And then I was getting her directly to the hospital.

"I just didn't want them to tell me it was just a false alarm again." Her lip stuck out in a pout, and I leaned forward to drop a kiss on her forehead.

"Everything is going to be okay, sugar," I promised her. "We're going to go meet our son, and then you'll get to rest."

She gripped my hand tight. "Promise?"

I ran my fingers under her chin, keeping those beautiful blue eyes on me. "Promise."

"Knock, knock."

I looked up to find my sister holding a stuffed wolf plush and a balloon, plus a bouquet of flowers. "Freya." I smiled. "Want to come meet your nephew?" My words were a whisper.

Eryne was asleep in the hospital bed—still tuckered out after a long labor and birth. It had been a long night, but we'd welcomed him this morning a little after six am. We'd both barely put him down since I'd cut the cord and the nurses had cleaned him up, not wanting to be apart from our little boy. I had him cradled against my chest, sitting in the chair next to my mate's bed.

Her parents had been by earlier, checking on us and doting on their first grandchild. I had no doubt my own would be the same once we made the trek up to Walnut Ridge in a few months.

"Oh, Bar. He's adorable." She kept her voice low as she came in, setting the gifts on a table. "I can't believe I'm an aunt." Freya came over to stand next to me.

"Meet Ronan Conrad Lockwood," I said, looking down at my sleeping son and his fiery red hair. He was so small, but already so fierce. "Want to hold him?"

She nodded, and I transferred him into her arms. He let out a little cry as I settled him into Freya's grasp, but just blinked up at her, his blue eyes taking in his aunt. "Maybe Mom will finally lay off of me about finding someone and having kids of my own now," she said, rocking him slowly.

I chuckled, shaking my head. "Fat chance of that. I give it a few months before she's asking Eryne and I when we're having the next one." I looked over at my wife.

She'd already expressed her desire to give Ronan a sibling one day—she'd grown up as an only child, and didn't want our child to experience that same loneliness.

"Mmm." Her eyes blinked open, sleepiness melting off her face as her eyes met mine.

"Look who came to say hi, Sugar," I said, standing next to her bed and indicating to my sister. She was cooing over our baby, talking to him in a low voice.

Eryne sat up, and I helped reposition the pillows behind her back. I pressed a kiss to the top of her head, inhaling her sweet apple scent.

"Hi." She smiled at my sister. "Thank you for coming."

"Of course. I had to come meet my new little nephew," Freya said, tracing a finger down his little button nose. "He's so perfect, you two."

My wife smiled up at me. "I think so, too." She let out a happy sigh. "But I might be biased."

"Just a little," I agreed with her. But we'd had multiple nurses tell us he was one of the cutest newborns they'd ever seen.

Ronan let out a wail of dissatisfaction—like he knew we were talking about him and wanted to be the center of attention. "Let's go see mommy, huh?" My sister carried him back over to the bed. My chest warmed as she placed our baby back in his mother's arms, and he immediately stopped crying.

"I'll let you three be alone," Freya said, hugging me tight. "I just wanted to come check in. I'll be in town for a few days before heading back to Walnut Ridge. If you need anything, just let me know."

I dipped my head. "We appreciate it. And you."

There was a wistful look in Freya's eyes as she glanced at the hospital bed. Eryne was lost in her own little world with our son, cooing over him softly, and I walked my sister out, not wanting to interrupt their quiet little bonding moment.

"You're welcome here whenever, you know," I said, turning

towards her as the door closed behind us. "Pleasant Grove is a great place to live."

She shook her head. "I love living in Walnut Ridge. My life is there. But I miss you, too."

"I know." I wrapped my arms around her again, giving her another hug. "Love you, Freya."

"Love you, too, B." She pulled away. "I should let you get back in there. Take care of your mate and pup."

"I will." I still couldn't believe this was my life.

That I was so lucky to have her—as my wife, my mate, the mother of my child. That she wore my mark on her neck and gave me that sweet smile every time she saw me.

I was the luckiest wolf alive to have my witch as mine, and I'd never forget that.

ERYNE

It felt like I was seeing a whole new side of Barrett watching him with our son. Watching him cradle him against his bare chest in the hospital, asleep in the chair next to my bed, made my ovaries want to burst.

And the way he would whisper softly in Ronan's ear, so tender and sweet, like he was telling him the best kept secrets of the universe? This was everything I'd ever dreamed of, and yet so much more.

Delivery had been *hard*. There was no sugarcoating that. I'd cried, and when I didn't think I could keep going any longer— when all I wanted was to sleep, Barrett had been the one to hold my hand, to whisper in my ear that I was doing so good, that he was so proud of me, to just push one more time—just one more, and then he would be here.

The moment they'd placed him in my arms, it felt like everything had fit into place, like a perfect puzzle. This little life that we'd created, complete with that fuzzy red hair. I felt like my heart was living outside of my body now, watching my husband—my mate—snoring softly with our newborn.

My boys. My perfect valentine's day gift. What more could I want?

Grabbing my phone, I snapped a photo of them, changing my wallpaper to the photo. Barrett opened his eyes as I put my phone back down, resting back against the pillow.

"Have a good nap?" I asked him, reaching out for the baby. I wanted my own snuggles, to inhale his sweet baby smell. I couldn't get enough of it.

He stood up, placing Ronan into my arms and then slid into the bed beside me. It was a tight fit with both of us—mostly because he barely fit in the bed—but I snuggled into his body as I let Ronan latch on to my breast. The first time I'd tried to nurse him, he'd had trouble with it, but after the lactation consultant came in, he seemed to be doing better. I ran my hand over his soft red baby hair as he drank my milk.

"Fresh from the tap," I joked.

"You're amazing," Barrett said, rubbing his thumb over my shoulder. "Both of you."

I hummed. "What do you think he'll be? A witch, or a shifter?"

My mate gave a thoughtful noise. "Maybe both. We'll know within a few months, in any case. Most shifters will shift for the first time when they're only a few months old. They can't control it at this age. How long does it take for witches to show their abilities?"

"A few years, maybe?" I guessed. I hadn't really been around that many toddlers to experience their haywire magic. I'd have to ask my parents to tell me more about when I'd been little.

"He'll be the best of both of us," Barrett said, reaching down to brush his hand over Ronan's cheek. "Witch and wolf. The world the way it should be."

It was everything we'd dreamed of when we'd first discussed breaking the old barrier. A world where mates weren't closed off from each other. Where who we were—who we loved—didn't matter.

All because a wolf and a witch fell in love.

"Love you, sugar," Barrett said, pressing a kiss to my forehead. "Every day, I'm thankful for those wraiths for bringing me here. For bringing me to you. Thankful that I fell completely under your spell. You bewitched me, and I'm so grateful you're mine. That the fates thought to give you to me." He ran his finger over my ring, the one he'd given to me that Halloween night. It had been early, but I'd never doubted his love for me. Never once.

"I love you, Wolf-Man," I responded, getting choked up as I felt all of his love pour into me. "This—you and Ronan—is everything I've ever wanted and more."

We stayed like that for a long time—him holding me in his arms, me holding our newborn in mine—our perfect little family.

The perfect blend of two worlds. Witch and wolf shifter.

Two hearts beating as one.

Thank the fates.

The End.

Want more Eryne & Barrett? Follow the link below to sign up for my newsletter for a peek into their pumpkin patch visit in the future: https://dl.bookfunnel.com/5kbi9jll2m

The Witches of Pleasant Grove will return in 2026 with *Eternally His,* a vampire x witch romance.

acknowledgments

To Hannah, thank you for everything. I cannot say enough how much I appreciate you being my emotional support human at events, my alpha reader, and my go-to hype girl.

To Olivia, the purple to my pink: thank you for never stopping to shout at me from the moment I first said "I think I want to write a wolf shifter book" and asking for it. (More still to come, I promise.)

To Meagan, for being my best friend and my support system as I was writing this—I love you and am so glad to have you in my life.

To Cat, my bolts buddy and my monster romance girl: thank you for loving Eryne. Always grateful to have you in my corner and for your never-ending support and friendship.

To Senny, thank you for the beautiful cover. I always love working together, and I am truly so in love with this one.

To Lana, thank you for being the biggest inspiration and such an amazing friend. I am constantly in awe of you. Thank you for letting me slide into your DMs until we became friends. ILY.

To Maren, my author bestie: truly, I don't think I'd be here without you. I am endlessly grateful for all of your mentorship, support, and advice. Love you long time.

To Mom, thank you for traveling all over the country with me and being my assistant at almost every event, for all the support you give me. Thank you for letting me live this dream every day.

also by jennifer chipman

CONTEMPORARY ROMANCE

Best Friends Book Club

Academically Yours - Noelle & Matthew

Disrespectfully Yours - Angelina & Benjamin

Fearlessly Yours - Gabrielle & Hunter

Gracefully Yours - Charlotte & Daniel

Cousins Coffee Club

(Best Friends Book Club Generation 2)

Uniquely in Love - Ellie & Owen

Wildly in Love - Quinlan & Sawyer (coming 2026)

Seattle Seals

Unexpected Icing - Sophia & Rhodes (coming soon)

Castleton University

A Not-So Prince Charming - Ella & Cameron

Once Upon A Fake Date - Audrey & Parker

A North Pole Christmas

Elfemies to Lovers - Ivy & Teddy

PARANORMAL ROMANCE

Witches of Pleasant Grove

Spookily Yours - Willow & Damien

Wickedly Yours - Luna & Zain

Bewitchingly Hers - Eryne & Barrett

SCIENCE FICTION ROMANCE

S.S. Paradise

A Love Beyond the Stars - Aurelia & Sylas

A Passion Beyond the Galaxy - Kayle & Leo (coming soon)

about the author

Originally from the Portland area, Jennifer now lives in Orlando with her dog, Walter and cat, Max. In her free time, you can find her with her nose in a book or going to the Disney Parks. She loves writing romance heroes who fall first and hard for their women. Jennifer writes Contemporary Romance, Paranormal Romance, and Sci-Fi Romance.

Website: www.jennchipman.com

- amazon.com/author/jenniferchipman
- goodreads.com/jennchipman
- instagram.com/jennchipmanauthor
- facebook.com/jennchipmanauthor
- x.com/jennchipman
- tiktok.com/@jennchipman
- pinterest.com/jennchipmanauthor